Perfection isn't all it's cracked up to be.

Stacey Barlow-Barrett has the perfect life—or, at least, the illusion of one. She's married to the man her parents approved, and she's making it work. But keeping up appearances is wearing her down. Her husband, Jace, wants to start a family. Her former lover, Mason, is a business associate she can't cut off, and he twists the knife at every opportunity. Trying to make everyone happy—everyone except herself—has her on the verge of a breakdown.

When Jace's best friend moves in, everything that seemed tenuously tolerable is now completely unbearable, and Stacey realizes something is very wrong in her marriage. Jace is keeping up appearances too, and it's at Stacey's expense.

Mason is the only one she can turn to for help...if he can forgive her for marrying Jace while the sheets were still warm from their last encounter. And even if he does forgive her, and she does dig her way out of the mess her marriage has become, Stacey may not be ready for what he needs in return: love.

Books by Laura Browning

Winning Heart

The Barlow-Barretts: An American Dynasty
Bittersweet, Book One
Balancing Act, Book Two
Remember Me, Book Three
Broken Heart, Book Four

Published by Kensington Publishing Corporation

Broken Heart

The Barlow-Barretts: An American Dynasty, Book Four

Laura Browning

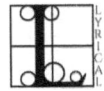

LYRICAL PRESS
Kensington Publishing Corp.
www.kensingtonbooks.com

Lyrical Press books are published by
Kensington Publishing Corp. 119 West 40th Street New York, NY 10018

All Kensington titles, imprints, and distributed lines are available at special quantity discounts for bulk purchases for sales promotion, premiums, fund-raising, and educational or institutional use.

Special book excerpts or customized printings can also be created to fit specific needs. For details, write or phone the office of the Kensington Special Sales Manager:
Kensington Publishing Corp.
119 West 40th Street
New York, NY 10018
Attn. Special Sales Department. Phone: 1-800-221-2647.

First Electronic Edition: October 2013
eISBN-13: 978-1-61650-488-5
eISBN-10: 1-61650-488-9

First Print Edition: October 2013
ISBN-13: 978-1-61650-846-3
ISBN-10: 1-61650-846-9

Printed in the United States of America

To Stacey, for finally finding your own voice. I'm glad I could give you a happily ever after.

Chapter 1

Avoiding him was nearly impossible. Wherever Stacey looked, Mason Hatch was in her line of sight. Since she was attending her brother Brandon's wedding, she couldn't leave, but she sure wished Jace would stick by her side this once. She scanned the room, but her husband was nowhere to be seen.

"Hubby MIA again?" Mason's voice was as smooth as silk in her ear. The fact he simply echoed her thoughts didn't make his intrusion into them any more palatable. "I could tell you where to look, but I don't think you'd like what you'd find."

"Stop it!" Stacey hissed between clenched teeth. Every time she encountered Mason, he made some cryptic remark about her husband. Stacey was tired of it, in part because she had enough doubts concerning her marriage. But not today. She refused to have them today. Today was supposed to be perfect. Jason had made love to her last night, had tried once again to talk her into starting a family. She wanted children. She did, but something always held her back. She couldn't stall too much longer, doing so wasn't fair to either of them, yet the mere thought of a divorce in her oh-so-Catholic family made her shudder. God, was she really contemplating divorce? Her mother would flip.

"Just trying to make conversation among these Virginia purebreds," Mason purred, once again barging into her brain. Why was there always a hint of amusement in his voice, as if he were actually laughing at her? Yes, she had been unfair to him, but had his contempt been there all along? Had he always regarded her with a smirk?

She sneaked a glance, finding her heels brought her nearly eye-to-eye with him. He was not short by any means, she'd simply inherited every bit of the Barlow-Barrett height and her mother's slenderness to boot. How often she had wished for even a touch of her younger sister Preston's curviness and her infinitely more diminutive height.

"Why can't you single out someone else to talk to?" she demanded, knowing she sounded as petulant as she felt. "Don't you have a date?"

He arched one dark brow, his eyes glittering like obsidian. "Perhaps I'm conducting a scientific experiment."

"Oh? And what would your experiment be?" She didn't want to continue this conversation, but she had no defense against his goading, had never been able to resist it, and that was what had gotten them in trouble to begin with. He was the match. She was the kindling.

"To see if there's actually a living, breathing woman still left under your high-class brittleness, or has the rarified air of your married life already drained it away?"

It shouldn't hurt. Not anymore, but it seemed she could still bleed if pricked. And Mason was stabbing deep with his verbal needling. She stared into his still cynically amused expression. "Fuck you," she whispered, her lips barely moving because she felt so frozen.

"The F-bomb, baby? In public?" He laughed, letting his gaze drop along her body. "Been there, done that."

Before she could think of any response, he had walked away, leaving behind only the deep contempt with which he'd stared at her. Stacey stood at the edge of the laughter and the crowd, feeling more isolated than if she'd been standing alone on the deck of her sailboat somewhere in the middle of the ocean. She swallowed and stuck her chin up.

A Barlow-Barrett must always stand straight and hold her head high. It had been one of the hardest of her mother's lessons for Stacey to learn as a gawky teenager. Taller than her peers, what she'd wanted to do was slump. As she did now, right before she slunk away into some dark corner where she could lick her wounds in private. But there was never any privacy in her family. They were in the spotlight whether they liked it or not.

Stacey needed to move. If she continued to stand here on her own, she would draw attention, something her mother would never forgive. Feeling some disgust at how tied she still was to pleasing her parents, Stacey moved back among the guests. No one would be able to fault her for not circulating, not making people feel welcome. The entire time she nodded, smiled and made appropriate comments, one part of her brain was detached. Nearly a half hour passed before she saw Jason return to the ballroom in the company of a man she had seen once or twice at various functions she'd attended recently with her husband. They were both tall, attractive men--perfect foils for one another. Jace's dark hair appeared slightly ruffled, but his companion's short blond locks were in perfect order. Even as she looked at them, she saw the two men laugh before they gripped hands and parted company. Her husband looked more relaxed than he ever seemed to be with her.

Jace headed her way, a smile curving his generous mouth as he saw her. Cupping her elbow a moment later, he leaned in and kissed her lightly on the cheek. "You look lovely, Stacey, as always." His compliment sounded impersonal as his gaze skated over the gathering. "Everything going all right? No outbreak of pole dancing by the bride or her guests?"

"Jason!" Stacey admonished. "Lucy is a wonderful person. You know the dancing was only to support herself until her art career got going."

He grimaced. "Still, darling, a stripper, no matter how noble the cause, is not exactly our kind of people."

"You pay too much attention to what other people think," she shot back, then realized the same applied to her.

Stacey remembered the day she and Brandon had plucked Lucy from the bay after her dinghy capsized. She'd been prepared to think badly of the woman until then, but after meeting her and getting to know her, Stacey had realized how lucky Brandon was. She opened her mouth to defend her brother's bride, then shut it. She didn't want to create any dissension with her husband, not when it seemed things might be going better between the two of them. Besides, her defense would do nothing to change what was so ingrained as to be second nature to him. Anything or anyone different was hushed, hidden or looked down upon.

"People like us have to, darling. Have you thought any more about what we discussed last night?" Jason's hand rubbed the small of her back, his head bent solicitously to her.

Her stomach fluttered with nerves rather than desire. "I don't know, Jace. I… Can you give me a little more time?"

Displeasure flitted across his aristocratic features before he once again assumed the urbane smile he wore at all social functions. "We're Catholic, darling. Babies are expected. You'll turn thirty next month, so you're not getting any younger."

She wasn't getting any younger? As if her eggs were any older than his sperm? But Stacey didn't say anything. Once again she heard her mother's voice, like a metronome of patrician aphorisms. As a Barlow-Barrett, you must support your husband. Lord, she was trying, but it seemed more and more that she was the only one in this marriage with a legitimate career, and getting damn little support of her own.

"I'll think it over," she finally muttered. It would be an easier decision if you'd ever give me an orgasm or even look me in the eye while we make love. It might be on the tip of her tongue to tell him so, but it would never actually leave her mouth. She wouldn't dare. Not with Jace. Not like she had with Mason. She'd been able to say anything to him. She glanced nervously again and found the man in her thoughts still watched her, this time from across the room, and he still wore an expression of cynical amusement.

Tilting her chin, she pasted a smile on her face and turned to her husband. "I don't know why I said that, darling. Of course I want to have children. I had just thought we could wait until the excitement of the wedding was over with. You know, so it would be easier to change my lifestyle--more exercise, less alcohol, maybe cutting back on my client list."

Jason was smiling again. This time he leaned down to kiss her lingeringly on the lips. Sometimes he seemed more demonstrative in public than he was at home. Stacey relaxed a bit, noticing for the first time the tanginess of his aftershave. She sniffed. "Is that a new cologne?"

Her husband laughed. "Mmm. Yes. Do you like it?"

She shrugged. "It just seems different."

He glanced around the room once more, almost as though he were searching for someone. "I hope a lot of things will be different, Stacey, better."

She looked at him in some confusion, but the approach of an old friend of the family prevented her from questioning what he meant.

* * * *

Mason ground his teeth as he watched Winchester laughing with his wife. If what he suspected was true, Stacey Barlow-Barrett--oops, Winchester--was in for some serious disillusionment, but he wouldn't be the one to burst her bubble of domestic bliss. In fact, he'd already dropped too many hints over the last couple months on those occasions when running into her at the gallery had been unavoidable. It would be better all the way around if he put her where she belonged--in the past-- and moved on with his life. So why was it so damn hard to do?

When his date, an aide for a senator he counted among his clients, stepped off the dance floor, he handed her a fresh glass of champagne and set his arm around her waist. If the gesture was more intimate than their first date called for, he wasn't ready to apologize for it now. That could come later when he dropped her safe and sound at her door with a peck on the cheek and returned to his penthouse alone.

There was only one woman in this room he'd had the urge to make a commitment to, and she was taken. Mason sneaked one last look at

Stacey. How many people were truly aware what passion lurked beneath her cool, blond exterior? He seriously doubted her husband was one of them.

Mason turned his gaze to the bride. Lucy Cameron danced, a bit stiffly, in the arms of her father-in-law, Alexander Barlow-Barrett. Only the elder Barrett could make a professional dancer appear ill at ease. The guy was the poster child for puritanical American capitalistic dynasties. It amazed Mason that already three of Barrett's children had found their own ways to rebel. Brandon had just married Lucy, a former exotic dancer. The eldest Barlow-Barrett, Seth, had quit the family's newspaper empire to run his own small town paper on the Delaware coast, and the sister, a couple years younger than Stacey, had beaten them all--bearing a child out of wedlock, becoming a veterinarian and finally settling down with a horse-trainer husband. Mason discounted the two youngest siblings. Phillip was too focused on his legal career and the girl apparently wasn't old enough to instigate her own rebellions yet, so only Stacey remained--the dutiful daughter. God damn her.

Mason could still feel her hips arching against his and hear her crying out in passion. Fuck. He set his drink aside and nabbed his date's, setting it aside too. "Let's dance," he growled. It was a fast number, which suited the hell out of him. Maybe if he worked up a sweat, he could work out the lust he still felt for the eldest Barlow-Barrett daughter, lust he no longer had a right to feel.

"Are you having a good time?" he asked his date.

She nodded, her glance darting around the room. "This is like being at a who's-who of Washington powerbrokers. God, Mason, how did you get to be friends with people like the Barlow-Barretts?"

Mason laughed. "Trust me. I'm no friend of theirs. Lucy Cameron, the bride, is one of the artists my gallery represents. Most of the time her husband is torn between punching me in the face or thanking heaven for me."

His date's only reaction was a slightly puzzled smile. Just as well. He didn't want to go into explanations of his not-so-willing role as cupid. He still kicked himself for that, but then anyone could look at Lucy and Brandon and see there would never be anyone else for either of them. When the song ended, another male guest claimed his date. He glanced around the dance floor and saw Winchester escort his wife onto the floor. Mason felt only relief, but when he saw Winchester's friend take over on the next song, a slow number, the only thing he could think was fuck no.

* * * *

Stacey had hoped to dance the slow song with Jace. She needed to feel him next to her, needed reassurance that everything was all right with their world. Now she was in the arms of Justin Worthington, one of Jace's closest friends. She hadn't realized who it was when she'd seen them together earlier. Jace had mentioned Justin a lot, but it had always seemed to her there was an edge of tension to him when he did and, until today, she had never met him.

"I'm so happy to meet you," Justin told her now. "Jace talks of you constantly."

Stacey gave him a look she was sure must be slightly puzzled. "Really? He's mentioned you too. I can't believe we haven't met before now."

His grip on her hand tightened slightly. "I've been working out of the country until recently."

She nodded. "I hate you missed our wedding. I know Jace wanted you there. It must have been a disappointment not to be able to share the celebration."

Justin smiled, his green eyes twinkling. "Now I'm in the area, maybe we'll be able to remedy that."

Was it her imagination, or had he pulled her slightly closer? As he turned her in time with the music, his thigh brushed against hers. Now she was uncomfortable. By no means did she consider herself a prude, but she could have sworn more than his thigh had touched her. Just about to open her mouth to ask him to hold her less closely, the sight of Mason tapping her partner on the shoulder had her clamping her mouth shut. She wouldn't mind a rescue, but exchanging Justin for Mason was like jumping from a campfire into a forest fire.

"May I cut in?"

Justin smiled graciously, but something in the way the two men eyed one another made Stacey catch her breath for an instant.

"Certainly." Justin smiled at her and said, "I'm sure we'll be seeing a lot more of each other, Stacey."

It was only when Mason spun her back into the crowd on the dance floor, and she caught a whiff of the spicy bite of Justin's cologne, that she realized Justin wore the same scent her husband did. Stacey shook her head slightly. Maybe that was how Jace had discovered it. After all, it was obvious the two men had re-established their long-standing friendship.

"Are you all right?" Mason's rumbled inquiry caught her off guard so she nearly stumbled. He caught her, his hand on her hip where, to her chagrin, he left it. The tingling it sent along her nerve endings filled her with guilt.

"Yes. Get your hand off my ass."

He moved it to the small of her back, his thumb stroking her spine through the silk of her evening dress. "So exactly why I love you. You appear to be such a lady, but you have a mouth like a sailor."

"Mason," she muttered. "Please don't. This one night, can't we have a ceasefire?"

"I didn't start this war, Blondie, but I'm willing to negotiate terms." His expression was inscrutable.

"There are no terms, Mason. I'm married. I won't be unfaithful to my husband."

"How old-fashioned of you. I hope your spouse is equally reciprocative."

"Stop it." Stacey felt as though he took her heart and twisted it in his grasp. "I'm sorry things didn't work out between us."

Mason put his mouth next to her ear. "Don't be sorry, baby. You were one of the best fucks I've ever had...and had...and had."

She couldn't control the gasp, the hurt stabbing through her, nor could she control the way she jerked away from him. Aware their sudden cessation of dancing would attract attention, Stacey put a hand to her mouth. "Excuse me," she said loud enough so the other couples dancing could hear. "I feel ill."

Without giving him a chance to grab hold of her again, she rushed from the dance floor and out of the ballroom in search of the sanctuary of the women's lounge. She longed to simply break down, but she knew her mother, knew her family. Someone would be in here in a moment, and she needed to have a believable story to cover behavior that had drawn unwanted attention. Rushing into one of the stalls, she slammed the door behind her, stared at the toilet and let out a defeated sigh. From years of practice, she leaned over, stuck a finger down her throat and gagged before she brought up the contents of her stomach.

"Stacey, darling?" It was her mother's voice. "Are you ill?"

She leaned one hand against the marble wall then grabbed a wad of tissue. "It's nothing, Mother."

"You're not pregnant, are you?"

There was such a wealth of hope in her mother's voice, but all Stacey felt were manacles tightening another notch around her wrists and throat.

* * * *

Mason had endured all he could. Even for Brandon and Lucy's sake, he couldn't stay here any longer. He was making himself miserable, and he'd made Stacey quite literally sick. He watched the doorway through which she'd fled, had seen her mother follow her, and waited now to see them return. As much as he wanted to get the hell out of there, he wouldn't until he was sure she would be fine.

What the fuck had he been thinking? How could he have said that to her? It would be better all the way around if he made sure to avoid any contact with her. She had made her bed the moment she'd accepted Jason Winchester's engagement ring. If her marriage now turned out to be something other than what she'd hoped, it was none of his concern. As soon as he saw her return to the ballroom with her mother, he located his date, making the excuse he had plans to sail early the next morning.

After dropping off the senator's aide, Mason drove past the house where he and Stacey had met. It was nearly two years ago now. And how pathetic was that? He was still lusting after a woman who'd dumped him so long ago. As the Porsche idled outside the brownstone, Mason remembered seeing her for the first time. Tall and willowy, dressed in a conservative suit with her hair pulled back into a neat bun, she'd turned her Barlow-Barrett haughtiness on him, thinking he was nothing more than a delivery boy. He'd set her straight in pretty short order, right before he'd eased her tight skirt up, shoved her lacy underwear to one side and taken her on the dining room table. Even remembering it now, so long after the fact, his cock swelled and his balls throbbed.

That was what pissed him off more than anything. He knew, given half a chance, he'd do the same thing again, married or not. But no matter how bitter he was, he wouldn't be the one to disillusion her about her husband. That was a journey she'd have to make on her own.

* * * *

They were going home. Finally. While Jace drove the Jaguar, Stacey leaned her aching head against the rest and stared out the passenger window. She wanted nothing more than to be able to take off the fancy clothes, let down her hair and soak in her tub with a glass of seltzer water in hand. Instead, in the side mirror, she saw the headlights of Justin Worthington's car. Jace had invited him for a drink. Stacey sighed. Her husband caught her hand.

"Are you feeling better, darling?"

"Yes." Did she have a choice? Without even asking, he had invited his friend to their home, so no matter how she actually felt, she would still need to play hostess for their guest.

But of course, she was positive none of what was going through her mind showed on her face when she smiled and welcomed Justin inside. It would go against everything she'd been taught to be less than gracious to a guest. When she started to remove the silk shawl from around her shoulders, it was Justin who took it from her. His grin was charming. "Allow me."

"Thank you." Stacey watched as he folded it carefully and laid it across the arm of the chair near the steps. It helped redeem him a bit in her eyes. Jace was never so careful with her things. Stacey hated disorder. Justin was obviously a man who did as well. Perhaps she had only imagined his penis brushing against her thigh while they danced, but even so, she supposed she could excuse him. After all, it wasn't necessarily something a man could control, was it?

"Sherry, darling?" Jason asked. At her nod, his glance moved to Justin. "And you, Justin? Still drinking Remy Martin?" At the other man's nod, Stacey watched her husband splash some of the cognac in two snifters. After handing her the glass of sherry, he delivered one of the snifters to Justin. Stacey settled herself on one end of the couch, a bit unsettled when Justin seated himself in the chair nearby, close enough his knee nearly brushed hers.

After a sip from her sherry, she steeled herself. "So, do you also know Brandon?" She was trying to figure out how Justin had become one of the guests at the wedding, although she couldn't remember seeing him at the church.

He laughed. "The groom? No, I don't know either your brother or his lovely bride. I happened to show up at the club, thinking I might get a decent, quiet meal there, when I ran into Jace. He invited me in to join the festivities."

She smiled and darted a glance at her husband, who seemed to be watching them both with unusual intensity. When she raised a brow at him, he shook himself and smiled. "You know, it's uncanny, darling. There is an amazing resemblance between the two of you."

Justin laughed. "Coincidence, Jace, I can assure you. I don't believe any of the Worthingtons, other than me, have ever traveled east of the Mississippi. That would certainly preclude any chance of our actually being related."

Stacey laughed, but she had to admit, Jace was somewhat accurate. Both she and Justin had blond hair of a similar color, though his was closely cropped while hers was confined in a sleek French twist, the way her husband liked it. They were of a similar height, particularly when she wore heels, and even his build was slender, though she had a feeling from having danced with him he was a lot stronger than he might initially appear. "You are too funny, darling. To even imagine Alexander Barlow-Barrett might have strayed…"

Her father was far too uptight and upright. She had spent a lifetime trying to live up to his strict ideas of what was right and wrong. And even though she had done everything she'd ever been asked, had gone to the right schools, participated in the right sports and married the right man, she sometimes couldn't help but feel she was more of a disappointment to him than the children who had thrown everything back in his face.

Jason laughed. "You're right. How absurd. So, tell me Justin, how are the renovations going on your condo?"

The other man grimaced. "None too well, I'm afraid. Everything is torn up. The contractors have mentioned having me relocate for a month or so until they get the heaviest work out of the way."

Before she realized it, Stacey impetuously invited, "You must stay here, Justin. We have plenty of room, and I know the staff get bored with only Jace and me rattling around in this big house. We bought it with plans for the future..."

He touched her hand. "I wouldn't want to intrude. You two haven't even been married a year."

Jace set his glass aside. "It wouldn't be any intrusion. We'd love to have you, wouldn't we, Stacey?"

She had regretted the impulse as soon as the invitation had left her mouth, but she could hardly take it back now. What had she been thinking, particularly when Jason had made it plain he wanted to get busy starting a family? But the invitation had been made, so she smiled and nodded. "Of course you must move in here while the work on your place is finished. I won't hear of anything else."

His hand stroked her forearm. "That's very generous of you, Stacey." His gaze shifted to Jason, though his hand remained on her arm. "Thanks, man. You're a real friend to share your home with me. I should get home, leave you two to get to bed."

* * * *

Jason prowled his study long after Stacey had gone to bed. After tossing back another brandy, he slumped into the chair behind his desk, rubbing his aching temples. He couldn't believe Justin had actually come. He'd emailed him just two days ago, knowing he was on yet another business trip, but too upset over the news he'd gotten to consider the consequences of contacting him.

And Justin had come back. Jace's throat tightened. He'd surprised him by appearing at the wedding. As soon as Jace had seen him, he'd dragged him into the deserted men's locker room where Justin had wrapped him in his arms. They'd always been so careful, so discreet. Would they be able to continue if Justin was under the same roof?

Restless, Jace popped out of his chair again. He pulled shut the door to his study so Stacey wouldn't overhear and called Justin--his best friend and the man he loved more than life itself.

Chapter 2

In the week since leaving the wedding, Mason had retreated to his office no less than three times to avoid dealing with Stacey. His assistant could handle her. Left to him, he'd tell her to find another gallery, but his clientele and hers overlapped to such an extent it was impossible. And truth be told, he often had to recommend her, because she was a damn good interior decorator.

He'd just made the absolute dumbass move of getting involved. What had started out as incendiary sex had morphed into something more for him. Unfortunately, the same couldn't be said for Stacey. While he had found a vibrantly passionate woman beneath the buttoned-down blueblood exterior, when push came to shove, she'd fallen right in line with whatever life plan had been laid out for her from birth on. The right man with the right pedigree had produced a ring, popped the question and she had accepted.

God knew, when it came to pedigrees, Mason Hatch was nothing more than a mongrel who'd been rescued, bathed and groomed. He might not be on the streets anymore, but it was where his roots were.

And right now, seeing her bring in Justin Worthington to look over their inventory had nearly sent him straight back to the hard-talking, hard-hitting years of his youth. Mason wanted nothing more than to pound his fist in Justin's golden good looks. A glance at his watch told him he couldn't hide out any longer. He had a lunch meeting with an artist whose work could be an asset to the gallery based on what he'd seen. If he didn't leave now, he'd be late. His gaze narrowed on the proprietary hand Justin placed at the base of Stacey's back, as if he'd already moved in on those marriage vows she'd tried to tell Mason she held so sacred. His stomach turned in disgust. Apparently putting hands on Stacey was permissible if the family tree dated back to seventeenth-century America.

Whatever. Mason couldn't accurately trace his family history to more than a barely remembered mother. He'd always suspected the name Hatch was an invention of some smartass social worker to imply something about his origins.

Stacey glanced over from the painting she was showing Justin as Mason stepped from the staircase into the front hall. He nodded to her, his gaze dropping for an instant to the hand Justin rested right at the top of her butt. It surprised him when she blushed.

"Justin," she said, drawing the other man's attention. "This is Mason Hatch, the gallery owner."

It was all he could do to stifle the growl that instinctively rose to his lips, but he shook the other man's hand. "I hope you're finding everything you need?"

"Yes, thank you, Hatch." Justin's tone set his nerves on edge, so similar to the one Stacey had used the first time she met him.

Mason switched his narrowed gaze to Stacey. "How's your husband, Stacey?"

"Busy." There was something in the shift of her eyes that made his nerves jangle. Not his business. Whatever problems she had, she'd chosen. He looked once more at the tall blond with her. "Nice to have met you, Worthington. Will you be here long?"

"Permanently, I hope."

Mason smiled. "So is Stacey helping you decorate?" Maybe he was simply a client.

Was Worthington's smile a bit smug? "We're not quite to the finishing touches, though she is making a few suggestions. My condo's under renovation right now. Stacey and Jace have graciously allowed me to move in with them temporarily."

Mason's glance flew back to Stacey. Now she did shift uneasily. "How...cozy." Mason smirked--on purpose. He glanced at his watch. "I hope you'll excuse me. I'm on my way out to a lunch meeting."

* * * *

"You've slept with him, haven't you?"

Justin's quietly worded question hit the silence following Mason's departure as loudly as if he'd screamed it. Stacey stepped away from her husband's friend, her hand fluttering to her throat. "Wh-what did you say?"

Justin's smiled widened, showing off the dimple in his cheek. "Hatch. You've had sex with him. He gives off the testosterone of one very possessive male."

Stacey clutched her purse in front of her. "I don't think this is something open for discussion, Justin."

He shrugged. "Whatever. Jace has never been a very possessive man. I doubt it would bother him."

She felt like she had to provide some explanation. What if Justin said something? "We...went out a couple of times before Jace and I got engaged."

"It's okay, Stacey." His tone was reassuring. "I'm sorry. None of my business. It just seemed odd. The guy was throwing off real vibes like he was ready to mark his territory or something, like some common cur. "

She smoothed a hand over her sleek hair. "I can assure you there's nothing between us. It ended when Jace and I got engaged."

Justin smiled. "I've embarrassed you. I'm sorry. Let me take you to lunch so I can make amends."

Stacey wanted to refuse, but she couldn't find a decent way to do so. In the past week, Justin seemed to be right there whenever she turned around, whether they were at the house or somewhere else. Last night, she'd heard the two men laughing in Jason's study long after she had gone to bed. Ever since Justin moved in, her husband seemed to have forgotten the whole discussion of starting a family. Now Stacey was stuck in the middle of Justin knowing something her husband didn't, and her almost inbred need to be a good hostess. It left no room to graciously avoid lunch. "That's kind of you, Justin. Thank you."

As they sat at a secluded table in a quiet corner of a restaurant in Georgetown, Stacey tried to hide her surprise when Justin took her hand. "I don't want there to be any awkwardness between us. Jace and I are such close friends. We've known each other since we were kids. I want you to be a part of our friendship too."

She opened the menu, using it as an excuse to slide her hand free from his. Truthfully, though, she had little appetite. Knowing she needed to respond in some way, she smiled. "I'm glad you two are so close. Jace humors me and comes sailing with me, but I know his heart's not really in it. He'd rather be..."

"Fishing." Justin grinned. "We've been trout fishing on my parents' ranch, even taken a few trips to Canada. He's got enough sixth sense when it comes to finding fish, he could be a river guide."

Stacey laughed, once again relaxing. It was difficult to imagine the always buttoned up Jason Winchester roughing it in the wilds out west. Maybe she was being too hard on Justin. He did seem to be good for

Jace. Her husband had been so much more relaxed this week. Maybe that would translate into their bedroom too. Stacey could only hope.

"You never did explain where you were that you couldn't get back for the wedding. You and Jace are so close, it's difficult to imagine you wouldn't have been his choice for best man, and I'm sure he would have been more than willing to fly you back--that is, if you weren't in the middle of a war zone."

Justin chuckled. "Not exactly. I was working on my family's land holdings in Australia. They're running cattle there as well as here. Jace did call me, but there was no way I could get back. You two had already set the date, so." He shrugged.

Stacey patted his hand. "It's okay. I understand how that is. Barrett Newspapers has always been the same way for my father and my brothers. Well, not Seth anymore, but Brandon stays busy. He managed to carve out time for a honeymoon, but I know he'll have to hit the ground running once they get back."

The waiter stopped at their table and took their orders. When all she ordered was a salad, Justin raised his brows. Once the waiter departed he looked at her, green eyes serious. "Shouldn't you be eating more if you and Jace plan to get pregnant?"

Stacey's hand rattled against her water glass. "He told you that?"

Justin laughed. "Well, yeah. He seemed pretty open about it. Is it a big secret?"

She recovered with a smile after she sipped from her water. "No. I guess not. It's just I hadn't even had the chance to mention it to my family." She waved her hand. "Never mind. I'm being silly."

Justin ran his fingers along the weave of the tablecloth. "Please don't take offense, Stacey. It just seems, with me in the house, I might be cramping your style. If you'd like, I could go out this evening…grab dinner and a movie some place and give you and Jace some alone time."

It was incredibly thoughtful, not something she would have ever given a guy credit for imagining, certainly not based on the knowledge of her own three brothers. "Thank you, Justin. That's kind of you."

He caught her hand and squeezed gently. "No problem."

* * * *

Jace's cell chirped with Justin's ringtone. A client had just left and he had an hour before the next one arrived. Relaxing back in his chair, he twisted toward the window and watched the traffic roll past on the street below. Warmth filled him. Justin had always been able to do that.

"What's up?"

"I finished lunch with your wife."

"Did everything go okay? Does it seem like she likes you?" Jace knew some of his anxiety was bleeding through, but this was so important. He heard Justin sigh on the other end of the line.

"Jace, things don't have to be this way. You know what it's like with me on the ranch. It could be the same way for you. Come out. We could have a life together. You could let Stacey go."

Jace rubbed his temples, the tightness starting again in his neck and shoulders every time he considered his future. "Christ, Justin, you know I can't do that. My father may be gone, but my mother would have a stroke--literally, I'm afraid. You're asking the only son of a staunch Catholic family to admit he's gay? I'm already in agony every time I try to have a normal relationship with Stacey."

"And you know I will stick by you no matter what, Jason. I love you, man, but this is killing you, and it's taking a toll on Stacey too. Can't you see she still loves that other guy?"

Jace ground his teeth. "He's not right for her."

"Listen to you. You don't really want her, yet you don't want her to have anyone of her own? You're better than that."

"I need her, Justin."

"As your beard? Without her knowledge? It's not right."

"I need her to have my baby. If I had at least one child…" Jason sucked in a shaky breath. "I could do it then. I could come out."

The line was silent for a moment. When Justin spoke again, his tone was resigned. "You know I'll help you any way I can."

"Thanks, Justin." After saying goodbye, Jace shoved his phone back in his pocket and squeezed his eyes shut. He'd made such a mess of everything. He'd panicked and created a situation that seemed to get more and more out of control.

* * * *

"There. What do you think?" Stacey turned to Justin with a smile as she surveyed the dining room table. She had candles set, her best silver and china placed and the lights dimmed.

He leaned against the doorjamb and grinned. "Perfect. Jace will love it." He stepped forward and kissed her on the cheek. "Good luck, Stacey." He winked. "I'll be back later."

Stacey felt guilty for the resentment she sometimes felt toward Justin. She gave him a kiss on the cheek and a quick hug. "Thank you for the suggestion and the help."

He waved it away and left the room. A moment later, she heard the front door shut. After checking on a dinner she and Justin had cooked after they'd dismissed the staff for the evening, Stacey hurried upstairs to change. Even here, Justin had surprised her, by suggesting what she wear. While Stacey would have gone for a short, vampy dress, Justin had suggested some silky lounging pajamas instead.

She bathed and perfumed before slipping the pajamas over her bare skin. No bra, no panties. She wanted to make this as easy for Jace as she could. A moment later, she heard the automatic garage door. Racing down the stairs, she waited across from the door he would enter to take his briefcase.

She smiled when he looked a bit confused. She took his case and stood on tiptoe to kiss him on the lips. "Welcome home, darling. Dinner is almost ready. Why don't I get you a drink, and you can change into something more comfortable."

"What's all this?" He held her away from him for a moment and smiled. "Mind you, I'm not complaining."

"We have the house to ourselves for the evening, so…" She smiled with what she hoped was a seductive look. Shit. She'd never been any good at this.

Jace pulled her into his arms again. "So you're seducing me?"

She leaned her cheek against his chest. "Is it working?"

"Yes. Pour me a scotch. I'll get a shower and be right back."

Stacey was elated. Maybe now they could get things going so she would finally feel like she had a marriage. Although they had been man and wife longer than either of her brothers had been with their spouses, Stacey often felt clueless when it came to her marriage, particularly whenever she and Jace were around the rest of the family. She had done everything her parents had asked, so why was this still so difficult?

But now things were changing, and whether she wanted to admit it or not, Justin Worthington had been a big help. She would have to find some way to say thank you. She reiterated that thought when Jace entered the living room clad only in a pair of sleep pants hanging low on his hips. She couldn't believe how receptive he was being to her overtures, so different from the times early on in their marriage when she had tried something similar. It was as if he'd become a whole new man ever since Brandon's wedding. Stacey could only thank her lucky stars.

Dinner went splendidly, Jace even feeding her bites of dessert and leaning in for kisses in between. When they left the table, he grabbed her hand as she headed for the living room.

"Let's go upstairs, darling," he murmured.

Yesss! Stacey returned his grip with a soft squeeze.

* * * *

Mason had taken clients to dinner. After dropping the couple at their hotel, he had decided to stop at a bar not far from his penthouse on the way home. Not in the mood for company, he'd found a quiet corner in the back where he could observe people going in and out. It was right after ten when he saw Justin Worthington walk in--alone. He had seen the man several times during the week, each time either in the company of Jason Winchester or Stacey. Did this mean Stacey and her husband were actually spending time together?

Mason swirled the bourbon in his glass, his brows drawing together as he tried to force away the image of the two of them. Did she do the same things with Winchester she had done with him? He tossed the bourbon back, nearly choking. Imagining her with her long legs wrapped around her husband and her slender hips undulating against his nearly made Mason crush the glass.

"Would you care for another, sir?"

He wiped the frown from his face. The waitress had done nothing wrong. "Yes, thanks."

He stared at Worthington. The man was engaged in conversation with another man at the bar. There was something in his manner that made Mason feel ill at ease. It was nothing he could put a name to, which bothered him even more. As he continued to watch the blond, it dawned on him that he resembled Stacey in a lot of ways. Both long-legged and lean, they also shared the same shade of hair. While Worthington's eyes were green instead of gold, they also had the same angular features.

Whatever.

Mason shivered as he sipped the new bourbon the waitress had dropped at his table. A life on the streets followed by four years of exposure to the opposite end of the spectrum as a scholarship student at Harvard had left him with a very cynical view of society. There were dregs rich and poor, and their economic status had very little to do with the content of their character, to steal a line from a great American. Justin Worthington might not be the dregs, but he and Jace Winchester were hiding who and what they were. He wasn't sure yet why, but he had a very strong suspicion--one making him half sick. When Worthington left a half-hour later, Mason slapped a couple bills on the table and followed him. From the shadows outside the Winchester brownstone, Mason watched the other man quietly let himself inside. Mason sighed heavily.

Maybe he was being paranoid. Hell, maybe he was turning into some kind of sick Stacey stalker because he sure as shit couldn't get her out of his head. And now he had to wonder exactly what Justin Worthington was doing staying there.

* * * *

Stacey sat in the hot tub on the back deck, determined to keep the mood going. Jace had made love to her as usual. He had seemed to get satisfaction from their coupling, but she couldn't say the same. Not that he would know. Stacey had gotten very good at making him think she was climaxing even while her mind detached from what was going on. He had his arm around her shoulders now, so Stacey snuggled a bit closer to his side. He rubbed her shoulder.

"Would you like a drink, darling?"

"Yes," she murmured, "that would be nice." He rose from the hot tub, not bothering to wrap a towel around his slender hips. He had a pleasing build, lean, not muscular like Mason, but still handsome.

Stop. Stacey didn't want to think about Mason right now, but she realized every time her husband made love to her, she fantasized, remembering what it had been like with Mason. It was the only way she could make her "climaxes" realistic. With a sigh, she stared off into the darkness. This wasn't right. She shouldn't be thinking about another man, a man she hadn't been with for nearly two years. There must be something wrong with her. Jace certainly seemed to find their married life satisfying, so what was her problem?

Maybe she should consider seeing a therapist. Her mind cringed from the very idea. A Barlow-Barrett always keeps her private life private. Somehow, Stacey doubted seeing a shrink went along with that particular maxim from her mother.

She looked over at the French doors leading to the deck as she heard Jace return, then quickly sank lower in the hot tub, her eyes widening in shock. Behind her nude husband was Justin Worthington with only a towel tucked around his hips. Stacey's glance darted from Justin back to Jace. She couldn't very well ask what the hell was going on.

"Justin just got home, darling," Jace told her with a smile. "I knew you wouldn't mind him joining us. After all, we're all friends, all adults." There was an underlying tone telling her more clearly than words she was not to contradict him. And of course, how could she anyway? Doing so would create a scene.

Stacey swallowed and tried to smile. She wasn't a prude by any means, and the bubbles hid a lot. She did, after all, owe Justin for his help. "Of course I don't mind." She hoped she didn't sound as uncertain as she felt. "Please, join us."

Justin eased in on her other side before stripping the towel from himself and letting it slap onto the deck. Now he was naked too. With her. With her husband on the opposite side--and her in the middle. Stacey swallowed, feeling more than a bit uncomfortable and not liking the situation Jace had forced on her.

"Thank you, Stacey," Justin murmured. "Did you have a nice evening?"

Chapter 3

"Yes. Thanks." Justin's question served as a reminder, whether he meant it that way or not, she owed him for giving her some time alone with Jace.

"Here, darling." Jace handed her a drink. "I made you a Cape Codder. I know how you like cranberry juice."

She took the highball glass and drank. He eased back in beside her, leaned over and whispered in her ear. "Don't be embarrassed, darling. You're lovely, but you're my wife. Justin respects our marriage. He would never do anything we didn't want him to."

What an odd thing to say. Still, she nodded and took another gulp from her drink. She wanted to tell him how mortified she was that he would simply bring Justin out here without giving her a chance to put on any clothing. Screwing up her nerve, she opened her mouth to say so.

"Stacey has been such an incredible help," Justin leaned forward to tell Jace. "We've got almost everything picked out for my place, so once the drywall is in, we can begin painting. I don't know what I would have done without her."

She smiled, feeling a tad sick. This must be some alternate universe because it surely wasn't the life Stacey Barlow-Barrett had been reared to live. She could almost picture the look of horror on her parents' faces--probably all of her siblings as well--if they could see her now. When the two men tapped their glasses against hers and toasted her, she drank once again.

God, how could she protest when they were both being so nice? She would come off like such an uptight bitch. Instead, she listened as Justin told them where he'd gone to eat and the movie he'd seen. She continued to sip her drink, but then feeling a bit woozy, Stacey reached behind her to set the glass on the edge of the tub. When she nearly missed, Justin caught the glass and grinned at her.

"Oops! What did you do, Jace, make her drink a bit too strong?"

Stacey turned her head to look at her husband, who raised his brows. "I didn't think so. You okay, Stacey?"

"Yeah. I guess I'm tired." Maybe this was the way to escape.

Jace smiled at her. "I'll help you to bed. Be a gentleman, Justin. Look the other way. I'll be back in a few minutes."

Her husband wrapped her in a towel and tucked one around his own hips, then settled his arm behind her back. "You sure you're okay, darling?"

She nodded but regretted the action as her head swam a bit. "Yes. Maybe I had a bit too much to drink between dinner and in the hot tub. I'm so sorry, Jace. Don't mean to embarrass you."

"Shh. It's all right. We had a good evening together. Just get some sleep."

He dried her off and tucked her in. He'd never been quite so solicitous, and she was touched. Stacey stroked his cheek. "Did you enjoy the evening?"

He kissed her forehead. "It was wonderful. You're wonderful."

She smiled as she drifted off. Maybe she was worried about nothing.

* * * *

Stacey awoke the following morning with a hangover almost as bad as some of the ones she'd experienced in college when she had sown a few cautious wild oats. And God! She had dreamt the most bizarre things. She shook her head. A little sex and a little alcohol and she was absolutely done in. With a board of directors meeting at Barrett Newspapers on her agenda, she couldn't do what she truly wanted, which was to take a couple ibuprofen and bury her head beneath the blankets. After showering, she felt a bit better, but was still vowing never to mix the variety of liquors she'd drunk the night before--wine with dinner, sherry afterward, and then the vodka in the drink Jace had made.

After wrapping her damp hair in a towel, she began slathering moisturizer on her legs, her movements slowing as she looked at the bruises on the inside of her thighs. She didn't remember Jace being so rough while they'd made love. Fingertips brushing the marks, she shook her head. They didn't hurt, and she supposed it had been worth it. Maybe now she could get him to focus on the sexual side of their marriage, on making babies and making her forget a dark-haired, dark-eyed man who'd made her body sing with passion.

They were just love marks. Jace had gotten enthusiastic--for a change.

Still feeling a bit rough, she took a cab to Barrett's headquarters for the monthly meeting. Her father had stepped back into his role as chairman after a heart scare earlier in the year, so Seth would only be here today to attend the meeting, no doubt with Brandon's proxy in his pocket since Bran was still on his honeymoon with Lucy. Stacey twisted her wedding and engagement rings. Maybe she could talk to her new sister-in-law about the bruises. Never one to have close girlfriends, Stacey suddenly found herself in need of some female advice, but the newlyweds wouldn't be back for another week.

"Good morning," Seth greeted her as she stepped off the elevator. He arched one thick, golden brow over keen eyes so similar to her own. "You feeling all right?"

Stacey closed hers for a moment and sighed. "I had a little too much to drink. Does it show?"

"No. It's just I know you pretty well. Problems?"

"No, in fact I'd say the opposite."

Seth smiled. "Glad to hear it. Tessa mentioned you seemed somewhat stressed at the wedding, but we had to leave before she could talk to you, so she could nurse the baby." Taking her hand, he tucked it through his arm and walked with her toward the boardroom. "Mother thought you might be pregnant."

"If you're asking me, Seth, the answer's no. If you want to know if we're considering it, then the answer's yes."

His gaze was searching as he patted her hand. She was surprised when he didn't greet her comment with assurances about how great that was.

"I ran into Jace at the club. He introduced me to your houseguest."

"Justin's staying with us while his condo's being renovated," she felt for some reason like she needed to explain. The whole time, an image of him sitting next to her in the hot tub burned its way through her brain.

"Mmm. Jace said the two of them were close friends. Had you ever met him before?" Seth's questions seemed casual, putting her on instant alert. Seth never asked anything just to make conversation. He was perfectly content to be silent if he was in a good mood, or growl like the lion he resembled if he wasn't.

"No. Justin said he'd been handling his family's holdings in Australia, so he wasn't here during our engagement or for the wedding." She absently twisted her rings with her thumb.

Seth smiled and touched her cheek. "You know you can talk to me if you have any problems, Stace. That's what big brothers are for. Next to knights in shining armor, we're the number one dragon slayers."

She laughed, feeling lighter than she had in a couple of weeks. "I love you, Seth."

"Same here, kiddo."

Stacey sat next to him during the board meeting, trying hard to concentrate on the treasurer's report, but it seemed to her the comptroller droned on and on. She began to feel a bit like Charlie Brown listening to his teacher. Everything became a series of blah, blah, blah.

Along with everyone else, she voted her approval of her father's return to actively run the company, and Seth's resignation as acting CEO. She knew her brother was anxious to get himself and his family back to their home on the coast, back to the paper he'd had to leave in the hands of his small, but capable staff. She enjoyed the excitement of her interior decorating and design business, but sometimes she thought she'd prefer the quiet of a house along the bay, someplace where she could let her hair down and find out for once who Stacey Barlow-Barrett was.

* * * *

Jason started in surprise when Justin walked into his office, carefully shutting and locking the door behind him. He was even more surprised when he walked right around the desk, pulled Jace to his feet and kissed him. He responded, as he always did, but eventually pulled back enough to ask, "What are you doing here?"

"I've found a doc in New York who will see you over the weekend."

Jace shook his head. "It's no use, Justin. Come on."

Justin knelt in front of him. "Give it a shot, Jace. What can it hurt? It would give you a chance to have your own child."

"I'm supposed to go sailing with Stacey."

"Tell her something came up. This guy's a male fertility specialist. He's doing me a favor because he's a friend of the family. You owe me this, Justin. You know I'm willing to help if I have to, but this might make it unnecessary. Please."

Justin's hands were moving along his thighs, making it difficult for him to think, making his heart pound with desire. How much easier would everything be if he could manage to look his family in the eye and admit the love of his life wasn't Stacey Barlow-Barrett? It wasn't any woman. It was Justin Worthington and it had been ever since they'd first seen each other at summer camp when they were teenagers.

* * * *

Mason congratulated himself as he drove to his house nestled beside a quiet cove. He had gone an entire week without seeing Stacey. Oh, she'd been inside the gallery a time or two, but Mason had made sure he was occupied elsewhere--like in his office with the door closed--and had managed to avoid her.

Now he was going to enjoy the weekend. He'd spend the night in his house, then sail the dinghy around to the marina tomorrow morning. From there he'd take his big boat out. Maybe spend the night anchored in some isolated cove. He sighed in anticipation of the relaxation. He'd never sailed a day in his life until he went to Harvard, then in looking for a job that would allow him to earn some spending money, he'd landed a spot helping to crew for a weekend sailor. As soon as he'd seen the wind in the sails and felt the roll of the deck beneath his feet, he'd been hooked. It had taken some time to get his own boat, but he'd built his way up just like he had with his business, buying a smaller craft in need of restoration that he'd eventually sold for larger and larger vessels.

At the last minute, Mason changed his mind about the house and decided he'd head straight for the boat. Recalling how he'd gotten started sailing had increased his longing to simply do it. After a stop to stock groceries, he hit the marina right at dusk. As he made his second trip from his car to the boat, he glanced over at the next row of slips to the boat he knew belonged to Stacey. A light was on. Was she there with her husband? Somehow, he doubted it. He'd heard through Lucy and Brandon that Winchester wasn't keen on sailing, although he did enjoy fishing, so apparently it wasn't a seasickness issue.

So was she there alone? Feeling pathetically like a stalker, he sat on deck with a beer in one hand, watching her boat. A short time later, the light went out, and it was only Stacey who appeared on deck. She hopped off the boat, her long legs left bare by her shorts, striding toward the marina office, ice bucket in hand. Oh yeah. Now he had an excuse, and by God he would take it. After spending time trying to avoid her, Mason was determined to run into her here where there was no one else they knew, no prying eyes to watch. No husband to be the excuse not to talk to him.

He wanted answers. After nearly two years, he wanted to know what had made her turn from what they had to the jackass she'd married. He prayed to God it had been more than a pedigree dangled in front of her. Hell, he'd have more respect for her if she told him she'd married Winchester for his money.

He nearly changed his mind when he saw her turn from the ice machine. Her shoulders were slumped, as if she had admitted defeat or simply caved in. Before he could say anything, she spotted him standing a few feet away. The evening breeze lifted her hair, which hung loose for once, the tips just brushing the swells of her breasts. It was like watching a set change at a theater production. The narrow shoulders squared, the chin lifted, and her expression cloaked itself in the same haughtiness he'd seen the first day they'd met. But this time was different. This time, Mason knew there was a passionate woman underneath her brittle veneer, a woman who right now was in pain.

"Stacey, how are you?" He asked the usual social kiss-off question, but he wanted to know, didn't want a throwaway answer.

But it was what he got.

"Fine. Thank you for asking." She started forward to move past him. "If you'll excuse me?"

He stepped into her path. "No, I don't think I will. Excuse you, that is."

She wouldn't look him in the eye, which might have been the very reason he noticed the faint circles, like bruises, in the delicate skin below her golden irises.

"Please, Mason," she whispered, "I can't take your sniping. Could you...please, could you just not?"

He took another step closer. "I don't want to...snipe. What's wrong, honey?"

He watched the muscles in her throat work as she gulped. She raised her free hand to smooth a lock of hair off her face, and he noticed the tremor in her hand.

"Talk to me, Stacey."

Her lips pressed together, and she shook her head. "I-I can't, Mason."

He didn't want her to go, needed to find some way to keep her near him. "Are you taking your boat out?"

She glanced behind her to where it rocked. This time her chin quivered. "I was supposed to." Her voice was a whisper again. "I've got some logistical issues. Jace was supposed to crew, but something came up at the last minute..." Her voice trailed away. Mason could imagine what had happened, but he bit back his response. She turned a bright, brittle smile on him. "But hey, I still have a great weekend away from the capital."

"Come with me," he offered.

She started to shake her head. "It wouldn't..."

"We'll do day sails. I'll come back in tomorrow night. I was going to spend the night anchored in a cove, but we can come back so you can sleep aboard your boat. No strings, Stacey. Just a chance to relax."

He was tempting her. He could see it in the way her eyes darted longingly to his boat. There was nothing better than feeling the wind and the tilt of the deck.

"She's fast," he added. "Faster than Bran's boat. I've beaten him both times he's challenged me."

He watched her thumb twisting nervously at her wedding and engagement bands. Finally, she smiled. "I'd like that."

"Come on over at eight. We'll spend the day on the water."

She nodded, said good night and padded back toward her boat. It was only then he noticed she was barefoot. Sexy. It was something out of the norm for the always-correct Stacey Barlow-Barrett Winchester. Maybe the woman he'd made love to was still in there somewhere.

* * * *

She nearly chickened out a dozen times. But in the end she went, because she was a Barlow-Barrett, and she couldn't resist sailing on a boat whose captain had twice beaten Brandon in a race. No one else in the family could do it, even their father.

She put on her suit, covered it with a polo shirt and shorts, slipped her bare feet into deck shoes and shoved her hair inside a ball cap before slipping on dark glasses. If she kept the sunglasses firmly on her nose then Mason wouldn't be able to see the circles under her eyes.

Stacey realized as she traversed the distance between their boats she felt freer than she had in the past couple weeks. And then she felt a stab of guilt. She shouldn't feel free with her husband away. She tried to tell herself it was simply because she would be sailing and it had been such a long time, but in her heart she knew the relief was in being away from both Jace and Justin. Her disappointment the previous evening hadn't come from the fact her husband would be elsewhere, but that she would be limited in where she could sail without someone to crew, and she hadn't felt like hiring a stranger. It made her uncomfortable. It seemed like people available to hire were invariably men, and she didn't want to be on the water for hours with someone she didn't know. It was like asking to be assaulted.

A gull wheeled overhead, and a few other sailors were preparing to depart for a day out on the waters of the Chesapeake Bay, but Stacey had eyes for only one of them. Mason was on deck, his dark hair lifting in the morning breeze. Feet planted firmly apart, he sipped from a mug of coffee and watched her approach. When she reached the side, he held out a hand to help her aboard.

"Good morning. I didn't think you'd show."

He still held onto her hand, and Stacey felt heat. She gulped as warmth flooded her from head to toe. He'd always affected her like this. Why this man? Why not her husband? She pulled her fingers from his, dug them in the pocket of her shorts. "I did almost chicken out," she admitted. "Several times."

"But you're here."

What to tell him? How much could she admit without feeling like she was betraying Jace and their marriage? Stacey stared out at the water, so calm here in the marina, but she knew out on the bay, it would be much more turbulent. "I needed this time here…sailing." She turned to look at him again. "Do you ever feel like you're losing touch with yourself?"

"Yeah." Mason stuck his hand out. "Come on. Let's get out on the water. You captain, I'll crew."

She shook her head. "No. I'm only a mediocre sailor. You call the shots. I want to see what you can make her do."

She laughed, feeling suddenly more carefree than she had since… before her engagement. Guilt assailed her. Stacey ducked her head and went to work, doing her best to complete every task he gave her as quickly and thoroughly as possible. Once they were out on the bay, tacking a course southward, Mason grinned at her. "You're a helluva crewman."

She grinned back. "I've had plenty of experience crewing, first with my dad and sometimes with Brandon."

"What about your eldest brother?"

"Seth?" Stacey shook her head and laughed. "He's never sailed for speed. He's as likely to float around in the middle of the ocean while he daydreams. I never understood that because he was always so serious and driven other than when he went out on his boat."

Mason glanced sideways at her. "It must be his safety valve, like a pressure cooker. It's yours too, isn't it, except you want speed."

"Yes."

"You know, I can be an ear if you need to talk." He kept his eyes on the horizon ahead of them. Stacey watched him, wishing more than anything she could pour it out, but doing so would cross the line, especially with Mason. If he knew… No, she couldn't go there, even in her thoughts.

"I can't, Mason. It's not something I feel comfortable discussing… with anyone."

His gaze narrowed on her. "Okay. Enjoy the day. I can give you that much. Make yourself comfortable. She can pretty well sail herself until we get to the cove I had in mind. We'll anchor there and have lunch."

Stacey nodded before going forward to perch near the bow. She wrapped her arms around her bent knees and simply enjoyed the feel of the wind and the sun on her face. Periodically she had to tuck tendrils of hair the wind had pulled loose from her cap back beneath it, and she enjoyed that too. Jace always wanted her hair sleeked into a French twist or a snug knot at the back of her head. Going with her feelings for a change, Stacey whipped off the cap and let the wind simply blow through her long hair.

She wanted the sun on her skin, and a moment later, she peeled her polo shirt off to reveal the top of her very conservative bikini. She'd leave the shorts on for now, but she already felt her tension ease, which made her wonder at how circumscribed her life had become when simply letting her hair down and showing her bikini top became such a big deal.

* * * *

When she took the cap from her head and shook out her golden blond mane of hair, Mason groped on the shelf in front of him until he found his sunglasses. After slipping them on, he could ogle her to his heart's content without her knowing it, and most of all without making her uncomfortable. When she crossed her arms and grabbed the hem of her shirt, he felt his groin seize, then begin to pulse. His throat went dry when she pulled her shirt off to reveal the black bikini top she had on underneath. God knew he'd seen skimpier bikinis and he'd seen tops filled to overflowing, but he'd never seen one filled out quite so perfectly for him.

Jace Winchester had to be the biggest freaking idiot in the universe. No way would he leave a wife like Stacey alone on the weekend. In fact, he hadn't left her alone. She was here with him right now, but damn it, he wasn't about to cross the line, not when he'd realized her wedding vows actually meant something to her. Too bad the same couldn't be said... No, he so wasn't going there. He would simply enjoy the gift he'd been given and try to make sure she was able to do exactly what she'd said she wanted to--get in touch with who she was.

"Want to see what she can do?" he called to Stacey.

She turned her head and laughed. "I'd love to. Does this mean I should hang on?"

Mason grinned. "You got that right."

He eased the mainsail out to run the boat before the wind. As she gained speed, he glanced at Stacey. Hair blowing into a tangled mass of golden strands, her face was alight with enjoyment. This was a woman he had never seen before. He'd seen more than enough of the buttoned-down Barlow-Barrett lady of the manor and not nearly enough of the tigress she'd become during their sexual encounters. But this woman--laughing, giddy and almost girlish in her enjoyment--was someone Mason didn't know. He stared now, drinking her in just in case she disappeared, and wondered how he could keep this Stacey around. She was captivating.

As he watched, she made her way back to his side. "Please--may I take the wheel? Just for a few minutes? I want to see what she feels like."

"Have you ever sailed like this?" he asked, wanting her to try it, but not wanting her to take on too much.

"No."

"Then why don't I stand behind you and hold the wheel too, until you get a feel for it." When she arched a brow, he held up three fingers. "Scout's honor. I'm not playing you here."

She stuck her hands on her hips. "Were you ever a scout?"

"No. But believe it or not, Stacey, I do understand honor."

Her mouth quirked. "I'm beginning to realize."

She slipped between him and the wheel, her hair fluttering against his cheek as he put his face near hers. This would put his honor to the test. But not for long. In next to no time, she was handling the boat as if she had always done it. Although he knew she sailed, she'd admitted she wasn't an adventurous helmsman. Mason eased away, his eyes glued to the pure joy radiating from her.

"God! No wonder Bran loves this so much," she commented as her face lifted to the sails.

"We'll need to change course to reach my destination. You want to try it?"

For a moment, he saw eagerness in her expression before it faded. "No. Maybe not this time."

He took over from her, sad she didn't have the confidence to try, but encouraged by the fact her response indicated there might be a second time. "We'll slip into a cove that's normally pretty deserted other than a few shore birds. We can go swimming if you'd like."

She remained standing near him. "I'd love to." Stacey tucked a few strands of hair behind her ear. "Thank you for this, Mason."

The look she gave him was almost shy. When his heart clenched, he began to realize how little they actually knew about each other. Two years ago, they'd been consumed with getting the clothes off each other so they could have sex. But lust hadn't been enough. She had gotten engaged to someone else, and any chance they'd had to form a deeper relationship had ended.

He'd like to get to know her better, but the feelings he still harbored for her made it difficult, because along with the passion was the pain from her rejection. She had completely blindsided him with her sudden engagement to Winchester, destroying his trust.

He altered course and tacked toward the cove where he'd anchor. Stacey helped, doing what he asked without question. She'd stuck the baseball cap back on her head to keep her hair out of her face. As she worked, he saw the play of muscle across her arms and shoulders. Slender, she might be, but she wasn't weak. From what Mason had heard regarding her family, they'd spent most of their summers along the coast sailing or swimming.

They both stripped to suits once the boat was secure and went over the edge. Stacey cut through the water with the ease of someone as comfortable in the sea as on it. What amazed Mason even more as he watched her through the afternoon was how much freer she seemed, as if a heavy weight had been lifted from her shoulders.

As they finished lunch, he offered casually, "Let me take you out to dinner tonight. Just friends. There's a great oyster bar not far from the naval academy."

"I know it. It's been years since I've been there."

She hadn't said no. "We could split a pitcher of beer, have some oysters..."

"Okay."

Mason grinned. "Great! Why don't you sail back and I'll crew?"

"Oh, I couldn't..."

"Yeah. You can, Stacey. You've got the feel of her. Sail like you would your own boat."

Chapter 4

They were back in the hotel room. Jace slumped on the mattress edge. Defeat dragged him down. Justin sat next to him, but Jace couldn't even bring himself to reach out to him.

"I told you I would help, and I will," Justin said quietly. "I'm sorry there doesn't seem to be another way."

Jace swallowed, and swallowed again. Knowing he needed to say something, he finally choked out. "I feel like such a loser."

"Oh Christ, baby. You are so far from that. Look, getting the damn mumps wasn't your fault."

Jace shook his head. "It sure feels like it was. And you have no idea what a mess I've made of this whole thing."

"Then tell me."

Jace looked into Justin's deep green eyes, feeling like he was once again standing in the middle of the evergreen lined trout stream flowing through the Worthington ranch. He knew he had to come clean, at least with regard to part of it--the part that truly concerned Justin.

"When you left for Australia, I was hurt, devastated. I'd convinced myself I would lose you. You'd be on the other side of the world while I was stuck here running a business I never truly wanted." Jace took Justin's hand, twining their fingers. "I panicked. We've always been so careful. You've always understood why I wasn't ready to come out. My parents were never as understanding as yours."

Justin pulled his hand free, but only so he could put both of his on either side of Jace's head. "Tell me, babe. Tell me what happened, so we can work it out."

"I hit on a guy at a bar here in the district."

"Aw, Jace."

"We hooked up. It was supposed to be quick, anonymous, but the guy somehow figured out who I was, and I panicked he would out me, so

I called Stacey. We'd had a few pretty platonic dates in high school. I thought if I was in a relationship with a woman, no one would believe this guy if he did say anything.

"My mother was ecstatic. Not only was I finally dating a woman, I was dating the highly suitable daughter of one of her best friends. The pressure was intense, but I wasn't getting anywhere with Stacey, wasn't even sure I wanted to, and the pressure from my family was only getting worse. Then my hook-up surfaced."

"Please don't tell me you gave him money."

Jason sighed. "I did, trying to stall him while I figured out what to do."

"Then he could come back any time."

He shook his head. "I hate to admit this because I still only feel relief when I think about it--the guy was killed in a traffic accident on the beltway--but by then I was engaged to Stacey. With both our mothers already planning the wedding of the century, I was trapped."

The silence stretched for a bit. Justin rubbed his hand over Jace's shoulders, the touch helping him relax until Justin spoke again. "You said you weren't getting anywhere with Stacey. How did it change to getting engaged?"

Jason almost blurted the entire truth, but closed his eyes and said, "I asked and she said yes."

* * * *

Guilt gnawed at her while she sailed Mason's boat back toward Mac's Marina. She shouldn't be having so much fun, feeling so relieved, without her husband along. She glanced over her shoulder to where Mason lounged in the stern. He grinned at her and she smiled back. He was so much more relaxed here than at the gallery. Her encounters with him in the city were always so intense. First, when they'd jumped all over each other, then because he always went out of his way to stir her temper.

The man she'd sailed and swam with today was much kinder than the Mason she was used to. She wished… She didn't want to finish the thought, but she had scarcely any control over it. She wished she'd seen this side of him before agreeing to marry Jace. The thought was disloyal, and Stacey knew it wouldn't have mattered, in the end. She had been so determined to do what her parents wanted, so determined to avert any scandal. It was useless thinking anyway. She was married.

So why had she agreed to have dinner with him? At least the oyster bar he mentioned was a pretty small place. Her friends would be a lot more likely to hit some of the upscale places, if any of them were even on the bay this weekend. And she knew she wouldn't run into Jace or Justin.

They'd decided to go fly fishing along the New River when one of their college buddies' cabins became available on the spur of the moment. Jace had invited her, but Stacey hated any fishing that wasn't on the ocean. Too many mosquitoes and too much humidity. He knew she detested it, so she wasn't sure why he'd invited her to begin with.

Maybe to get me in a hot tub with Justin again? She shook her head, her attention lapsing enough that one of the sails flapped.

"Everything okay, honey?" Mason asked.

"Yes. Sorry."

By the time they reached the marina, it was already after five. "You want to grab a shower and I'll meet you in an hour?"

"That sounds good." Stacey told him. Back on board her own vessel, she used the bathroom next to the main cabin. The boat had been an engagement gift from Jace, though she knew Seth had given him a lot of advice on finding the right fit. For any of her brothers, it would have been a cinch to sail on their own, but she didn't have the same amount of experience they did, so she usually had someone crew. Brandon had always been a good choice when he was in town, but now he and Lucy were married, she probably couldn't count on him being available. After all, he had his own boat. Jace sometimes came unwillingly, but she'd always found those excursions turned tense. He was slow to do anything she asked, which made trips frustrating.

Today, she'd had a blast. Mason was an excellent helmsman and equally good at crewing.

After slipping on slacks and a neatly pressed button-down shirt, she started to put her hair into a knot at the back of her head. As Stacey stared at her reflection in the mirror, she slowly let her hands drop. Running her fingers through it instead, she scooped it back off her face and simply left it loose.

When she climbed topside, Mason stood on the dock, leaning against one of the supports, his own hair tied back at the nape of his neck. He straightened. "You look great. Ready?"

"Yes." She took the hand he held out to help her onto the dock and walked easily next to him toward the parking lot. She liked the fact they were nearly the same height, so for once she wasn't dwarfed. Amazingly, she discovered it didn't make her feel gangly or awkward. It made her feel safe. Brandon, Seth, Jace…and now Justin always seemed to loom over her. This was nice.

Mason handed her into his Porsche before sliding in on the driver's side. After starting the sports car, he glanced over at her. "You're okay with having dinner with me? I mean, it won't be a problem, will it?"

"No." Jace was hours away fishing. Even if he heard something, it wasn't like it was anything scandalous. She saw Mason a lot in the course of her work. They were business associates who'd spent a friendly day together. That was it. "I have to tell you, after a day out on the water, I'm starving."

Mason chuckled. "Me too." He put the car in gear and pulled out of the parking lot heading into downtown Annapolis.

The restaurant was exactly as Stacey remembered it, small and dimly lit, housed in an older building with plenty of ambiance. The crowd was light, and despite her assurances that going to dinner with him was not a problem, she was relieved to see no one she knew. As promised, Mason ordered a pitcher of beer and two glasses along with a bucket of raw oysters.

He made no attempt to start a conversation until after they'd taken the edge off their hunger and thirst.

"Have you heard anything from the newlyweds?" He plunked another empty shell in the bowl on their table.

"No. They took off in Brandon's sailboat and have been pretty much incommunicado other than quick emails from their ports of call to let us know they're okay."

"Lucy told me they were choosing between the sailing honeymoon or returning to Colorado."

Stacey nodded. "I think they're planning to go out there this winter when they can go skiing." She shook her head. "Lucy's got a lot more guts than me. I don't think I could go back anywhere near where their plane crashed."

"Lucy is an amazing woman," Mason commented. Stacey felt a twinge of jealousy for her sister-in-law, then immediately dismissed it. He was basically affirming what she had already voiced. "But then she had a tough life where she had to learn early on to make the best choices for her."

Stacey stiffened. She took a quick sip of her beer. "Are you implying the only way people learn how to make tough choices is by having a difficult childhood?"

Mason leaned back in his chair, his dark eyes narrowing. "I think it forces kids to grow up a whole lot faster."

Laura Browning

"Speaking from personal experience?" There was a bitchy tone to her voice even she could hear.

Mason finished his beer and set the mug on the table with a decided click. "Yes. I am. I've never tried to hide who I am or where I came from. The circumstances of my birth are not my fault, but I can take credit for who I've become."

"And I can't? Is that what you're saying?"

He crossed his arms across his broad chest. "I think you'd have to admit your parents have had an influence on the choices you've made."

"Is that so wrong?" Stacey knew she sounded defensive, but she couldn't help it.

Mason leaned forward, tried to take her hand in his, but she jerked it away. Lips pressed together he responded, "It is when you're forced to make choices that make you unhappy."

He was uncomfortably close to a truth Stacey wasn't ready to acknowledge to herself, let alone him. "There's nothing wrong with the choices I've made. I have a wonderful life."

"Why? Because you dumped me just so you could get the Winchester diamond on your finger? Was it what you wanted or simply another item on the list of things Stacey Barlow-Barrett should do?" He arched one brow at her.

Stacey took a quick sip of her beer. "And what is that supposed to mean? You arch your eyebrow. Why don't you come right out and say what you're thinking, Mason? I've never before seen you show any hesitation when it comes to speaking your mind."

He leaned forward again and put his elbows on the table, bringing his face uncomfortably close to hers. "All right. If the choices you've made have led to such a wonderful life, then why is it you're down here alone for the weekend and your husband is God only knows where?"

"He's trout fishing. It was a last minute opportunity, and he loves fly-fishing. I couldn't stand in the way…"

"Even though he'd already promised to come with you? It sounds to me like you're the one making the sacrifices. You've had to take in his… friend. I take it Justin went with him?" She nodded. "So your groom of less than a year is off fishing with his college buddy while you're stuck on your boat, not even able to get out because you needed Winchester to crew."

Stacey pushed her beer away from her and fumbled for her purse. "My marriage is not open for examination, especially not by you. Jace and I have a wonderful relationship. We're even trying to start a family."

She had the fleeting satisfaction of seeing his face go pale beneath his tan. His lips parted as if he wanted to say something, but then he clamped them tightly together. After slapping a couple of bills on the table, Mason stood. "Let me take you back to the marina, Mrs. Winchester."

The ride back was silent. Stacey stared out the window, wanting to say something to ease the tension between them, but not knowing how to begin or even what to say. He walked her to her boat, made sure she was safely aboard and turned away. She had to do something.

"Mason?"

He stopped but didn't turn. "What, Stacey?" There was weary impatience in those two words.

"Thank you for today. I had a wonderful time on the bay."

He glanced at her. "I did too. I'm sure I'll see you around." He walked away, but she noticed instead of returning to his boat, he headed for the parking lot. He was leaving. She felt as alone as she had when she'd first arrived Friday evening.

* * * *

A family. She was going to have Winchester's babies. Mason's jaw clenched as he slid behind the wheel of the Porsche, barely resisting the childish desire to spin his wheels as he left the parking lot. But no. He kept his temper and headed south toward his house. He didn't want to be anywhere near Stacey tonight. Even his boat a few slips over was too close. He'd spend the night at his house then head back to town in the morning.

After turning the Porsche into the dark drive, Mason let himself inside. He switched on the light over the stove so he could see his way around while he got a glass from the cabinet and grabbed a bottle of bourbon. When he'd splashed enough in the glass to satisfy him, he grabbed the heavy crystal and downed it in a couple of gulps. To hell with sipping, drunk was what he wanted.

He carried the bottle into the living room and flopped back on the couch. Kicking his feet out of his Sperrys, he leaned into the corner, propped his feet up and unscrewed the cap. After a couple swigs, he laid his head back and closed his eyes.

All he could see was Stacey as she'd been on the boat that day, her hair blowing in the wind, her smile and her laughter as carefree as he'd ever heard it. Most of the time, she seemed as uptight as the first time he'd seen her. But even then, Mason had felt the overwhelming tug of attraction for the cool blonde and her ice maiden beauty.

She'd stared down her nose at him with her golden eyes as if he was nothing more than a servant to do her bidding. Boy, had it pissed him off.

"If you'll bring the items in," she'd told him in a haughty tone, "I'll be able to tell you where they go. I seriously doubt your boss wants you loitering on his time."

He'd looked her up and down. "I don't answer to the boss. I am the boss."

She'd refused to believe him of course. But after their initial exchange had ended in some incendiary sex, he'd been unable to get her off his mind. He'd gone out of his way to see her, and her client's home had been an ideal meeting place. Had it been wrong? Hell yes, and that had been part of the fascination--but not all. Every time he'd put his hands on her, held her, made love to her, the emotions he thought he'd had such control over had flared, singeing him.

Mason took a long swallow from the bottle. It had seemed like a fairytale. He'd wanted to believe it was, but he should have known better. Fairytales didn't happen to men who'd had a whore for a mother and no father, only his mother's pimp, who had viewed Mason as just a unique addition to his stable.

Yeah, he knew about well-heeled men like Jason Winchester. Knew what they hid behind their expensive lifestyles and their Ivy League educations. At the core they were as rotten as an apple infested with worms.

But Winchester was the one with Stacey. Mason shuddered. He had to find a way to get her out of there.

* * * *

Stacey lingered around the marina as long as she dared on Sunday, but she never saw another sign of Mason. She felt like she should apologize, but for what? Tell him she was sorry she was trying to make her marriage work? That she was willing to give Jace the baby he so seemed to want because sometimes she wasn't exactly sure about her relationship? But the most frightening thought was she needed this marriage to work with Jace because she was in love with another man, one she couldn't have, one her parents had made more than plain was not acceptable.

And Stacey Barlow-Barrett never did anything unacceptable. The one time she'd tried, it had nearly ended in disaster.

Finally deciding Mason would not be back and knowing she couldn't wait any longer, Stacey loaded her duffel bag in the back of her car and headed back to Georgetown. As soon as she entered the house, she realized Jace and Justin were already back.

"Stacey?" Jace called from out on the back deck. "Come join us, darling, we're in the hot tub."

This time she wore her bikini. The two men weren't quite so inhibited. Stacey kept her eyes averted from her husband's friend as she slipped into the water.

"Did you have a nice time, darling?" Jace asked.

She smiled a bit uneasily. "Yes. I just puttered around the boat." Something made her not want to mention her day with Mason, almost as if talking about it would spoil it in some way. "What about you guys?"

Justin grinned. "We caught a couple fish, but released them. It was a great weekend, though, wasn't it, Jace?"

Her husband nodded. "Wonderful. Very relaxing. Would you like a drink, Stacey? I was going to make some margaritas."

"Sure," she smiled, "but just one."

Alone with Justin, she shifted. His green-eyed gaze was guileless as he looked at her. "So did you sail?"

"Some. Mostly I worked around the boat, sat on deck."

"Jace worried you might not go out without him to crew. Did you find someone else?"

"A friend there at the marina. It was fun."

Justin raked his fingers through his short hair. "Look, if my being here makes you uncomfortable…"

"No," Stacey protested, not wanting him to feel awkward.

He relaxed. "I noticed the bathing suit and everything…"

"I'll probably take it off later," she assured him, not intending to do any such thing if she could gracefully avoid it.

He smiled, his expression as innocent as a choirboy. "I'd be happy to look the other way. I don't want you to feel inhibited because I'm here."

Stacey smiled, feeling like she was being expertly backed into a corner. If she refused, it would seem she didn't want him there. Justin turned his back, and she felt like she had little option. She would take her top off, but that was it. As she set the bikini top on the deck, she said, "You can turn around."

Jace returned then with a pitcher of margaritas and three glasses already filled. He handed one to her and then Justin before setting the pitcher on the edge of the hot tub and grabbing his. Leaning forward, he smiled at them both and raised his glass. "To good friends and a fabulous future. Cheers."

Stacey drank. There was more salt than she cared for around the rim. Jace seemed to keep forgetting she liked hers without. She had to admit, the hot tub felt good because she was a bit sore tonight from sailing and swimming Saturday with Mason. As she chatted with Jace and Justin about their fishing trip, it seemed her glass was always full. Finally, after her fourth yawn in a row, Stacey giggled. "I hate to be a party pooper, but I can't seem to stop yawning."

"I'll take you to bed, darling," Jace said, setting his glass aside. As he stood, Stacey noticed he was already semi-hard. She giggled again.

"Jace, I'm going to go sleep."

She saw him wink at Justin. "I'll be back later, bro. Enjoy yourself."

Stacey tried to stay awake as Jace laid her on the bed and began to kiss her. As he usually did once things got hot and heavy, he turned her onto her stomach and raised her hips. She was feeling fuzzier and fuzzier, her head swirling with a dizziness that seemed to increase the sensations because she'd swear he felt different than normal, his thrusts deeper, his hands gripping a little harder…but she didn't want to question it. Jace was finally showing more interest in her. That was good, wasn't it?

* * * *

The following day turned into a real bear. It seemed she was running behind all day long. When she parked out front, Jace's car was already there. He'd gotten home early while she'd still been at Congresswoman Stanczewski's house, where they'd spent the last couple hours matching paint and fabric samples. At least Justin was nowhere to be seen, she thought as she set came inside.

"Stacey," he greeted her coolly from the doorway of his study. "After you put your things down, come in please. I have something we need to discuss." Without another word, he turned on his heel and stalked out of her line of vision. Sometimes, his mannerisms reminded her of her father…and not in a good way.

Looking around cautiously, she set her purse and her briefcase on the chair near the stairs. She would collect them later to take to her own sitting room so she could finish the drawings for the congresswoman to approve. From the silence, she guessed Jace had sent the staff home for the evening already, which usually meant they were going out to eat, but somehow, it didn't feel right tonight. In fact, this didn't feel right at all.

Smoothing her hands along the sides of her skirt, she stepped forward and spotted him standing near the fireplace, a frown drawing his dark brows together.

"Why were you out Saturday evening with Mason Hatch?" he demanded with no preamble when he saw her.

"We ran into each other," she began. "He's a business associate. You know that."

"People saw you together, Stacey. Friends saw you. Said it looked more like two lovers having a quarrel." He stepped forward and grabbed her wrist. "How do you explain that?"

Her heart beat heavily. "You know how he is, Jace. We were discussing some business and we disagreed. He made it personal." He still had hold of her wrist in a grip bruising in its intensity. When she tried to free herself, he snatched her closer, jerking her off balance. A gasp of surprise and fear escaped her. "Jason!"

"Did you think I didn't know about the two of you?" he demanded, his eyes narrowed to slits and his mouth thin.

"There's nothing between us…"

"Maybe not now," he interrupted. "And I emphasize maybe. But did you actually think I didn't know why you were in such a hurry to accept my proposal?"

Stacey struggled to get her wrist away from him. "Let me go…"

"Word got 'round, darling, despite your parents' best efforts. While you had already started dating me, you were fucking the gallery owner." He'd bent her arm behind her back at such an awkward angle, she couldn't move without injuring herself. She'd always known he had a temper, but she'd never seen it directed at her. "Accepting my proposal was just a way to stop the scandal after someone said they saw you inside a client's house…"

"Stop it…you're hurting me."

"Jace." Justin spoke quietly from the doorway. "Let her go. You're not doing yourself or her any good."

Her husband's eyes lifted to stare at the man behind her. Never had Stacey imagined she would be grateful for Justin's intrusion. Jace's hold relaxed. She twisted free and moved several feet away from him, hands shaking so badly she could barely wipe the tears from beneath her eyes. Justin was there in front of her, a handkerchief in his hand. When she tried to take it from him, her hand trembled so much, he closed his fingers around hers.

"Let me," he murmured. Stacey stared into his green irises as he blotted the tears from her face and tucked the handkerchief back in his pocket. "Let me see your wrist."

He had it in his grasp before she could tell him no, and it hurt too much to pull away. "I'm fine."

He looked back into her eyes. "You need ice on this. Get some ice in a bag, Jace. Do it now. You could use some cooling off too." He glared at her husband. A moment later, she heard his footsteps as he left the room. "He loves you a lot, you know. You hurt him."

"Nothing happened," Stacey whispered. "And he hurt me."

Justin shook his head, touching his fingers to her cheek. Stacey barely repressed the urge to pull away. "You should have told us yesterday you'd gone sailing with Hatch. The whole scene just now could have been prevented."

Stacey eased her hand from his and stepped back. So now it was her fault? And what was with the us? What stake did Justin even have in this?

Jace returned, looking contrite, an ice bag and a towel in his hand. "I'm so sorry, darling," he murmured as he handed it over. "There's no excuse other than being worried about you with someone like Mason Hatch. I guess I don't realize my own strength."

She took the offered items from him and even murmured an acceptance of his apology, but in the back of her mind was the niggling thought there was no sincerity behind his words. He simply sounded like he'd rehearsed lines in a play. "If you two will excuse me, I'm going to go upstairs and lie down while I ice this." She left the room and started up the steps, but realized halfway she'd forgotten her purse and briefcase. Slipping back down, she gathered them and turned to go back upstairs, pausing when she heard Justin speak.

"Jace, don't be a fool. You'll ruin everything you're trying to do."

"I don't want her fucking other men."

"Would it really be such a big deal?" Stacey nearly gasped when she heard Justin's callous remark.

"Yes," Jason bit out. "My family expects suitable grandchildren, not some bastards sired by a man who doesn't even know who his parents are."

"Then you'd better make sure you smooth things over, so you'll have the opportunity to get her pregnant."

Stacey had heard enough. She ran silently upstairs and into her sitting room to drop her purse and briefcase. So far there hadn't been any opportunity to get her pregnant because she had yet to go off the pill, a fact she hadn't yet told Jace. Acting on instinct, she opened her purse and transferred her birth control pills to her briefcase--something she had always kept locked so it wouldn't open inadvertently and spill paint and color samples everywhere. As she snapped it shut again and spun the combination, she felt sick. Was this what her marriage had become? Had it reached the point where she was half-afraid of her husband and hiding birth control pills from him so she could continue to take them?

She stared at her reddened wrist as she put the ice back on it. No matter what she might have hoped, there were already major problems with her home life and her relationship with her husband. For an instant, she recalled her day on the bay with Mason. He hadn't sniped at her, hadn't belittled her abilities. He'd encouraged her, praised her and made her feel like she could do whatever she wanted.

Stacey slumped in a chair, resting her wrist on her leg. As she stared at the ice pack, her eyes clouded over. Was avoiding a scandal, trying to protect her family and Mason, worth this? She blinked the tears away and took a deep breath. Mason had built a thriving business that depended on word-of-mouth, as did hers. Barrett Newspapers could survive almost anything, behemoth that it was, but Phillip might be another matter. He was building a law practice, had political ambitions. There was so much more at stake than a few incriminating pictures and her reputation.

So how in the hell could she hide the bruise?

Chapter 5

Mason didn't see Stacey until the middle of the week, and then only because he heard his assistant talking to a work-study student in the outer office.

"Something's going on with her. She was showing a client some stoneware in the back gallery when a delivery guy came in and let the door slam. She jumped so much she would have dropped the plate she was holding if the client hadn't caught it."

His assistant's tone was disbelieving. "Stacey Winchester? The ice-maiden?"

Mason closed the document he had open on his laptop and set his hands flat on his desk.

"Yes," the young woman interning with them confirmed. "She was shaking so much she had to excuse herself. I followed her to the restroom because I thought she might be ill." The girl's voice lowered, but Mason could still hear her. "She was wiping her face with a paper towel, and on her wrist, she had this terrible bruise…"

He didn't wait any longer. Mason slipped out the other door to his office, the one leading right out onto the landing overlooking the lobby below. Stacey stood there with the congresswoman's assistant. As she concluded her business and shook hands, Mason stepped to the railing. "Mrs. Winchester?"

Stacey looked at him, her face pale and faint shadows below her eyes. "I was ready to leave. I have an appointment with another client."

"Five minutes. That's all I need. Stay there. We can talk in the fine art room." He began moving even before he finished speaking because she looked like she was preparing to bolt. As he reached her side, he put a hand to the small of her back and half-guided, half-pushed her toward the room, shutting the door behind them unceremoniously.

"Mason," she protested. "What the hell are you doing? I need to leave."

"Show me your wrist."

She eased one hand away from him. "I don't have to…"

"Show me your wrist, damn it!"

She made a face as if she didn't have time for his antics, but he saw the fine tremor in her hand as she held the wrist in such a way it was still half hidden. "I tripped on board my boat Sunday and hit it. It's nothing."

He grasped her coat sleeve and pulled back the material. "Try a different lie, Stacey. That bruise encircles your whole wrist. It didn't come from a fall."

She snatched it away from him, and when she failed, glared him right in the eye. Tilting her chin she said, "Where it came from is none of your business. You're neither my husband nor my lover, so you have no right. Now, please, let me go."

Mason felt his blood boil, but seeing the purple marks on her delicate skin, he swallowed his temper. Chances were she'd already been frightened enough. After releasing her wrist, he jammed his hands in his pockets. "I apologize. You're right. It's not my place, but Stacey, if you need help…"

"I don't," she bit out. "Excuse me. I'm going to be late." She brushed past him, dressed in a classically tailored suit, not a hair out of place-- every inch the society lady she was, except for the bruise on her wrist.

Mason stared after her, his eyes lingering on the entry even after she was gone. He pulled his cell phone out of his pocket. It was tempting to call Lucy, who he knew would answer when she saw it was him, but he hadn't yet become so desperate he would interrupt a woman on her honeymoon, even if he had the feeling the groom would forgive him since it concerned his sister. No, during his years on the street, Mason had made friends in all sorts of unusual places.

"Detective Jones, please." Mason didn't have to wait long before the line was answered.

"Jones."

"It's Mason. I need some help."

"Anything you want. I owe you."

"You quit owing me a long time ago, but I can use a favor." He went on to describe what was going on. "Look, I need someone extremely discreet. These are some high-powered families we're talking about, and nothing needs to get out unless Stacey wants it to."

"Call John Smith."

"Right. Next you're going to tell me Smith is the guy's real name."

"It is. I'll text you his number when we're done. If anyone can find out what you need to know, he can."

"Thanks, dude."

"Like I said. I owe you."

Now all he would have to do was sit back and be patient, but patience had never been one of his strong suits. He would find a way to get her out, make her see what was happening. To get his mind off Stacey, Mason jogged back to his office and poured himself into his work. He had a couple of artists he was courting, and he was taking a look at more paintings than he had in the past. Although he would still keep his bread and butter in three-dimensional art, he had a lot of clients in the market for paintings to help decorate. It only made sense to be able to supply them himself instead of outsourcing to other galleries.

* * * *

Jason had been going overboard trying to make up. When she arrived home, another florist's box awaited her on the side table in the front hall. Stacey looked at it with near trepidation. She wasn't ready to simply forget what had happened even if he and Justin were treating her like a queen. Justin had taken her to lunch, then Jace had called late in the afternoon to see if she would be amenable to a quiet dinner, just the two of them.

She agreed. For one thing, it must mean Justin was going to make himself scarce. Maybe if it was only her and Jace, they could really talk, really work some things out. She stepped into the kitchen to see the cook and the housekeeper putting the finishing touches on dinner.

"Don't you do a thing, Mrs. Winchester," the housekeeper scolded. "Relax and get ready for dinner. We'll have it ready to serve once Mr. Winchester gets here and we'll leave you to it."

Stacey was tempted to ask the housekeeper to stay, but not wanting to be alone with her husband would seem strange. Besides, she knew the woman had a husband of her own she no doubt wanted to get home to, so Stacey stayed silent, simply smiling vaguely before she carried her briefcase and purse upstairs. Before she stepped into the shower, she swallowed her birth control pill and carefully placed the container back in her briefcase. This was something she'd have to confess to Jace. Soon, just maybe not tonight.

She'd finished her shower and changed when she heard a knock on the door. Jace had brought her a glass of wine as he came upstairs, kissing her lightly on the forehead as he handed it to her.

"You know," she murmured, "I should cut out the alcohol if we're trying to get pregnant."

He touched her cheek. "You don't drink much, Stacey, and it helps us both relax."

She smoothed a hand over her still-sleek hair. "Jace, I have a favor to ask."

"What's that?"

"When…I mean if…we make love tonight, could you…could we do it facing each other?"

He looked uncomfortable. In fact, she would swear he looked pale. "You don't like our lovemaking?"

Oh God, she hadn't meant it as a slight to his prowess as a lover, and she certainly didn't want to make him mad. She smiled at him. "Never mind… I'm being silly."

He smiled and held out his hand. "Come. Let's eat."

Jace kept her wine glass filled throughout dinner, then afterward handed her a glass of sherry before sipping on his brandy.

"This was lovely, Jace," she murmured as they headed upstairs. "You know I don't mind Justin staying with us, but it is nice to have some private time."

He led her into their bedroom. "I have an idea how we can use our private time."

To be fair, he attempted to keep things face to face, even spending more time than usual caressing her, but at the last moment, he turned her and entered her from behind. Stacey didn't protest. She'd had enough wine, she was feeling a bit too relaxed. Once he'd finished and pulled out, she simply stretched out and fell asleep. Sometime in the middle of the night, he woke her, again pulling her bottom to him. She started to turn her head, but he held her in place with one hand while he thrust deeply into her, his movements almost angry as he pushed toward orgasm.

"Jace?"

"Shh, darling," his voice came from somewhere above her. "Go back to sleep." She felt the bed shift and realized he must have risen. She should say something to him. He'd never taken her twice in one night before, not even on their wedding night, but the thought was lost as she slipped back into sleep.

The next morning, she found bruises on her hips. Stacey touched the small bluish marks, wondering if she should say something to him about being a bit gentler. He was sitting at the breakfast table with Justin when she came downstairs.

"Oh, darling," Jace said with a smile. "I'm glad I caught you before you left. I thought with this weekend being your birthday we could go to the beach house, spend the weekend there and celebrate."

"That sounds marvelous, Jace." She turned and smiled at Justin. "I spoke with your contractor yesterday. They should finish by the end of this week. Did you want me to go ahead and hire a painting crew to do the colors we discussed?"

"Yes. I see no reason to hold off."

She smiled, feeling more confident discussing her area of expertise. "Who knows, maybe we can get you moved in before fall."

* * * *

Justin waited until the door shut behind Stacey before he spoke. "Don't ask me to do it again, Jace. It's not right. I told you I would do anything to help you, but I have to draw the line at what happened last night."

"It would be so much simpler."

"For whom? For Stacey? Jesus, Jace. That was rape! I won't do it again. Is it supposed to be simpler for me? I have no interest in sex with a woman. I'm out of the closet back home. I want you to come with me. I want us to have a relationship. And if you think it's simpler for you, you're fooling yourself. If you insist on living this lie, I will agree to help, but only under certain conditions."

Justin looked almost frightened as he asked. "And what are those?"

"She must be aware of your fertility issues and agree to have me as a sperm donor."

"Okay. I can live with that."

"And she needs to know about us."

"Justin, let's not rush into this."

"We've been lovers for more than ten years. There is no rush."

Jace's hand shook slightly as he sipped from his coffee cup then set it aside. "We'll take her to dinner Thursday evening. I'll talk to her after."

It wasn't as soon as Justin would like, but it would do. He crossed to Jace's side of the table and bent to give him a hug. "Come upstairs, Jace. We have time before we have to leave."

Jace nodded, getting gracefully to his feet. Justin's heart ached. Jason Winchester wasn't an easy man to love, so hemmed in by his upbringing and his nearly paranoiac fear of admitting to the world he was gay. Nevertheless, Justin did love him. Somehow, he'd convince him to leave this behind, to come out to the ranch. Justin had his own parcel of it and an older brother already busy creating little Worthington heirs, so the pressure to be anything other than who he was had never been an issue.

What he wouldn't do was a repeat of last night. He burned with guilt even thinking about it. Stacey was a beautiful woman, and she deserved to be happy, but it would never be with Jace, if only he could make Jace see.

* * * *

Mason couldn't help it. In a complete reversal from before, he was now trying to see Stacey every chance he could, and what he was seeing, he didn't like. Already slender, she had lost weight she couldn't afford to lose. Every now and then, he would catch an expression of weariness on her face when a client wasn't looking at her, as if she weren't sleeping well at night. Something was definitely different. Stacey loved her work, and as long as he'd known her she always brought an overabundance of energy to everything she did.

Thursday afternoon, his assistant poked her head in the door. "Mason, there's a Mr. John Smith to see you." Her tone clearly showed she didn't quite believe the name. Big surprise, neither had he.

Mason stood. "Great. Show him in."

The detective was as nondescript as his name. Not an ugly man by any means. In fact, he was handsome in an understated kind of way, but definitely not a man who would stand out in a crowd. Mason supposed that was exactly the quality a client would want in a good detective. He held out his hand, and Smith took it with a firm grasp.

"Mr. Hatch. It's a pleasure to meet you."

"Call me Mason," he responded and gestured to a chair. Rather than going back around his desk, he sat in the chair across from Smith. "I take it you have something to report since you've gone out of your way to see me personally."

Smith nodded. "Yes, but I have a couple of questions I was hoping you might be able to help me with."

"All right. I'll try."

"First let me tell you what I've discovered so far. You asked me to find out more on Justin Worthington. I can tell you, his family connections are legitimate. His parents have large land and cattle operations both in the western United States and Australia. He has an older brother whose primary responsibility is running the ranch out west. Worthington was indeed out of the country during the time of the Winchesters' engagement and wedding. He has only recently returned. Right now, he's working here in the capital, part of a cattlemen's lobbying group."

"And his connections to Winchester?" Mason prompted.

Smith pulled out a tablet computer and opened his notes. "They met at summer camp in their early teens. Both attended the same camp in subsequent years. There were also a few other occasions when they visited each other. In college, they became roommates. Worthington, like Winchester, dated women, but on only a casual basis. Neither man has had a serious relationship with another female until Winchester married Stacey Barlow-Barrett."

Mason tapped his pen on his desk. "Are you saying in a roundabout way what I think you are?"

Smith set the tablet on the edge of the desk and leaned back. "Look, I'm going to be completely up front with you. Jones told me your background, so I know nothing I say will come as a shock. I'm bisexual. I've had a male lover a lot longer than a wife. If you believe the adage 'it takes one to know one,' then what I'm seeing with Justin Worthington and Jason Winchester is exactly what it appears to be--an intimate sexual relationship, though I don't think Mrs. Winchester is aware of it."

Mason leaned back and expelled a loud breath. "It's what I suspected. Tell me something, if I'm not being too personal, does your wife know about your lover?"

Smith smiled. "We have a unique relationship. We live together. This isn't what's going on here."

"But Justin Worthington is staying in their home." The idea Stacey would take part in such a triangle was making Mason slightly sick. It was one thing to think of a menage in theory, quite another when it concerned the woman he loved.

Smith leaned forward, his brown eyes narrowing. "I don't know what your interest is in this--I'm assuming it's Stacey Winchester--but what I need to know is do you believe she would be a willing party to a three-way relationship?"

"No." Mason could say so without any doubt whatsoever in his mind. "She is most emphatic about honoring her marriage vows. The whole Barlow-Barrett family wears their Catholicism on their sleeves, so to speak. In fact, she told me this last weekend she and Jason were trying to start a family…" When Smith looked surprised, Mason stopped. "What? Why does that surprise you?"

Smith picked his computer back up and scanned through his notes. "The last summer Winchester was at camp, he contracted mumps and had to be quarantined. There's every likelihood he's sterile."

Mason didn't like the picture forming in his head. It was no coincidence Winchester wanted to start a family right at the point where Justin

Worthington entered the picture. He looked at Smith. "I want you to keep digging."

Smith nodded, tucked his tablet back in the pocket of his jacket and stood. "If I find out anything more of significance, I'll give you a call."

Mason stood, shook his hand and escorted him to the door. "Thanks, Smith."

After the detective left, Mason returned to his desk, sat heavily and spun his chair to stare out onto the busy street. Now what the hell did he do? Deciding he needed to let Stacey know something, he started to call her but disconnected. What was he supposed to say? Hi, I've had a detective following you. That would be a good opening line, guaranteed to win her over. Not. She would hang up on him before he could even get to what mattered. It wasn't exactly like they'd parted on the best of terms. No, he needed to talk to her in person. She was usually in the gallery on Fridays. It seemed to be a good day for getting together with her clients, so he would have to talk to her then because she was equally unlikely to meet with him in person if he requested it.

Shit. Mason scraped his hair off his face and tucked it back into a ponytail. If he was lucky, business would keep his mind occupied until then, but the rest of the day was fairly slow. Mason had plenty of time to think over Stacey's situation--and the best way to approach her. He kept recalling the bruising on her wrist, how down she'd seemed the previous weekend and finally decided he would need to be subtle. She had looked so fragile earlier, Mason's gut clenched remembering.

He had an artist he was taking to dinner that night, a painter who was just beginning to make a name for himself with his portraits. Mason felt like he could give the artist a real boost, but it would also increase his business as well. Once the painter's portraits caught on, demand would increase for his other work as well--and that would be what Mason exhibited.

They discussed business over pre-dinner drinks before being shown to their table in the dining room of the expensive Georgetown restaurant he preferred to use for business. After placing his order, Mason sat back, his body tensing as he heard a familiar laugh. Gaze going to the door, he saw Stacey enter the dining room with Winchester on one side and Worthington on the other, but it was Justin who had his hand resting familiarly on the small of her back.

He and Smith had it wrong, Mason realized, his jaw hardening. There was no cover up, no lying going on. It seemed perfectly obvious to him Stacey knew exactly what was going on between her husband and Justin

Worthington and was a willing partner in it. And if she was looking a little fragile, then maybe it was simply due to an overactive sex life. He averted his gaze, looking at the table while he swallowed the fury boiling inside him. The thought of her with both men made him sick, but at the same time, he couldn't keep his thoughts from straying down that path. Did they pair off for privacy? Do it together? The images made him want to gag.

He looked at the young artist. "Excuse me for a minute."

He needed to step out and compose himself, but God Almighty, he had to walk by their table to get outside. There was no way he could simply walk past without saying anything. Too many people in the district knew them, would know there was some issue if he didn't stop to speak to her. It could hurt his business and Stacey's.

Fury barely in check, he stopped at the table, noting the way Worthington had his hand on her arm. "Good evening. Good to see the three of you." When Stacey didn't meet his eyes, he shook the men's hands. Finally, she extended her hand, and he shook hers as well. The faint tremor there made his gaze once again dart to her face, but the brittle, social Stacey he so disliked was firmly in place, her expression not betraying what her handshake did. She wasn't nearly as happy as she appeared.

Mason stepped out of the dining room and into the bar for a moment. He raked his hand through his hair, concern once again mixing with anger. Something wasn't right with the whole picture. Winchester nearly ignored his wife. Worthington appeared to pay her far more attention. In fact, had he never seen the three of them before, he would have to assume Stacey was married to Justin, not Jason.

He felt sick.

Taking a deep breath, Mason readjusted his tie and checked his BlackBerry. There was a message from Smith. When he opened it, the text was simply Smith's number and a message to call him first thing in the morning. Mason sighed and pressed his lips together in frustration. If it was something important, he needed to know now, while Stacey was here. Acting on impulse, he dialed Smith's number, but got dumped into his voicemail. Damn.

Mason shoved the phone back into his pocket and headed back to the dining room. He nodded at the people he knew, but didn't stop until he reached his table.

"Sorry about that. I had a call concerning some personal business I had to take."

By the time he and the painter parted ways, both men were satisfied with the deal they'd worked out. Mason would refer clients to him for portraits, and he would provide the gallery with some of his work and suggest clients use Mason's gallery. Mason had taken a cab to the restaurant rather than driving, and now he decided to walk back to his penthouse. Fresh air was a commodity that had felt in short supply in the restaurant's dining room.

Once home, Mason decided he would call Smith first thing in the morning. Only after he had the latest from him would he make any attempt to contact Stacey. It was time to tell her what he knew and see what her part in the whole affair might be. If she was happy with her situation, then so be it, time for Mason to move on and put her in the past for good.

The idea of cutting loose the emotions she'd stirred hurt. The idea of her with someone else still hurt. But Mason didn't need the kind of head job sticking around would bring. He'd had enough of psychological games before he finally took to the streets as a kid. As a successful businessman, he no longer had to put up with anyone messing with his head or his heart.

* * * *

Stacey wanted to shrug away from Justin's hand on her back as they entered the dining room, but one glance around told her there were simply too many people they knew, her clients as well as some of Jace's. Her husband would never forgive her. Her mother's voice drummed in her head. A Barlow-Barrett never creates a scene. Stacey supposed never creating a scene applied both in public and in private, and she could certainly see her mother living up to that, but she was finding it increasingly difficult to do so.

Jace had never been overly attentive in public. Open displays of affection embarrassed him, but when it reached the point where it seemed Justin was her escort and Jace merely along for the ride, that was too much. Still she smiled. She was a Barlow-Barrett, so even though she might have her own rebellion started in private by continuing to take her birth control pills, she wasn't ready to bring it out in public. In fact, she wasn't sure she would ever be ready, and it frightened her to think her existence could go on like this forever. The poster child for passive-aggressive--that was her.

"It was thoughtful of you, Justin, to take us out to celebrate my birthday early," Stacey told him, feeling guilty for the resentment still burning inside her toward him and her husband.

Justin leaned closer, resting his hand over her forearm. "I know you'll want to celebrate the actual day in private, so I figured you wouldn't mind a littler earlier public celebration. Jace is such a close friend, and I feel the same way about you, so it's my pleasure."

It was all Stacey could do not to cringe. Mason chose that moment to stop by their table. She saw his eyes rest for a moment on Justin's hand, and she couldn't meet his gaze as he shook hands with both men. Finally, knowing she had no choice, she offered him hers. God, she was shaking again! She almost snatched it back, but knew she couldn't, not when they were in such a public place. Instead, she pasted the expression on her face her mother had drilled into her from girlhood, the social mask concealing every worry or problem. She was good at it. She watched Mason's eyes harden, saw the faint tightening of his generous mouth. When he turned away from her, she wanted to yell at him to take her with him. She was instantly ashamed that even the thought she needed rescuing from her own husband had crossed her mind.

Dinner passed in a haze. Justin and Jace were both attentive, but their conversation seemed to flow over and around her rather than including her. She drank more wine than she intended, something happening to her a lot of late. Stacey was sure she would awaken yet again with the groggy, hungover feeling she hated after a night filled with bizarre dreams. By the time they left, she was grateful for Justin's supportive arm at her back.

For once, she went to bed and slept without any of those disturbing feelings of waking in the middle of the night wondering what was happening to her. She had slept so soundly, she hadn't even awakened when Jace came to bed. When she did rise the following morning, it was with a faint headache.

Knowing she had a busy day ahead of her, Stacey went ahead and packed a bag for the beach, leaving it inside her closet, so all she would need to do when she came home was change clothes, then grab it and go. It was her hope getting a solid couple of days on their own would help them clear the air about a few things, like her continued unease at the thought of having children at this point in their marriage.

She kissed Jace goodbye, disappointed when he turned his face so her lips brushed his cheek, and gave Justin what she hoped was a sincere smile of farewell. Then she was out the door and on the go until nearly lunchtime. When her phone rang, her heart sank when the caller ID showed it was her husband.

"Darling...I'm so glad I caught you. I have a client who's had to reschedule for later in the afternoon, so I will be a little late getting to the beach house."

"That's okay," she assured him, relieved he was only running late. "I'm swamped too. Why don't we meet there? It might save some time."

"That's a marvelous idea. I promise I'll be there in time to take you to a late dinner."

Stacey smiled, feeling better than she had in ages. Jace sounded sincerely apologetic that he would be delayed. With a bit of free time after lunch, she ran by the house to grab her bag. She could always change once she got to the beach. Everything was going according to plan. In fact, she finished earlier than expected in the afternoon. Good thing, too, because she realized she'd forgotten to stuff her bathing suit in her duffel bag. It would be easy enough to swing by the townhouse, change clothes and grab her suit, then head to the beach. She would still have time to get the beach house opened and aired out. Stacey hated spending the night in places that had the feeling of having been shut for an extended period of time.

She used her key to get in, disarmed the alarm, set her briefcase and purse down and kicked off her heels. As she did, her gaze took in two other briefcases--Jason's and what she had to assume was Justin's. Her gaze slid to the hall tree, where their suit coats hung as if put there in a hurry. Good. Maybe Jace had finished earlier than expected and they could travel to the beach together. Strange, though, he'd left the alarm armed... And why hadn't he called?

As she padded along the hall, she became aware of the sounds coming from his study. Heavy breathing followed by a low moan, then her husband's voice thick with more passion than she'd ever heard in it. "Fuck. That feels so good. Just like that. How the hell am I going to get through a weekend without you?"

Was he in there with another woman? Without giving herself time to think, to remember all those Barlow-Barrett gentility maxims her mother had drilled into her, Stacey swept into the room ready to give her husband and his girlfriend a piece of her mind. Screw passive-aggressive. She wasn't the daughter of a newspaperman for nothing.

Jason was sprawled in one of the chairs near the fireplace, his tie askew, his shirt partially unbuttoned and his lover kneeling between his legs giving him a blowjob. Except it wasn't a woman. It was Justin.

"Oh, shit!" Stacey swayed and thought for a moment she might faint. She blinked, hoping she was hallucinating, but when she opened them again, both men were on their feet, tucking in and zipping up. Stacey turned, wanting nothing more than to get out of there as quickly as possible, but as she reached the doorway, Justin grasped her arm.

"Wait, Stacey!" he implored. "Don't leave. You need to hear us out."

She jerked her arm away from him and spun to face him, her hand snapping out and slapping him across the cheek. "I don't need to listen to anything you have to say. Get away from me. You disgust me!"

Justin held out his hands and backed away a step, but it just gave Jace room to get by and block the doorway. "Stacey, I don't know what you saw..."

She laughed, an edge of hysteria in her voice. "What I saw? I saw you having your cock sucked by our houseguest while you moaned how you couldn't get through the weekend without him." She drew in a couple of breaths, trying to calm the pain and rage coursing through her.

"Stacey..." Jace muttered.

She glanced between the two men, an eerie calm now suffusing her. "This isn't anything new, is it?"

It was Justin who replied. "No. It's been going on since we were teenagers. We had hoped... Well, it doesn't matter now what we'd hoped."

"You're right about that." She took another deep breath. "I can't deal with this right now. Please let me out of here."

Jace moved toward her, acting like he wanted to take her in his arms. Stacey recoiled, pushing past him. She grabbed her briefcase and purse and fled down the steps to her car. Before she gave herself any time to think, she was behind the wheel and heading out of town.

She managed to make it to the outskirts before she had to pull over. Standing on the shoulder of the highway, she braced one hand on the hood of the car as she bent over and vomited.

* * * *

Mason had called Smith first thing in the morning, and what he'd discovered had Mason immediately trying to reach Stacey. Jace and Justin's fishing trip had been anything but fishing. According to Smith, the two men had visited a fertility specialist in New York. Both men. God. Were they somehow coercing her into bed with Justin so she could get pregnant? His stomach turned.

He got her voicemail.

"Stacey, it's Mason. Give me a call as soon as you get this message." He hung up and tried to concentrate on his business, but couldn't get her off his mind. Stepping out of the office, he looked at his assistant. "If Stacey Winchester comes by, I need to speak with her. Even if I'm out of the gallery, find some reason to stall her and keep her here until you get in touch with me so I can get back."

He hated to sound so melodramatic, but he knew Worthington had no reason to see the fertility specialist unless Jason had asked him to, and it could only mean he wanted him to play some role in fathering a child. Mason couldn't envision Stacey being willing to agree. But did she have to be willing? Did she even know?

When he didn't hear back from her, and she didn't show at the gallery, Mason went so far as to drive past her house. In desperation, he finally called her home number, something he'd found in the gallery's files though he'd never used it himself.

Just when he thought the answering machine would take the call, Jason answered the line.

"Winchester residence."

"Winchester, it's Mason Hatch. Sorry to disturb you at home. Something's come up at the gallery concerning one of Stacey's clients. Is she available?"

"We're going away for the weekend, Hatch. I'm sure whatever it is can wait until Monday."

Mason rolled his eyes, thinking quickly. "Normally, I would tell the client the same thing, but they're leaving town this evening..."

"That's too bad. Stacey left early, and I'm getting ready to follow her now, so you've missed her. I'd say if she's not answering her cell phone, then she doesn't wish to speak with you."

"If you would let her know I called."

"I'll make it the very first thing when I see her," was his sarcastic response. Winchester disconnected with a pronounced click.

"And fuck you too," Mason muttered to the dead line. He recalled the way Worthington had rested his hand at her back and then on her arm at the restaurant last night. "Hell, what am I even worrying about? She's probably getting ready to go away with both of them. Screw this." Mason snapped his laptop shut and stepped into the outside office. "I'm done. If you wouldn't mind, lock up, I'm going to spend the weekend on the bay sailing, fishing and knocking back a few beers, not necessarily in that order or priority."

He'd put her behind him. He had to. His mind replayed the day she'd arrived and flashed the Winchester diamond in his face. He'd pulled her into another room and shut the door.

"What's going on, Stacey?" he'd demanded, pointing to the ring.

She'd raised her chin, her ice maiden air firmly in place. "Nothing, Mason. I'm engaged..."

"The hell you are!"

"I've accepted Jason Winchester's proposal."

"You were dating him while you were screwing me?"

Her face had paled. The silence had dragged. "Yes. Jace and I have a lot in common. I've known him since high school."

Mason had felt such fury he'd wanted to hit something. Hit her. He sucked in a deep breath as everything inside him twisted into a knot. He laughed with a bitterness he hadn't felt in a long, long time.

"So what was I? The boy toy to play with until you found someone acceptable to Mommy and Daddy?"

She said nothing, simply raised her chin and stared at him from those golden eyes of hers--looking down her nose at him as she had the first day when she thought he was the delivery driver.

"Go to hell, Stacey." And he'd walked away from her without looking back.

He wanted to do that again, but doubt still niggled at him.

* * * *

"Jace!" Justin protested. "You have to go after her."

"She needs time to cool off." The truth was Jace didn't want to deal with this. He felt his world collapsing around him. For a short time, he'd thought he could have it all, a marriage that appeared to be happy and normal while he still maintained his relationship with Justin. His sterility had blasted those dreams out of the water.

He wasn't ready to come out, but he knew right now, the chances of him staying in the closet were pretty well shot.

Justin grabbed his shoulders and spun him around to face him. "Jace. Enough is enough. This isn't fair to any of us. You're living a lie that's eating away at you. Stacey's clearly in love with Mason Hatch, so I'm not even sure why she's in this marriage to you, and I just want to live my life with the partner I love."

Jace blinked back tears. "She's married to me because I blackmailed her and her family."

Justin's hands fell away and he stared at Jace. "Please tell me you're joking."

"She was meeting Mason Hatch. We'd started dating, hadn't discussed being exclusive, and I discovered she was screwing Hatch in some of her clients' houses. At the same time, my anonymous hook-up was squeezing me, so I squeezed her. I got pictures of her and Hatch, threatened to make them public."

"How did you expect to get marriage out of that?"

"They don't know it was me. But I knew how her parents would react, how she would." Jace felt tired, beaten. "Death over dishonor and all that. I popped in with an offer of marriage and I'm sure they saw it as a way to save face, a way to separate her from someone they would consider unsuitable."

Justin spun away from him, stalking over to the window and staring out into the street. "What's happened to you, Jace?" He swept his arm around the room with its antique furniture and Persian rugs. "The guy I fell in love with was happy with a fly rod and a flannel shirt. He wanted what I wanted--a life where we could be free to love each other. But this person you've become? I don't know you. I don't know this man who is so afraid to admit he's in love with me, another man, he would resort to blackmail to hide it?"

"Justin--"

"No! I don't want to hear anything else right now. I need some space."

Justin grabbed his suit coat and briefcase and slammed out the front door. Jace stared at it, willing it to open again, willing Justin to come back in and tell him he didn't mean it. But it stayed shut, and Jace's world unraveled.

* * * *

It was only when Stacey pulled into the parking lot of the liquor store in Annapolis she realized she'd left Georgetown without her shoes. After putting the car in park, she leaned over into the back seat and found her deck shoes in her duffel bag. Okay, so she wouldn't be making any fashion statement, but that wasn't her purpose for this visit. She fully intended to buy a big bottle of bourbon and get as rip-roaring drunk as she could.

After all, this was a celebration. She'd married a man who would much rather spend time with his male lover than her. And wow, didn't that take her self-esteem to new and unheard of lows. She walked into the store, heading for the bourbon section. As she scanned the bottles, her brows drew together. Who knew there were so many? She usually left purchasing booze to Jason or the housekeeper. And when Stacey did drink, it was usually wine or something after dinner. But this was a special occasion, and one she intended to do right. How many times could a woman honestly say her life was completely and totally fucked up beyond all recognition?

"May I help you, ma'am?" a man who looked to be in his fifties inquired politely.

"I need a bottle of bourbon."

"Are you looking for something to sip or to use in mixed drinks?"

Hmm, now that was a question. She didn't plan on mixing it with anything else, but she also wasn't planning to sip it. Still, if she was going to get herself rip-roaring drunk, then it would have to be something smooth going down. "I need a good sipping whisky."

"Let me suggest the Blue Silk. It's a single barrel bourbon with a very smooth taste, but the price is reasonable."

"Great," Stacey replied. In truth, she didn't care. She planned to drink it shot after shot. The only thing she knew about bourbon was Seth and Brandon both enjoyed it. If it was good enough for her older brothers, it was good enough for her. She paid cash, took the bottle in its brown paper bag and headed back to her car. She'd go to the marina, get on her boat, put her feet up and start knocking back the booze. She'd drink toasts all evening until she passed out. Here's to the life that had led her to marrying a man who couldn't give her an orgasm and apparently spent the few times he did fuck her fantasizing about his male lover.

Once on board, she set the bourbon on the counter in the galley, then stripped off her suit right there, slipping shorts over her lacy briefs and pulling a t-shirt on without bothering with a bra. She didn't even want to think about her body but couldn't help it. Tall, slender with small boobs. Had Jason only married her because she wasn't the typical curvy female? Had she reminded him of a boy? Had she reminded him of Justin?

When a soft sob escaped her, Stacey grabbed the bourbon bottle and headed topside. Curled in the stern of the vessel, she opened the bottle and tilted it back, not even bothering with a glass. Just so she wouldn't completely forget all her mother's Barlow-Barrett strictures, she held her pinky out from the neck of the bottle.

"There, Mother, see how correct I still am?" Stacey tipped the bottle back and swallowed another mouthful of the liquor, expelling a sharp breath. As the sun began to set, she considered the idea of trying to find some dinner, but she was too drunk to go anywhere and knew the only thing on board were some crackers and Cheese Whiz. She glanced at the marina office. She might not be able to drive anywhere, but she could at least grab a snack from the machines. Stacey stumbled below deck and dug out some change, laughing when quite a bit of it bounced over the floor. She'd clean it tomorrow.

Getting off the boat wasn't as easy as it usually seemed. For some reason, the dock and the boat were moving more than normal and it took her several tries to get her legs coordinated with the whole idea of stepping off the deck and onto the dock. Stacey stumbled a bit, laughed and headed to the snack machines.

Shit. When she drew close, she could see Mason standing at the ice machine. "Of all the gin joints in all the towns in all the world…" she muttered.

Mason turned. "She walks into mine," he finished. His gaze traveled over her from head to toe. "Jesus, Stacey. I've been trying to find you all day."

She weaved slightly as she concentrated on putting her money in the coin slot. "Here I am."

Mason stepped over to her side. "And you're drunk, honey." He looked toward her boat. "Aren't you supposed to be at the beach? Is Winchester with you?"

"No." She gazed at him, with narrowed eyes, trying to make his blurring face steady. "You're so handsome, Mason. Why didn't I marry you?"

"Now, that is the question of the year. Where's Jason, honey? He shouldn't let you wander around in this condition."

Stacey waved her hand. "I don't want to discuss him." She tried desperately to focus on Mason's face. "Would you like to come over to my boat for a drink?"

"Oh, I suspect you've already had enough for the two of us. Why don't I walk you back? Is Winchester already there?"

"Not coming." Stacey laughed, finding the double entendre immensely funny. Jace truly wasn't coming as far as she was concerned. After seeing him with Justin today, she realized Justin had been Jace's fantasy every time he'd made love to her. She stopped abruptly, and Mason nearly ran over her. Swiveling her gaze sideways to peer at him, she demanded. "Do I look like a boy?"

He looked confused. "Not at all."

"Do you like men too? Is that why you fucked me?"

She could have sworn she saw Mason's Adam's apple bob a couple times before he pulled her face against his broad chest and tucked her body close to his. "Oh, baby! Is that what this is about?"

The dam finally broke. Stacey clutched Mason's shirt in her fingers as her hands clenched and unclenched. She couldn't even feel any embarrassment when the first sob finally escaped as a whimper. "I saw them," she mumbled. "Justin and Jason. They were in Jace's study…"

"Shh. Don't think about it, Stacey. Not now. I'll take it to mean you're on your own here?"

She nodded, but then quit when her head spun uncomfortably.

"Come on. Just lean on me. I'll get you back to your boat."

When he lifted her easily on board then jumped in beside her, Stacey murmured in protest. "I'm too heavy."

"No. In fact, you've lost weight. Come on. Let's get you something to eat."

She watched him move around the galley as confident as if it were his own boat, and in a matter of minutes he had a bowl of soup in front of her with some cheese and crackers to go with it. She watched him while she ate and realized he was watching her as well, his muscled arms across his chest. After eating most of what was in front of her, she felt physically better, but her thoughts tortured her.

"I thought he was being nice, you know, inviting his friend to stay with us while his condo was being renovated. But the whole time..." She gulped, stared at the table. Finally she could stand it no longer, she looked at Mason and whispered, "Make love to me, Mason. Please. I feel..." She couldn't go on. At the moment, she couldn't even process how she felt-- Dirty? Used? Humiliated?--maybe a combination of all of those.

Mason leaned over, took her hand in his and gently stroked her palm with his thumb. Her mind immediately compared the hard feel of his hands to the softness of her husband's. She wanted to plead with Mason again to make love to her, make her feel like she was a woman someone would want. His gaze was on their hands. When he finally lifted it to her face, his voice was a soft rumble of sound, "I would like nothing better than to take you back in your cabin, strip off your clothes and make love to you from now until Sunday afternoon."

Tears welled in her eyes. "But you're not going to, are you?"

"No. Not because I don't find you one of the sexiest women I've ever met."

Stacey snorted.

"Don't, Stacey. Don't be so hard on yourself because one man is more attracted to his best friend than to you." He carried her hand to his lips, kissed it then simply continued to hold it in his firm grasp. "I won't make love to you tonight because right now you've had too much to drink and you're upset. When we make love, honey, I want it to be because we can come together as equals, happy about what we're doing and why--not because you need comfort."

It wasn't what she wanted to hear. "Please," she whispered. "I need this. Don't you understand? I walked in and saw another man giving my husband a blowjob! You have no idea how I feel."

"Don't do this to yourself, Stacey. He's not worth it."

"He's my husband."

"You're right," Mason said. "And if I did what you want, it would be the very thing you said you wouldn't do--dishonoring your marriage vows."

"He did it." A dull headache began behind her eyes and she rubbed her temples in exhaustion. "Why did he even marry me?"

Mason stood and tugged her to her feet. "Come on. You need to sleep. I'll stay with you until you do, okay?"

Stacey rested her forehead against his neck. "Thank you."

"Don't mention it."

* * * *

After she'd slid her shorts off, he helped her into bed, covering her and then stretching out next to her. It probably wasn't the smartest thing he'd ever done. In fact, as the warmth of her lissome body reached out to him, Mason decided he had to be a complete masochist. She watched him from her golden eyes, and he stroked the tangled hair out of her face.

"Go to sleep, honey."

Between the booze and her emotions, Stacey's lids drooped in pretty short order, but even after she fell asleep, he stayed with her.

How the hell had they gotten to this point? All he'd ever wanted was to make her his. Now she was married to a man who--at best--was bisexual, and Mason had doubts about that. He also had concerns he hadn't even shared with Stacey. She was simply too drunk to hear it. But they would discuss it in the morning, once she was sober and aware. Something wasn't right, and he feared Jason had his own agenda for ensuring he had a child, a downright insane agenda. No way could he spring that scenario on Stacey in her present state. She was already teetering on the edge of hysteria.

At last, once the marina had settled into silence for the night, Mason touched his lips to her cheek and slid quietly from the bed. She moaned softly in her sleep, her seeking hand going to the warmth he'd just vacated.

Enough. He had to leave. No way in hell would he endanger her reputation. God knew he'd seen how vulnerable her family was to attacks by rival media. Brandon and Lucy had been proof plenty. Mason would not be the cause of something similar happening to Stacey.

* * * *

Jace had waited in his study throughout the afternoon, drinking scotch and watching the room gradually darken without either Justin or Stacey returning. He had already given the servants the day off, thinking they would be going to the coast, so the house was silent and oppressive. Bracing his elbows on his desk, he buried his face in his hands.

He needed Stacey as a cover. If he could produce one child from their marriage, he'd bear the censure a divorce would bring. Didn't Justin understand a child was his ticket out of town? He could leave, join Justin on the ranch and no one would give it a second thought because he would already have done his duty, already have supplied an heir to the Winchester name. Even if the child couldn't be part of him, it could be part of Justin.

But for any of his plan to work, he had to have Stacey back. Somehow, he would have to convince her it was all a mistake, just the heat of the moment. She was key because he knew she would protect whatever child came out of their marriage. She would see the baby was raised as it should be.

Jace leaned back in his chair, poured one more scotch and sipped. He knew where he could find her. She would run to her boat. He'd given it to her for their engagement, but right from the start, he'd been jealous of any time she spent on board. It was her sanctuary, and first thing in the morning, he would talk to her, convince her to come back. She was his wife, damn it, and she owed him some loyalty, some forgiveness.

Who was he kidding? She wouldn't come back willingly, but there had to be some way to make this work.

Chapter 6

She had expected her dreams to be filled with images of Jace and Justin, if she could sleep at all, but it wasn't the case. Mason filled her slumber with his smooth voice and dark eyes that never seemed to miss a thing. He had been kind. It was something she wouldn't have attributed to him, although he had certainly shown kindness to Lucy when the media had come after her and Brandon. There had never been time in her relationship with Mason to see a gentler side of him.

She stretched, blinking at the first light of dawn coming in through the window.

"So you're awake. Did your lover tire you out?"

She stiffened. Jace, not Mason. She rolled over and snatched the covers, though why she did, she had no idea. Mason had made sure she kept her briefs and her t-shirt on before he sat next to her and held her against him until she slept.

"Don't start, Jace," she mumbled. "Why are you here?"

He straightened from where he lounged against the doorframe. "We have a conversation to finish. Just you and me, Stacey, no one else to interrupt."

"I don't think we have much to say to each other," she protested, feeling vulnerable. Jason stood there in shorts and a polo shirt, and she was barely dressed. Even if his eyes were bloodshot, he was groomed and together.

"Maybe you don't, but I do. You want to sit there looking like the injured party? Get off it, Stacey. We both had reasons for this marriage. I had family members starting to question the fact I'd never seriously dated any woman. You needed some way to stop the scandal ready to erupt over you and Hatch. Oh, yes, I can see you thought I didn't know, but I did. Plenty of people did."

"The pictures..." she stammered, remembering the humiliation when she'd opened the envelope and seen the photos someone had taken of her and Mason inside her client's house. Even worse, they'd been sent to her parents. She stared at Jace as if seeing him for the first time. The note included with the pictures had made vague threats about going public, but had asked for only a pittance of money. Stacey never knew what her parents had done with the pictures or the demand for cash, but she did know the edict they'd given her: end the affair, find someone from their circle of social equals and settle down. Jace had arrived on the scene right on the heels of that with an engagement ring in his pocket. How convenient.

"You set me up," she whispered, sliding her legs out and standing. She hated being at a disadvantage. "There weren't plenty of people who knew. It was you. You set Mason and me up."

Her husband shrugged. "We both got we wanted. Your scandal went away, and so did the potential one for me. No one would question my marriage to you. We'd hung out together as teenagers. I even took you to the prom, so we were high school sweethearts who'd found each other again. It was so romantic, no one questioned the fact we hadn't actually dated for any length of time before my proposal."

Stacey felt sick to her stomach, and it wasn't the effect of a hangover. "I wanted our marriage to work. I liked you, Jace. I thought it would be enough, but it's not--for you or for me." She raked her hair off her face. "I want a divorce, an annulment...something. We can't continue this farce."

Jace's mouth thinned. "Oh, but we can, Stacey. Those pictures can still go public, and imagine the scandal now. You'll be the slut, and I'll simply be the poor, cuckolded fool. My goals are still the same. I want a child."

"Get rid of Justin," Stacey blurted. "Then maybe we can talk." Had she really said that? Why was she even having this conversation? She should be storming out, telling him to go to hell. After what had happened, she couldn't actually allow him to make love to her. Hell, it wasn't making love. It was simply sex, but she couldn't do it, not even for the sake of avoiding a scandal that might drag her, her family and Mason through the gossip rags.

Jace moved into the cabin, drawing closer to her. It was all Stacey could do not to cringe from him. "Oh, but darling, I can't get rid of him. You see, Justin is a very important part of this equation. He's got my back, you might say, in more ways than one."

"Stop it!" she hissed, revolted by his innuendo. "I won't have your lover as a part of our marriage."

He laughed. "But I need Justin to be part of it. The last summer I was at camp, I caught the mumps from a younger camper. Do you know what mumps can do to a young man?"

"Sterile?" Stacey barely mouthed the word, her stomach roiling with a sick feeling. "Then how…"

"I had hoped Justin could be more than just my lover, darling."

Her mouth fell open in shock. "That's insane! How can you ask such a thing? I won't do it."

He arched a brow. "Oh, but you already have."

Stacey thought back to the night Jace had taken her twice. The second time had been so foggy, so strange. She gagged. "What did you do to me?"

"I didn't do a thing, darling. You did. You started drinking like a fish. If you'd unwind a bit, the whole thing could be done completely above board. Is it so much to ask? To have a child with you?"

"You want me to stay with you and let your male lover impregnate me? You're crazy, Jace." When he stuck his hands in his pockets, she darted past him and made a run for the steps, but he was too quick. He grabbed for her as she put her foot on the first stair, knocking her off balance. Stacey twisted, trying to stay on her feet, but she crashed heavily against the stairs, smacking her ribs on the edge of one of them. While she gasped for breath, Jace grabbed her by the hair and hauled her to her feet. Clamping his other arm around her waist, he dragged her back into the main cabin.

"You know, I never liked your long hair, but now I can see it does serve a purpose. So, how long until we can find out if Justin was successful?"

"Never," Stacey ground out between teeth she'd clenched in pain. She was still having trouble taking a deep breath. "I never went off the pill!"

As soon as the words left her mouth, she realized she might have made a huge mistake. The fury on his face was frightening.

Jace shoved her back on the bed, jerking her arms above her head and ignoring her cry of pain as he leaned over her, pressing against her injured ribs. "You're my wife, Stacey! I've tried to be what you want. Why can't you give me what I want? A child. Is it so much to ask?"

"Jace," she gasped. "You're hurting me."

His eyes filled with tears and she had to look away. "I can't let you go, Stacey. I need you."

"Not like this!" She tried to twist away, but pain shot, sharp and hot, along her side. His grip on her arms was bruising in its intensity. She'd never considered him to be strong. He'd always seemed so lean and urbane compared to Mason's just-came-in-off-the-streets look, but Stacey was trapped. Between his iron grip and her injuries, fighting wasn't an option, so she begged.

"Please, Jace. Let me go."

Tears rolled down his cheeks. "I can't. If I make love to you like this, face-to-face like you want, will you stay?"

Everything in her cringed. "No, Jace. You have to let me go."

"I'm sorry, Stacey, so sorry. I can't. Just give me a chance."

She heard the zipper on his shorts release.

"No!" Stacey screamed.

* * * *

Mason awoke with an uneasy feeling. He hadn't liked leaving Stacey alone the previous night, but for his own sanity, he'd had to get some distance between them. He wanted her, but not when she was hurting and vulnerable. He wanted the Stacey he remembered from the weeks they'd been lovers. He'd never experienced such a degree of passion before. That was what he wanted, and he was willing to take the time to get it.

He stood and pulled on a pair of board shorts and a t-shirt, sliding his feet into flip flops as he puttered around the galley brewing coffee and making toast. He'd check on Stacey as soon as he had some java. For a second, as he waited for it to brew, he thought he heard a scream, but it was just after dawn and the seagulls were wheeling and diving, crying as they found and fought over their morning catches. It had to be that.

After wolfing a piece of toast with butter on it, he poured two mugs of coffee and headed topside. A glance over at Stacey's sailboat showed him everything was still quiet—well, not quite. It looked like the stairs below deck were open, so maybe she was already awake. Mason was sure she'd appreciate some coffee. Taking his time he ambled along the docks to the slip her boat was in. "Ahoy, Party Girl! You awake, Stacey?"

Balancing the mugs, he stepped on board. "Stacey?" A faint sound from below deck made him frown. No doubt she was feeling the effects of having overindulged. Setting the mugs on the shelf right next to the helm, he braced his palms on the metal stair rails and slid into the main cabin area. "Stacey, honey? You hungover?"

"Mason?" Her voice shook, and sounded so breathy he was sure she must be sick. He stepped through the living area and into her cabin, ready to provide her with some hangover relief. She was huddled into a ball in the corner of the bed near the headboard, her hair tangled around her head and her arms wrapped inside covers she had pulled to her chin. Her whole body shook, tears tracking slowly down her pale cheeks.

The unease he'd felt earlier blossomed into full-blown alarm. As he stepped nearer, she cringed farther back into the corner, her eyes almost rolling back in her head, like a wild animal at bay. "What's happened?" he whispered.

"Jace…" Her shaking increased until her teeth chattered uncontrollably. He reached toward her but she shrank away. "No! No, don't touch me," she cried, then what little control she still had deserted her and she broke into a low keening moan, making his stomach tighten in a different kind of alarm. In his years on the street, he'd seen the aftereffects of plenty of women getting beaten, raped or both. Hell, he'd felt those same things. The question was what was he facing in this situation?

He held his hands up. "Not going to hurt you. I'll stay right over here for now." He couldn't see any bruising on her face, but then Winchester was probably too smart to leave visible marks. "What do you want me to do?"

"Keep…him…away."

"Done, baby. He won't come near you again. Now I need to know where you're hurt."

She lowered the covers, keeping one arm against her side and across her stomach. On the other arm, the one holding the blankets, he saw angry marks on her wrists that continued onto her upper arm and disappeared beneath the sleeve of her shirt. The bruises were bad enough, but he was more concerned with the way she held her other arm, and the shallowness of her breathing.

"I can see the bruises on your arm. Are your ribs hurt?"

She nodded. "I fell." He lowered his head and looked at her. Surely she wouldn't still defend the bastard. "Trying to get away." She paused to take a couple of shallow breaths. "I think something's broken, Mason."

"Then we need to get you to the emergency room."

"I can't do that," she whispered between her chattering teeth.

Treading carefully, he asked, "Why can't you, Stacey?"

"It would cause a scandal."

Fuck a bunch of scandal was what he wanted to tell her right before he went after Jason Winchester with his fists, and that was just to start. Instead, he pointed out reasonably. "If you think your ribs are broken, you need to have an x-ray."

Stacey tried to smooth her hair and tuck it behind one ear. "But if I go to the hospital, then they might see the other bruises."

Mason closed his eyes and took a deep breath to control the urge to kill now bubbling inside of him. "Where else did he hurt you?"

She averted her eyes and looked around the room, anywhere but at him. Then with a faint attempt at putting on the social mask he despised, she finally looked back at him. "He tried to rape me, but it wasn't... he couldn't...I can't really explain."

Holy shit. What exactly had Winchester done? He needed to get her to a hospital.

"Mason?" she whispered.

"What, honey?"

"Can a husband even rape his wife?"

He dug his hands in the pockets of his board shorts. "Yes, he can. And it is a crime." He paused. "Even if it was simply attempted, honey."

She nodded, glanced out the window for a moment. As he watched, he saw her slowly gathering her inbred poise around her almost like a protective cloak. "I see. If I went to the hospital, would they have to report it to the police?"

Mason shook his head. "No. They'll want evidence though, in case it's needed later on." As she continued to stare out the window, as if she was considering the idea, he asked, "Would you like me to call your parents... someone in your family?"

"No. No," she said in a perfectly reasonable and polite tone of voice. "I don't think it would be a good idea right now, but I would like to go to the hospital." She turned her head to look at him, her golden eyes wide and wounded. "Can you take me? I don't want an ambulance or anything."

God, no. That would cause a scene. People might know. Mason clamped down on the bitter thoughts running through his mind. "I'll take you."

"I don't think I can walk. Would you mind carrying me?" Her quietness, her reasonableness was downright scary. He needed her to be something--pissed, hysterical, anything but so closed in she seemed not to have any emotions whatsoever.

"Yes, honey. I can carry you. I need to grab my wallet and keys. Will you be all right if I leave you for a couple of minutes?"

"Yes. Mason...I only have a t-shirt on. I'll need clothes."

"Oh, Jesus, Stacey." Mason sat at the foot of the bed. He raked a hand back through his hair. "Can I touch you? Just to make sure you're okay."

She shook her head. "Not yet. I can't hold it together if you do. Maybe later, okay?"

Still that terrifying calm. He nodded. "I'll be right back."

He sprinted back to his boat, exchanged the board shorts and t-shirt for jeans and a polo shirt, slipped on his deck shoes then grabbed his wallet, BlackBerry and keys. As he dashed back toward Stacey's boat, he glanced across the marina. Brandon was back. God, he should tell them. No. It was Stacey's decision. Too many people had told her what to do or made decisions that should have been hers to decide. Whatever she wanted, he would do.

When he got back on board, she sat on the edge of the bed with a sheet wrapped around her. She smiled faintly at him. "I read somewhere you're not supposed to change clothes, but I don't think I could anyway."

He grabbed her duffel bag and shoved her deck shoes back inside it. Found her purse too. "Why's that?"

"It hurts too much." He noticed her breathing was shallow and her pale skin had a faint sheen of perspiration, he assumed from having wrapped the sheet around her.

Mason clamped his lips together then spoke, "I'm going to take these out to the car then come back for you. Stacey, you should know, Brandon's boat's back. I could get him and Lucy over here if you'd be more comfortable with them."

"No. Please, Mason. I'd like your help. I can't see anyone else…not yet. I don't want them to know."

Something that had lain tense and hurting inside him since she'd told him of her engagement uncoiled. "I won't leave you," he promised, "and I will keep you safe."

"I know." And with those two words every single bitter feeling he'd harbored evaporated. He would do anything for her because she meant everything to him.

No one was up and about yet, and if anyone did notice them, Mason couldn't care less. He cradled her in his arms, her lower body cloaked in a bed sheet, along the docks to his car. After settling her in the seat and helping her with the seatbelt, he paused and softly touched her cheek. She didn't say anything, just leaned into his touch and closed her eyes. Mason gulped. As he walked around the car, he blinked to disperse the furious tears blurring his vision.

Jason Winchester would pay. He would see to it even if he couldn't convince Stacey to file charges. What frightened him was he had the feeling he didn't even know a fraction of what had been happening to her the past few weeks.

* * * *

Justin parked in front of Jace and Stacey's townhouse and simply sat in his car for a moment, staring at the front of it. The conservative, buttoned-up exterior reminded him of Jason Winchester. He remembered meeting him at summer camp when they were both rebellious fifteen-year-olds. While he'd worn faded jeans and scuffed cowboy boots along with his hair pulled back into a ponytail, Jason had sported a shirt and shorts that still looked pressed and deck shoes so white they'd nearly blinded him.

Neither one of them had wanted to be there, yet they'd recognized the inner struggle they were both going through, and it had drawn them together. They'd been unlikely friends the first summer, slowly relaxing their guards enough to admit their struggles with their sexuality. The second summer they'd been inseparable, but it wasn't until the summer before college they'd confessed what they felt for each other.

Justin still felt the same way. It would be easy to simply stew in his anger and disappointment over what Jace had done, but he loved him too much to hold onto his negative emotions. Jace needed help. Justin had been calling him since early this morning with no luck. The answering machine picked up the house phone, and his cell phone went right to voicemail.

Stepping out of his car, Justin palmed the house key Jace had given him and sprinted up the front steps. After unlocking the front door, he checked the alarm system, but it was already disarmed.

"Jace?" he called, but didn't get an answer. He checked the downstairs when he saw he wasn't in his study, but other than finding his car keys sitting on a tray in the front hall, there was no sign of him. Justin's gut tightened. Jace was not in a good place, hadn't been for some time. "Jace!"

He raced up the steps and along the hall to the master bedroom, but when he thrust open the door, the bed was smooth and neat. As he turned back into the hall, he heard a rustle from the guestroom Stacey had given him. Heart pounding because he wasn't sure what he might find, Justin opened it.

Jace lay sprawled across the bed with one arm flung over his face. His chest rose and fell with short, erratic jerks. Justin closed his eyes, trying to let calm flow through him. Somehow, he needed to convince Jace it was time to simply let go.

"Jason, babe, don't do this. Look at me."

The arm came off his face. He had scratches on his nose and near his eyes. It looked like a bruise was forming along his cheekbone. Justin slid next to him on the bed, leaning over to take a closer look.

"What the hell happened?"

Jace turned his head away, but not before Justin saw the tear trickling from the corner of his eye. "I found Stacey on her boat."

Everything stopped. Justin wasn't even sure he drew a breath. When his heart started beating once more, he whispered, "What happened, Jason?"

"I tried to convince her we could work things out."

Justin brushed a fingertip over the bruise. "Was that guy there? Mason Hatch?"

"No," Jace mumbled, "just Stacey."

Holy shit. As gently as he could, Justin turned Jace so he would have to look at him. "What did you do, Jace?"

"I wanted to show her I could be who she wanted, that we could make it work."

That hurt because what Stacey wanted didn't include him. She'd made her feelings plain. Justin took a slow, steadying breath.

He made himself bring a mental image to mind of the Justin he remembered from two years ago. The man expertly landing a trout, then laughing as he took the fly from its mouth and gently released the big fish back into the river. There was almost no resemblance to the man who lay next to him now. This man was conflicted, depressed. He needed help, and Justin feared things had gone way too far for both of them, if what he suspected had indeed happened.

He would deal with those complications later. Right now, he was going to get Jace cleaned and sobered up. Then they were going to sit and talk.

* * * *

The next few hours passed in a blur of examinations, x-rays and questions. The hospital staff was amazing, but Stacey wasn't in the mindset to appreciate it. She wanted it to be over with. She wanted Mason with her. And somehow, she would figure out a way to explain to him what had happened, not just to her, but to them.

A nurse helped her shower then dress once they were through collecting evidence, filling out questionnaires. Her ribs were badly bruised, and her other injuries were superficial enough she would recover quickly, at least physically. They wheeled her out to the waiting area. Mason rose to his feet, brushing his hands along his jean-clad thighs. Concern mixed with uncertainty on his lean face.

"Ready?"

"Yes."

From over her shoulder, the orderly pushing her wheelchair said, "If you'll bring your car to the entrance, I'll wheel her out."

Stacey waited until they were in the car, then, fingers picking at an imaginary piece of lint on her slacks, she stated, "I can't go back to the boat, Mason. I don't ever want to get back on it again. I don't even want to see it. Could you...would you take me to your house?"

His fingers tightened on the steering wheel. "Jesus, Stacey," he ground out. "You don't have to ask. Of course I'll take you there. Are you ready to talk to any of your family or do you need more time?"

The thought of ever telling her parents made her cringe. "Not today or tonight. Tomorrow. I need time to think." She glanced at him. "Did you mean what you said on the boat?"

"That I'll keep him away? Keep you safe? Yeah, honey. Every word."

"Good, because I'm going to hold you to it." She would ask him later about moving in with him. Not now. She couldn't do anything now. All she wanted was somewhere safe to hide. "They gave me some pain medicine prescriptions."

He glanced over at her. "We'll get them filled on the way. Stacey, I've already taken a call from Lucy wondering where you are. Can I at least tell them you're staying at my house and will talk to them tomorrow?"

"Yes. I want Seth and Brandon there, but mostly...I need Phillip."

Mason looked at her from the corner of his eye. Her youngest brother practiced law and already had a reputation as a litigator. "You're considering legal action then?"

Stacey closed her eyes. "I want to explore my options. Mason, am I strange for feeling so rational about this? Is there something wrong with me? I mean, he attacked me, tried to rape me. I should be falling to pieces, but I don't feel that way."

He pulled into the parking lot of the CVS and cut the engine. "Your feelings are yours alone. So whatever you feel right now, nothing's wrong with it, nothing's wrong with you. I think you're one hell of a woman, and whatever you decide to do, I'll help any way I can. If you want me to go kill the motherfucker, I'd even do that. In fact, I wish you would tell me to do it." Mason leaned against the headrest and closed his eyes. "I'd do anything never to see such an injured look on your face again."

Stacey's throat tightened with tears, but she wasn't ready to shed any more. She had to hold it together, not for her family, not for appearances, not even for Mason. She had to do it for herself. She clasped his hand and held onto it. Mason moved it to his knee, his thumb slowly stroking her fingers. His movements stopped and he went still.

"Your rings..."

"I won't wear something that never meant anything to begin with."

Mason nodded. "Give me your prescriptions. I'll get them handled."

She closed her eyes and tried to keep her mind blank while he was gone. Plenty of things needed to be done, to be figured out and strategized, but for now she wanted to back away from it and catch hold of the strength she knew was somewhere inside her. She needed it right now, and it had to come from her. Yes, she wanted Mason's help and his support, but ultimately she needed to dig deep. She'd seen Seth and Brandon do it, and God knew her sister, Anna, had been forced to do it after having a baby without the father there to support her. Now it was her turn.

Maybe that was the secret she hadn't known until now. They had all been tested in some way. She had thought simply always doing what she was asked had been the right road. As long as she towed the line, her life would be perfect, or so it had seemed. She had begun to doubt it when the pictures of her and Mason had arrived on the scene. Now she understood. It appeared the only way anyone in their family could find any measurable degree of happiness was by going through utter hell to get there. And right now, she could identify with the hellish part of the journey.

When Mason returned with a couple of bags, she glanced from them to him. "I grabbed a few snacks. We'll get food delivered today, and figure out tomorrow when we get there."

"I like you, Mason. I wish I'd told you a long time ago."

"I like you too, Stacey, and don't worry. You're telling me now."

She leaned her head back, closed her eyes and smiled slightly. She would be all right, maybe not right now, not today or even tomorrow, but eventually she would be.

Chapter 7

His house didn't have that closed up feeling a lot of oceanfront properties seemed to have. Mason used it nearly every weekend. Sometimes more often. With it being just south of Annapolis, the house was an easy drive from Washington, and being there eased his tension. When they pulled into the drive, he glanced over at Stacey. She was looking at the house, and it seemed to him she relaxed for the first time since he'd found her.

"It's beautiful, Mason. So quiet. You must love it here."

"I do. I hope you will too. You can stay as long as you like." He opened his door and glanced back at her. "Can you walk or would you like me to carry you?"

Her hands knotted in her lap. "I'll walk."

Slowing his pace, Mason cupped her elbow and steadied her. When they entered the airy great room, he said, "Make yourself comfortable, honey. I'll get you a glass of water so you can take your meds, then get a room ready…"

She looked at him. "Can't I… Please, I don't want to be by myself, Mason."

He sucked in a breath. "All right. I'll put your things in the master suite."

He jogged down the stairs and back out to the car, collecting the shopping bags, her duffel bag and purse before heading back in. Mason kept glancing from the kitchen into the great room as he got out the meds- -an antibiotic and some Percocet--and poured a glass of water. Worry swirled through him that she was way too calm. Stacey was burying a whole lot that would have to come out at some point. He hoped he would be able to help her put the pieces back together again after the explosion occurred because he was terribly afraid if she continued to exercise such tight control over her emotions, when she did finally crumble, it would be utter destruction.

"Here you go." He held out the glass and pills, ignoring the way she'd jumped a bit when he spoke. She had a right to be scared. After taking the meds, she handed the glass back to him. "If you'd like to lie down, I can get you a blanket…"

She shook her head. "Not right now. I'd like to go outside. Just sit. Would you mind getting hold of my brothers? But, Mason?" She touched his hand and he paused. "Don't let them come over now."

He smiled. "I'll block the door with my body as long as you'll nurse me after they beat me black and blue."

Relief flowed through him when she smiled slightly. "I don't think you'll have to worry about Phillip, but Seth and Brandon… You're on your own there. Stopping them is like trying to hold back a tidal wave."

"There are soft drinks in the fridge, and I left the snacks I bought on the counter." He couldn't help himself, he caressed her cheek with his hand. When all she did was turn her golden gaze to him, he smiled. "Treat this place as yours, honey."

He watched as she grabbed a bottle of sparkling water and made her way out onto the deck off the kitchen. Only when the door had shut did Mason pull out his BlackBerry. He had Brandon's cell in his speed dial. Seth and Phillip were another matter. He took a deep breath. These weren't going to be easy conversations. He'd already experienced firsthand how intense Brandon was when it concerned people he loved, but it was him he would call first. He needed numbers to reach Seth and Phillip.

The phone rang several times before Brandon finally answered. "I've brought your artist home safe and sound from her honeymoon. Jeez, man, what are you, like a watch dog?"

"Bran…"

There was a pause on the other end, as though Stacey's brother heard something in Mason's tone. "What's up?"

"Stacey's here at the bay house with me. Winchester…" Mason paused. There wasn't an easy way to break this. "Shit, man, he beat her, tried to rape her."

"I'm on my way."

"No! Wait! She's…she's all right. I found her this morning on her boat and took her to the hospital. Brandon, she doesn't want to see anyone today. She wants some time to pull herself together."

"So she's with you? I thought you had the hate-hate thing going."

Mason swallowed. "It's never been hate on my part. Listen, man, there's been some real messed up shit going on at her place, but I'm not going to discuss it without her permission. I need a number to reach Seth…also one for Phillip."

"Phillip?" He heard Brandon release a long breath. "She's going to go after Winchester? Stacey?"

Mason raked a hand through his hair. "She's going to do something. She also doesn't want to be anywhere near her boat again. I don't want to leave her alone. You think you and Lucy could get the rest of her stuff out of it and bring it with you tomorrow?"

"Sure. We'll do it today and get the boat secured."

"One other thing… In case she does pursue legal action, leave everything alone like…like bed sheets or any…torn clothing." Mason stopped, took a deep breath, then growled. "Damn. I want to go kill the motherfucker, Bran, just choke him with my bare hands."

"Easy, Mason. I'm right there with you, but either one of us getting tossed in jail is not going to do her any good."

He turned away from the window so Stacey couldn't inadvertently see him. Pinching the bridge of his nose, he grated out, "Be glad you didn't see her."

"Mason--thanks for being there."

The breath he sucked in was almost a sob, and he felt embarrassed. "I'll take care of her."

He got the phone numbers for Stacey's remaining brothers, but he waited a couple of minutes to calm down before making the calls. When he explained the story to Seth, he was a bit more under control. He'd have sworn he felt his cell phone burn with the fury coming over the line from the eldest Barlow-Barrett sibling.

"I'll be there. You will take care of calling Phillip?"

"Yes."

"What about our parents?"

"She doesn't want them to know anything right now, Seth. If it were my decision to make, the police would already be involved, but I'm letting her decide what she wants to do."

"That's a tough one. My inclination is the same as yours, but I know you're right. She needs to call the shots." Seth sighed. "Call Phillip. He can offer the best advice."

By the time he got off the phone with the youngest Barlow-Barrett brother, Mason's emotions had hit overload. After cramming his phone in his pocket, he went down the hall to the master bedroom and shut the door. He wanted to slam his fist into something, anything, but he couldn't do that. Such a violent release of temper would only scare Stacey. He paced back and forth in the room, raking his hands through his hair before he finally stood at the bank of windows overlooking the bay. Tears rolled down his cheeks. As he brushed them away impatiently, he noticed he hadn't even shaved.

He felt so damn guilty. The three saddest words he knew went through his brain over and over--if only I. If only I hadn't left her alone. If only I had gotten there earlier. If only I had tried harder to find her Friday morning.

A knock on the door interrupted him.

"Mason? Have you talked to them?"

He cleared his throat and scrubbed the heels of his hands over his eyes. "Yeah. I was going to grab a shower and shave. You need anything?"

"No," she said through the door. "I'm going to lie down on the couch for a few minutes. The painkillers are making me a little sleepy."

"Right. I'll check on you when I get done."

* * * *

Stacey stood at the door, her brow furrowed. Mason hadn't sounded like his usual self, but then that had pretty much been the case since last night. She shook her head and walked slowly back to the living room with its oversized couches and chairs. She liked this house a lot. It seemed to be a reflection of the Mason she was beginning to know--casual and comfortable with a touch here and there of brightly colored art. Stacey sat carefully on the couch then stretched out. Even with the painkillers, she was still sore, and as much as the hospital had assured her that her injuries from Jason's assault weren't serious, she hurt like hell.

Stacey stroked the smooth leather and smiled. This house opened a door on a Mason she didn't much know--but would like to. She recalled the first time they'd met. She'd been going through a house with a client, deciding where they would place some of the artwork awaiting delivery that afternoon. Her client had needed to leave, so Stacey stayed behind to take delivery. Mason had arrived driving the truck, and since he was clothed in jeans and a polo shirt, she'd assumed he was the delivery guy.

Finally fed up with her attitude, he'd whipped out his wallet and shoved his driver's license under her nose. "What name do you see on there, Miss Barlow-Barrett?"

Stacey had snatched the license then felt her heart sink as she read it. "Mason Hatch." The owner of Mason's, one of the most exclusive, sought-after galleries in the area. Knowing she'd had some serious backpedalling to do, she'd handed it back to him. "Please accept my apologies..."

"For being an insufferably stuck-up bitch?" Mason's eyes had narrowed into glittering slits. "I think what truly needs to happen here is you need to reexamine how you treat the people who work for you."

"I really don't think…"

"Shut up. It's my turn. I've listened to you try to lord it over me for the past half hour and kept my mouth shut because, you know what? You are my client whether I like it or not. But what I learned is you seem to have no regard for people you consider to be of a lesser social status than you. I don't care for that. Now what you need to ask yourself is exactly how you're going to do business without my gallery as part of the picture."

"What?"

"I don't do business with snobs. I've worked my ass off to get where I am, and sure, not having you bring clients in might cost me for a month or so, but it will cost you in the long run. My gallery's reputation is strong enough now to trump your Barlow-Barrett pedigree, so you can take that to the next DAR meeting with my blessings. While you're stroking your pearls and congratulating yourself on not mucking up your bloodlines, I'll be counting the cash from the clients who are still coming to me… just not to you."

"You insufferable bastard!" Stacey had hissed. "You have no right to speak to me in such a way."

"You're in our nation's capital, honey. We're in the land of free speech and equality. Just because my mother was a hooker and my father's unknown doesn't make you any better than me. So fuck you. Have fun explaining why I'm driving away with the rest of your client's shit." He'd shoved his wallet back in his pocket and spun on his heel.

"Wait!" Stacey had called after him, catching him at the door by the arm. As soon as she'd touched him, heat flooded her, desire flared and all she could do was gape at him.

His expression had been one of impatience. "Yes?"

Stacey had released him and taken a deep breath. "Could we start again? Look, I've been running late and haven't had a chance to grab lunch. Can I take you to the deli on the corner and bribe you with food?"

"I'd rather have sex."

Stacey had stared at him. Jumping his bones had already occurred to her, maybe it was part of the reason she had been so bitchy. He was right. She was a snob. She licked her lips nervously and inquired in a voice reduced to nearly a squeak, "Right here?"

Mason had arched a brow and smirked, challenge lighting his eyes. He'd stepped closer to her, crowding her back toward the doorway behind her. "No, the dining room table would be better."

Stacey's entire body had throbbed. Her purse and her briefcase had dropped to the floor as Mason's hands grabbed her hips and pulled her to him. His erection pressed hot and hard along her stomach and her body reacted, swelling and melting for him.

"I'm not doing this for business," she'd mumbled.

"Good," Mason had growled against her mouth right before he kissed the daylights out of her. In what had seemed no time, she'd been on her back on the dining room table, her skirt pushed to her waist. After covering himself with a hastily produced condom, Mason had held her butt in his hands and pumped his hips between her thighs. As their coupling intensified, he'd bent over her to kiss her again. "You are so fucking hot. Do you know how often I've watched you and wondered what you would feel like wrapped around me?"

Stacey couldn't have answered if she'd tried. She was too busy arching her hips in an absolutely mind-blowing orgasm. Before he'd reached his own climax, she'd come yet again. In the aftermath, they'd simply stared at each other.

He'd adjusted his clothes and offered her a hand off the table before surprising her by helping her straighten her own clothing. "How about lunch now, only I'll buy?"

It was like he'd flipped a switch, knocking her completely off guard.

The next two weeks had been amazing. Stacey had never reacted to any man the way she did Mason. They'd both had commitments that made going out in the evening impossible, but they'd managed to meet at clients' homes, once even in the storeroom at Mason's. The sex had been hotter than hot. They couldn't get enough of each other, but time hadn't been on their side. Right at the point when he'd finally asked her out on a legitimate date, the pictures had arrived at her parents' home.

She shook her head and sighed, staring at the abstract work he'd chosen to decorate his house on the bay. So many mistakes she'd made because she had lacked the guts to stand up for herself. And look what it had gotten her.

* * * *

When Mason left the shower, he'd pushed through the anger and pain at what had happened to Stacey so he was fairly certain he could keep himself under control. She definitely didn't need to be dealing with him going all weepy and unmanning himself--or the reverse, letting his anger out. He was afraid what might happen if he got his hands on her husband.

After pulling on clean shorts and a shirt, he padded along the hallway into the living room. She was curled on her side, her arm snugged protectively around the ribs he knew had to be badly bruised. As quietly as he could, he covered her with a lightweight throw and continued on into the kitchen. After checking the fridge and the cupboards, he put together a list and called a local grocer who would deliver for a fee. He decided to order in pizza for dinner. With a soft chuckle, he wondered if Barlow-Barretts even ate pizza or if there was some social rule barring them from such a middle class activity.

Mason grabbed a beer and headed to the dock in the backyard. He left the back door open with only the screen shut so he could hear Stacey if she called him. Pulling out his BlackBerry, he called his assistant at home and told her he was going to be taking a few days off to handle some personal business. She would be in charge in his absence, but he told her if she needed anything to call him.

"Everything okay?"

He sighed. "It will be. Look, if any clients call asking for Stacey Winchester while I'm out, tell them she's out of town for a family emergency."

"Mason? Does this have anything to do with what the intern saw?"

"Yeah, but I can't tell you more. Just feed people the lines I've given you."

"You got it."

After slipping the phone back in his pocket, he hefted the beer bottle and tilted it. The yeasty flavor of it slid over his tongue and down his throat. There was so much he wanted to ask Stacey, and didn't dare. As he stared at his dinghy bobbing in the water next to the dock, he also admitted he had a few things he would have to tell her, like hiring John Smith to check out Worthington and Winchester. There were so many obstacles standing between them he wondered if they could overcome them. He wanted to. He wanted her. And for the first time since she'd dropped the bombshell of her engagement, Mason began to believe a future together might be possible.

He'd just polished off the beer when he heard her scream. Flipping the bottle around so he clutched it like a weapon, Mason raced across the yard, taking the steps two at a time. As he burst into the kitchen, his gaze automatically zeroed in on the great room. She was huddled on the couch, her face pale. No one else was there. He set the bottle down, rubbed his hand over his hair to smooth it while he caught his breath, then walked toward her.

"What's wrong, honey? You were sleeping. Bad dreams?" She nodded, obviously struggling to calm herself. "I could sit next to you if it would make you feel better."

"Please." The request was made in not much more than a whisper.

He eased next to her and stretched an arm along the couch behind her. She sat, tension radiating off her like heat off a stove and the cover still clutched in front of her like a shield. "It's okay. You're safe. The front door is locked, so are the windows. I had the back door open, but I was right out in the yard where I could hear you. I won't let anything happen."

Some of the tension left her shoulders. She closed her eyes and sighed. "I don't want to be like this, Mason, afraid of everything, jumping at every sound or bad dream."

"You want to talk about it?"

She looked at him from the corner of her eyes. "Yes, but I don't know where to start."

He held his hand palm up and simply waited. She slipped her hand in his and he squeezed to give her encouragement. "You know you'll probably have to go through most of it again tomorrow. You can practice on me."

She smiled slightly and rested her cheek on her drawn-up knees. "You make it sound like rehearsing for a play."

He kissed her knuckles. "No, not that, but maybe a chance for you to get yourself together like you said you wanted." Tears glistened in her eyes. "Aw hell, honey. I don't want to make you cry."

She swiped at her eyes. "I wish…" She stopped and shook her head.

"What…what do you wish?"

"That I'd been strong enough to tell my parents to go to hell, strong enough to stand up for what I felt for you."

Everything inside him stilled. He sensed a lot more behind her brief statement, so much going on beneath the surface that he'd never actually known. He'd wrapped himself in his anger and hurt after she'd announced her engagement, so rather than press her for answers, he'd simply walked away with his heart broken but his pride intact. He stroked her hand with his thumb. It was getting to be a habit, but it seemed to comfort her, and it sure as hell steadied him. He could use that now because he had a feeling he was about to find out what had happened between them had layers he'd never suspected existed.

She turned her head and rested her chin on her knees. She no longer looked at him, but she didn't pull her hand away. "I remembered the day I met you before I fell asleep today."

"I hope it wasn't what made you scream."

Stacey actually chuckled, which was what he'd hoped to achieve. "No. You were right that day, Mason. I was a stuck-up bitch and I did look down on people I thought weren't my social equals. It was what I'd been taught all my life, but I'm not casting complete blame on my parents. I readily accepted the brainwashing, internalizing it like it was a gospel handed down from the mountain. And even though you were the most amazing thing that had ever happened to me, I couldn't shake the belief you weren't up to Barlow-Barrett standards. Mother and Father would never look at you with the same approval they gave to Jace."

Mason couldn't help the growl that erupted. Just the mention of his name made his gut tense and his temper heat.

"He had called me the night before and made arrangements to take me to dinner. I went out with him because we'd known each other since we were kids. Sure, we'd drifted apart, but he had been a friend through high school and on into college. He asked me out again, and I went, but I realized pretty quickly it was a mistake. The only thing occupying my thoughts was how much I wanted to be naked with you." This time she squeezed his hand, worrying her lower lip with her even, white teeth. "I had never done anything against my parents' wishes before you pushed me down on that table and fucked me silly."

Mason's eyes widened. It still surprised him with her aristocratic looks when she popped out with anything vulgar. He looked away to hide the slight smile he couldn't help.

"Yes. Laugh if you must, Mason. Here I was, an adult, and all I could concentrate on was trying to make my parents' happy. Jace made them happy. You wouldn't have, so I kept the two things separate, but the more I was with you, the more I realized it was you who occupied my mind. There was nothing official between us, so it was easy to keep playing the game of using him to hide you. Jesus, even when Jace kissed me, I thought of you so I could drum up some response. As soon as I acknowledged that fact, I knew I needed to end it with him. And the whole idea scared me to death."

"Because of your parents?"

She shook her head. "No. Because you didn't seem to be interested in anything more than sex. You never made an attempt to see me outside work hours, and I wasn't assertive enough to demand to know why. I'd always been taught it wasn't ladylike, so I waited when what I wanted to do was ask you out, drag you out, force you to be a bigger part of my life."

Mason frowned as he stroked her hand. "I never realized, and you wouldn't have had to force me into anything. You were almost aggressive in dealing with vendors who weren't getting the job done to your satisfaction, and never hesitated to give clients your opinion, so the idea you might be hesitant about us, about any of your personal relationships, never even occurred to me."

He blew out a puff of air. "I have to admit to being guilty of my own brand of snobbery. I hesitated to ask you out because I'd already convinced myself you'd say no. Then when I finally did and you agreed, everything went to hell. The next day you arrived at the gallery with that damn diamond on your finger and a phony fucking smile on your lips. I wanted to kill you."

"I know you did. I wanted to do the same thing...kill myself, that is."

"Huh?" Mason felt as if the world had somehow shifted, or at least his perception of it.

"The evening after I agreed to go out to dinner with you, I got a call from my parents. My presence was requested immediately. If you knew my family, you'd realize that's like being asked to come to the principal's office or being served a summons. Choice doesn't factor into it. So I headed to their house in Virginia, the whole time wondering what I might have done wrong. I never did anything wrong. Anna might have screwed up, but not me. I was the good child. I'd kept my association with you out of the public eye...or so I thought."

She turned her head and looked at him with her sad tiger eyes. "They had pictures Mason...of you and me...in my client's house...in their kitchen."

"Fuck me."

He remembered that day. He'd made an excuse to leave the office and meet her there. He'd no sooner gotten in the door than she'd dragged him back to the kitchen, pulling off his clothes as they went. Of course, he'd been doing the same thing to her. There was a window seat looking out onto the backyard. The secluded backyard. They'd taken turns going down on each other.

Mason could never get enough of her. She was like a drug in his system and he'd sworn he'd find some way to make it permanent. Deep inside, he knew her lady of the manor act wasn't all act. At her core, it was part of who she was, who she'd been raised to be. But right then, holed up in their client's still-vacant home, with his lips trailing across her stomach and into the nectar between her thighs, he forgot all that and simply lost himself to the God-awful lust he felt for her. He didn't even need to see her. Just the sound of her voice drifting to his office had been enough to make him want to drag her away from whoever she was with, drag her into his office, a closet--wherever he could get her alone and get his hands and mouth all over her.

He'd sat her on his lap there on the window seat of the house and loved her until she'd come again and again. He loved the way her long, blond hair tumbled over her bare shoulders, the way she arched backward with her eyes squeezed shut in pleasure so overwhelming she almost looked like she was in pain. He'd been right there with her every step of the way.

Still naked, they'd fed each other from the food they'd brought with them, and he'd taken her one more time, her long legs wrapped around his neck.

Then their fledgling relationship had exploded, leaving him wounded, angry and wondering what the hell had happened. At the time, all he'd been able to deduce was her inner core of arrogance had finally pushed her away from him, away from the guy with no pedigree, the guy with no true parents or really any family at all.

He stroked her hand now, realizing they had both become victims. "Oh honey, I'm so sorry."

She shook her head. "How could you know? It was bad enough my parents saw pictures of the two of us, but there was a note with them too. It demanded money or copies of the pictures would be sent to rival newspapers. I know now where those pictures came from."

"Winchester?" At her nod, Mason's rage stepped up another notch. "So what happened?"

"I guess my parents took care of paying off the money, but what concerned me was the demand they made of me in return. They would only make it go away if I dumped you and found someone of my own background. They wanted a committed, settled relationship, pronto."

"And Jace happened to be waiting in the wings with the family diamond."

She nodded. "I didn't love him. I never did, but I liked him. I thought it would be enough. Our mothers were friends. We'd known each other forever. I'd seen a couple of my sorority sisters turn social alliances into decent marriages. I thought I could do the same. I kept telling myself I was doing it for you, I was saving you and your business from a scandal that could ruin you. But the truth was, Mason, I was too weak to fight for the man I--" She stopped.

"The man you what?" he prompted, his voice hoarse.

She looked him straight in the eye. "The man I loved. I told myself it was lust, I would get over it, but I haven't," she whispered. "And every time I saw you I died a little more inside. I realized on my wedding night what a colossal mistake I'd made. Jace…"

"You don't need to tell me this."

She rubbed her hand over her forehead. "I do. I need you to know, please? I don't want there to be any secrets between us. I want you to understand. Is that okay?"

Mason chuffed, then nodded. He couldn't deny her, if this would help her in some way.

"He would never look at me. It makes such revolting sense to me now. He tried to talk me into cutting my hair, but failing that, he wanted it in a bun or a twist. He barely touched me, and when he did it was as if he was getting it over with as fast as possible, never like it was with us."

Mason couldn't stand it any longer. She had been so passionate with him, and he could only imagine how such coldness would have shut her down on so many levels. The past year and a half were now so much clearer. He needed to be able to offer comfort, and he hoped she could accept it.

"Come here, honey. Let me hold you."

She curled into his side, her cheek against his chest and her hand clenched on his shirtfront. With a deep sigh, she continued, "I thought there was something wrong with me, so I started faking it. He seemed happy, my parents were happy, so I tried to ignore the fact I wasn't. I was pretty good at it too, except when I had to see you. Then a few months ago, you started dropping these cryptic remarks. What was with that?"

"Just a feeling. I wish like hell now I had acted on it sooner. I'd seen him around town with Worthington. Then that day at the wedding, I didn't have any proof, I just knew. It's a guy thing. But I got proof."

Stacey pulled away a bit, studying him. "What do you mean?"

"After you came in with the bruise on your wrist…" Mason hesitated, but they were being honest, and she certainly wasn't holding anything back, so he needed to do the same. "I hired a detective. Not to follow you--Smith was getting information on Worthington and your husband for me. I was worried about you, honey."

She was silent for so long, her gaze focused straight ahead, that he began to get nervous. "What did you find out?" she finally asked.

"Background, mostly on Worthington. How the two met. That sort of thing."

"So, tell me." She turned her face back to him, and he was relieved to see her expression didn't hold any condemnation.

"They met in summer camp, attended the same camp for years, visited in between summers and eventually became college roommates. Neither one ever had a serious relationship with a woman until Jace and you. There were a couple of other things."

"Those were?"

"The weekend Jace bowed out of sailing with you to go fishing with Justin--they weren't fishing. They both visited a male fertility specialist in New York." He stopped abruptly as she began shaking again. "Stacey?" Mason tilted her face to his, and what he saw in her expression made him want to commit murder.

"That was why..." she mumbled, stopped and then continued to tremble. The control he thought he'd built crumbled like a tower of children's blocks tumbling under the onslaught of a careless hand.

"Oh God! Something else happened?" She didn't answer, but he saw it in her expression. Mason pulled her onto his lap, careful of her bruised ribs, wrapped his arms around her and simply rocked her.

"Jace wanted a baby," she whispered.

Mason remembered her telling him they were trying to start a family.

"I was uneasy with Justin in the house. I felt like the outsider when the two of them were together. I was not sleeping well, and I started drinking. One night... I thought Justin had made love to me twice, but that wasn't true. He told me this morning... It was Justin the second time."

He rocked her, stroking her hair and rubbing her shoulder. "Is there a chance you're pregnant?" He so didn't want to know, but he would stand by her no matter what.

"No. Something made me keep taking my birth control pills. I even hid them from Jace," she whispered. "When I told him... That's when he lost it this morning."

A shudder went through Mason. "I should have done more the minute I saw the bruise on your wrist. I've seen this before. I knew where it was going."

Her hand crept up, cupped his jaw. "It's not your fault. I have my own list of 'if onlys,' and trust me, it's much longer than yours. I feel so stupid." She laid her cheek against his shoulder and was quiet for a moment. "Mason?"

"What?"

"Does it make a difference?" Tension stiffened her body. "I mean..." She stopped and sucked in a breath with a hitch in it.

"I know what you mean. You don't have to say it. Not a bit of difference. Stacey, I love you."

She broke then, crying like her heart would shatter into so many shards it could never be fixed. He let her do it, let her get it out, and if his own eyes blurred, if he had to swallow a few times while he listened to her, then it was okay. People spent too much time trying to hide what they felt. "Get it out, Stacey. Get it out, honey."

"I hate them, Mason," she whispered at last. "Jace hurt me physically this morning, but the other…he and Justin…that's so much worse."

"It is. They violated your trust in the worst possible way."

"He told me if I didn't come back, do what he wanted, he'd leak the pictures."

Mason tilted her face so their gazes locked. "It won't happen. We'll make sure of it."

Chapter 8

Jace concentrated on keeping his hand steady as he poured coffee for himself and Justin. "I'm telling you, I'm fine."

"I think you need to get an attorney."

Jace smiled as he handed the mug to Justin. "There's no need. She won't do anything to cause a scandal."

"I still think we would both be wise to retain counsel. Jace, I'm going to get in touch with our family attorney. I'm sure he'd be happy to represent you too."

"She'll come around. We'll be able to make this work."

Justin shoved his coffee away and stood. "I'm going upstairs. Alone."

That finally penetrated Jace's haze. "I thought we could be together."

Justin's mouth thinned. "I'm here to give you support if you need me, but, Jace, until you get your head around this, I think it would be better if we gave each other some space."

Not even waiting for a reply, Justin spun on his heel and stalked from the room. Jace took a half step after him then stopped. Justin didn't understand. His family was so laid back, so supportive. He just didn't get the pressure Jace had always been under, and now Justin was simply adding to it. There had to be a way to fix this situation so he could keep Justin and still avoid humiliating his family. The Winchesters might never have been the most prolific at guaranteeing the family name would go on, but as far as Jason knew, there'd never been an openly gay male in the family. He released a long, heavy breath. He didn't want to be the first.

* * * *

Mason fed her pizza for dinner. While he had beer, she had sparkling water since she was on pain medication, but they drank from the bottles and ate the pizza with their fingers. The only other time in recent history Stacey could remember eating such an informal meal was when Mason had taken her out for oysters.

He gave her privacy to change clothes and get in bed, offered to sleep in a chair or on top of the covers if it was what she wanted. But it wasn't. She needed to feel his arms around her. She wished she could have handled more, but it was enough for now. And when she awoke in the morning and saw him watching her, it was more than enough. It was wonderful.

Stacey stroked his beard-roughened cheek, watched his dark eyes search hers with concern. "Thank you," she murmured.

He stroked her hair away from her eyes and ran his fingers around the shell of her ear. "Thank you for making one of my fantasies come true--waking next to you, seeing what you look like in the first flush of morning. And you're beautiful, Stacey, the most beautiful being in the universe."

"I wish…"

He put his fingers over her lips. "No wishes for what might have been. We're moving on together from where we are right now, not hiding, not running away. I can do it if you'll be there with me. Can you?"

"Yes. Would you kiss me…even with morning breath?"

His answer was to touch his lips to her forehead, the tip of her nose and then her mouth. She let her arms creep around his neck, felt his hands stroke and caress, but not confine her, and she relaxed against him. There was no fear with Mason. He brushed his tongue along the seam of her lips, and Stacey opened to him. As they continued to taste one another, his body shook. Stacey drew back, looked into his eyes.

"What's wrong?" she murmured.

Mason closed his eyes and took a deep breath. "It's just…I want you so much. I'm afraid I'll scare you."

"I'm not scared now." She leaned her forehead against his. "You could hold me next to you."

He bumped his forehead against hers gently. "I'm aroused. If I hold you…"

Stacey took a deep breath. Bad idea. She wanted to be comfortable with that, but she wasn't. "I'm not ready."

He kissed her lightly on the cheek. "Then I'll go get breakfast started. Why don't you shower and dress while I cook?" He rolled away from her. He was trying to keep her from seeing his arousal, but there was little hope of that. Stacey gulped and shut her eyes. Only once she heard him zip up his pants and the door shut behind him did she open her eyes again.

When she eased from the bed, she was relieved to find she wasn't nearly as sore today. While her ribs still hurt…the bruises on her hips and thighs were no longer painful. Once she was out of the shower, she opened Mason's closet, found a dress shirt and slipped it on before she pulled on the shorts from her duffel bag. Spying her purse next to it, she reached in and located her phone. With a deep breath, Stacey pulled it out to check her messages. There were six.

Feeling her stomach knot, she sat on the edge of the bed and connected to her voice mail.

"Darling." Jason's disembodied voice made her start to shake. "Where are you? Call, I need to know you're all right." She started to hit erase, but something held her back.

"Darling, we need to discuss what happened. I never meant to hurt you. Please call."

"Stacey, it's your mother. Jason is very worried about you. As his wife, I would hope you'd remember the consideration you owe him. I simply don't understand what's gotten into you. Please call as soon as you get this." She erased her mother's message.

"It's time to quit playing games, Stacey." Jason's voice was colder this time. "We need to talk. Don't be foolish."

A soft knock at the door preceded Mason opening it an inch. "Stacey? You decent?"

She paused the playback. "Yes. Come on in." As he stepped in the room, she added, "I borrowed a shirt. I hope you don't mind."

He grinned, his dark eyes warm. "Not at all."

She lifted her phone. "I had some messages, so I decided to check them."

His gaze roamed her face. "Why don't you bring it into the kitchen? I'll be there with you, and you can get a cup of coffee." He didn't need to add he didn't want her listening to them on her own. She understood and felt the same.

"All right."

She waited until she'd had a couple sips of coffee before continuing. The next message was another from Jace. She put it on speaker. "You have twenty-four hours to get in touch with me, Stacey, then those pictures are going public. I won't take the risk of waiting." She took a deep breath and punched save once again. When she glanced at Mason, his face was pale and his eyes nearly black with anger. He set his egg turner down and folded his arms across his chest.

"We'll stop him, honey. Don't you even worry about it."

Stacey took a deep breath, simply drawing strength from the idea of such unconditional support.

The last message was from her mother. "I must insist you call. Jason's told your father and me how upset you became at the idea of starting a family, how much you've been drinking lately. Darling, talk to us. If you need some time away, there are several lovely facilities not far from here…" Stacey punched save.

"Honey? Talk to me, okay? Don't hold it in." Mason sat next to her and took her hand in his. Only when she felt his steady grasp did she realize how much she was shaking. But this time it was from anger.

"I saved them, well, except for the first message from my mother. I don't know much with regard to the law, but maybe Phillip can use them." She tapped her fingers on the table. "I need to talk to my mother. He's pretty much told her I've gone over the edge because he wanted to start a family. Nice, huh?"

Mason put his hand over hers to still her tapping fingers. "Eat first, then call your mother."

She sighed. "You're right, because I'm sure I'll be so angry after I speak with her I won't be able to eat anything. I think I'm about to get a real feel for what Seth, Brandon and Anna have been through."

Mason arched a brow. "Haven't you already faced their wrath when you had to accept Jace's proposal?"

"Not really, because I didn't face their wrath, I caved in without a fight. All I got was the speech informing me of their grave disappointment and my responsibility to the family." Stacey stared him in the eye. "But this time I'm not giving in."

"Good girl. You want me to leave while you make your call?"

"No. I'd rather you were sitting right here. Do you mind?"

He released her hand and gestured toward her plate. "I'll do anything you need, Stacey, but first…eat. You've lost weight you can't afford to."

"I haven't been able to eat very well for a long time."

"And I go and make you sick at Brandon's wedding." Mason frowned.

"No, I faked that to get away from you," she had to admit, "but then I had to make myself sick because I knew my mother would come in after me, and I felt compelled to make the lie a reality. I've been such a coward, such a fool, lying to save a marriage that was a sham from the start."

"You're safe now, and I don't think you're a coward or a fool. Eat."

She stared at the fluffy omelet, toast and fruit. After she'd swallowed the first bite, she glanced at Mason. "You made this? It's wonderful."

He smirked. "I haven't always been some useless rich guy. I've actually had to work, and one of those jobs was as a cook."

"A cook, a sailor, an amazing lover and a knight in shining armor...are there any other talents I need to know about?"

He grinned. "I have a very checkered past, with some very shady friends. In fact, say the word, I can make a couple of phone calls and take care of Jace and Justin without incurring legal fees."

"As tempting as that might be, I think I'm leaning more to rocking his carefully constructed world, especially after the message threatening to make those pictures public. And I'm betting Phillip will do the legal work pro bono." Stacey continued eating, only becoming aware of Mason staring at her after she'd swallowed a couple more bites. "Do I have crumbs on my face or something?"

"Or something," he said quietly. "Are you sure this is what you want to do? I ask," he hastened to add, "because it seemed more in character for you to try to handle this as quietly and discreetly as possible. That's the person I've always known you to be."

Stacey set her fork to the side. "Mason, if you can stand the heat, I think I'm about to become the most rebellious Barlow-Barrett yet. I want out of my marriage. I'd like to do that as quietly and quickly as possible--that's where Phillip comes in--but if quiet isn't possible, then this could make Lucy and Brandon's media feeding frenzy pale in comparison."

"Does this mean I'm likely to see my bare ass in some newspaper?"

She laughed. "They'll blur it."

Mason arched a brow and smirked. "That's comforting, 'cause, you know, I've been worried I might be getting cellulite." When she laughed, he took her hand. "I'm with you whatever you decide you have to do."

Stacey nodded, then finished her food and took a final sip of her coffee before pulling her phone toward her. After taking a deep breath, she looked at Mason. "Here goes."

He set his hand on her forearm. "Are you planning on telling them what happened?"

She shook her head. In the back of her mind was the fear her mother wouldn't believe her. Stacey pressed her lips together, knowing she needed to say something. "I'm afraid to hear what her response would be. And God, Mason, who in their right mind wants to tell their parents their husband's lover raped her, or her husband tried to?"

Mason's mouth tightened into a thin line. "Jesus, Stacey. You don't know how hard it is for me to keep from hunting him down and killing him. I could still make those phone calls..."

In a strange way it was comforting to know he meant it. "Thanks, but no. I want all of us to get a turn."

Mason stood and gave her shoulder a squeeze. "In case I haven't said it yet today, you're a hell of a woman, Stacey. I loved you before, but I have to tell you, this tough, new you is pretty darn sexy."

She watched him begin taking care of the dishes as she dialed. It rang only twice before her father answered. "Stacey...are you all right?"

"I will be. Thank you for asking."

"Jason said you've been having some problems. He spoke to your mother, so let me get her on the line too."

There was momentary silence, and then her mother joined the call from a different extension. "Stacey, darling, wherever you are, let us know. We can send the chauffeur to drive you. I've already looked into a very nice facility not far from here. They have room and can take you now. It's very private, very discreet. No one need know."

Stacey felt her nerves set on edge. "Know what, Mother?"

"About this little problem you're having. Jason is so upset. He told us all the details."

"I'll bet he did. Would you care to hear what I have to say?"

"Darling, how much more could you really add? This facility has an excellent reputation. You'll be well in no time."

"Father? Do you have anything you wish to add?"

"I would rather hear what you have to say."

Bless him. Perhaps her brothers and Anna had affected him after all. It appeared her mother was a different matter. She had always adored Jace.

"Jace and I have been having some difficulties recently."

"He explained that, dear," her mother interrupted, "And you know your duty is to support your husband and provide him with children."

"Stop it, Mother!" Stacey finally snapped. "For once, would you listen to me?"

"There's no need to take such a tone..."

"There's every need. I am going to say this, and say this only once. I have left Jason. I will never go back to him again. I will not go into everything that's occurred because it is private, but I will tell you this: Friday afternoon I caught him in our home with his lover. I left and went to my boat. Saturday morning, he showed up. We had a disagreement about his relationship and the future of our marriage. He hurt me. Mason Hatch had to take me to the hospital." Dead silence met her. Mason had come to stand behind her, his hands gently massaging her shoulders. Finally, Stacey inquired, "Do you have any response?"

"Darling," her mother began in a soothing tone. "Just tell us where you are..."

Stacey interrupted her with a bitter laugh. "You know, I expected nothing different from you. So be it. I'm sure you'll be hearing more on this shortly, but it won't be from me. Goodbye."

She ended the call then turned off her phone. All she could do was sit there. Her mother would rather believe Jace than her own daughter. It was much more acceptable to believe her daughter had a drinking problem and was close to a nervous breakdown than to believe Jace Winchester had attacked her.

"Stacey?" Mason's hands stilled on her shoulders. "Are you all right?"

"No." She pushed her phone away from her and turned in the chair. Mason pulled her into his arms. "He made them think I'm having a nervous breakdown and have an ongoing alcohol problem." She clenched her hands into fists against his chest as pain seared her. "They believe him, not me. My parents believe the man who tried to rape me."

* * * *

Mason's throat tightened. He hugged her tightly and swayed to and fro. He'd never truly experienced what a family should be. After social services finally yanked him from his mother and her pimp, his childhood had been a series of foster homes and institutions--if he wasn't actually living out on the streets--so he'd become accustomed to distrust and disbelief from adults. Many times, in his case, the lack of faith had been justified. Although he didn't know the disappointment she felt now, he did recall the euphoria when a high school teacher had taken an interest in him early on, becoming his mentor. What she felt now must be the polar opposite.

"I believe you. Your brothers will believe you. Most importantly, should you decide to pursue it, I think the police and the courts will too." He wished he could offer more comfort, but she showed him it was enough.

Stacey took a deep breath and straightened away from him. "How long until my brothers get here?"

"A couple hours."

"Can we both fit in your dinghy?"

"Cozily, but yes. Would you like to go out? We'll stick to the inlet here so we can be back in plenty of time. You want to sail her?"

Stacey smiled. "I think I would. Maybe you can give me some pointers."

Mason waited for her on the back deck. She was handling this so much better than he'd expected. Despite what had happened, despite the reaction of her parents, she was standing up to it and showing him an inner strength he hadn't suspected. The strength was there, but the confidence wasn't.

When she stepped outside, her hair in a ponytail stuck through the back of a cap and a smile on her face, he couldn't help but smile back. God she was so beautiful like this--no make-up, his borrowed shirt, and shorts that left those long, tan legs bare for him to stare at.

When she reached him, he caught her wrist. "Come here," he murmured and tugged her to him, overjoyed to see how willingly she came. Tilting his head sideways to avoid the brim of her cap, he covered her lips in a quick kiss. "You're so sexy, just like this. I thought so the weekend you sailed with me, but even more so now with you wearing my shirt."

She laughed. "You're kidding, right? I have no make-up on..."

"I know. But you have no idea how mushy macho I go inside seeing my threads next to your skin. The only sexier sight was waking to you this morning and seeing the flush of sleep still on your face."

Her lips parted slightly, and his cock twitched. She was turned on. That look he knew all too well. He touched his fingers to the open neckline of the shirt, careful to keep the contact light and teasing even when what he wanted to do was lick her from head to toe and show her how good they would still be together.

"We'd better go sailing before I have to take a cold shower. Somehow, I don't think the brothers Barlow-Barrett would look kindly on me tenting my shorts for their sister."

She set a hand against his chest and looked at him, eyes wide with wonder. "I didn't think I would, but God, I want you. I'm just too tender right now."

He kissed her again, then took her hand. "Let's go. We'll both get our minds off what's still ahead and just enjoy the wind and the water."

As he'd already seen on his own boat, she was a better helmsman than she believed herself to be. It amazed him how someone from her background could have so little confidence in herself in so many areas. He wondered if it was a trait of all the Barlow-Barrett women or just her. As she guided the boat out, tacking with a natural instinct that kept everything moving with smooth efficiency, he finally commented, "You're a natural sailor, honey. Why do you have such a lack of confidence?"

She glanced at him. "I didn't always lack confidence. I mean, I wasn't as outgoing as the rest of the family when it came to sailing, but I was competent until Jace came along. He always criticized what I did and how I did it. There were plenty of times we ended up dead in the water, sails drooping, and I would be so embarrassed."

Mason grinned. "Sounds to me like you had a substandard crew. Now I, on the other hand, have crewed for some serious sailors. It's why I beat your brother when we race."

"Brandon was on Harvard's sailing team."

"And? So was I. Well, after I learned to sail."

Stacey shook her head as she looked at her sail. "I still can't believe you didn't learn how to do this as a kid. Lord, I feel like I've been sailing my entire life. The only one in the family who doesn't is Anna."

"Why didn't she?"

Stacey giggled. "It made her seasick. Poor thing. Even though I was insanely jealous of her, I felt sorry for her. Here the rest of us were, tall, blond and as comfortable on a boat as on land, and Anna was short, dark-haired and started turning green as soon as she looked at a mast bobbing in the water."

Mason studied her. "Doesn't sound to me like there was much for you to be jealous of."

She lowered her eyes as they both maneuvered through another tack. "She was short and curvy and incredibly determined to find her own way. I can't remember a time when she wasn't standing defiantly against Mother and Father. Good grief, she ran away from boarding school when she was a kid and hid out at Seth's school until someone ratted them out."

"Sounds like Seth didn't toe the line either."

Stacey laughed. "No. He stomped all over it, but he also had a sense of duty that wouldn't let him take off the way Anna did."

"And what about you?" Mason's voice was quiet.

"I wanted everyone to be happy, especially my parents. I did my best to please them."

He glanced at her as she adjusted course. "And let me guess, you never felt like you succeeded."

There was the faintest quiver in her voice. "No."

"Stacey...I'd like you to move in with me if you want it too. I'd like it to be as my lover...my partner, but it can be as friends if that's what you need right now."

She looked at him. "I need somewhere to stay. I refuse to intrude on any of my brothers, so I'll accept your offer, Mason. As for whether it's as a lover or a friend...can we play it by ear for now?"

"Yeah. I just wanted us to have something settled before I'm surrounded by Barlow-Barrett testosterone. Between their bullheadedness and my years on the street, it could get ugly over the next few hours. I have to admit, though, they seem like a pretty devoted fan club. You're lucky to have siblings like them."

"I know. Bran and I have always been good friends. He wasn't very pleased when I announced my engagement. In fact, he took me aside to ask if it was what I truly wanted. I guess I should have paid attention." She shook her head. "Let's not discuss it right now. Give me some tips, coach. How am I doing?"

He sat next to her, where she manned the tiller. "You're doing great. You have a great foundation. You need to be a bit more adventurous. Steer for the area off the point there. There's a good spot to drop anchor and swim."

"I don't have a suit on."

He grinned. "Swim in your underwear. There's no one around."

He held his breath, wondering if she'd blast him or freeze him, but neither one happened. After staring at him for several seconds, she laughed. "I will if you will."

"You're on."

Mason furled the sails, and Stacey dropped anchor. When she turned away, he stripped off his shirt and started shucking his shorts. Something made him pause. He caught her staring. The heat of her gaze scorched him, and his body responded. "God, Stacey, don't look at me like that."

"I'd nearly forgotten how beautiful you are," she whispered. "Always so suave and urbane around the gallery, but underneath as sleek and muscular as a jungle cat."

He kicked off his shoes and closed the distance between them. "Swim with me. I won't do anything else. I want your trust."

"You have it already." She turned her back to him and removed her shorts. As he watched them slide down her legs, his breathing quickened. Then she unbuttoned the shirt she'd borrowed and let it slide off her shoulders. Mason sucked in air on a hiss. The only line disrupting the smooth, bare skin of her backside was her panties. Before he could wrap his mind around the idea she was topless, Stacey stepped on the gunwale and dove in. He turned his back for a moment and adjusted his hardening cock.

For fuck's sake, Hatch! The woman had just been sexually assaulted by her husband. She needed time to recover, not someone breathing down her neck wanting sex. Stepping up where she had, he followed her in. She stroked lazily in the water not too far from him, her ponytail floating like molten silk behind her. He floated, watching her. When she unselfconsciously flipped onto her back to drift along, her breasts barely concealed by the water, Mason cleared his throat.

She opened her eyes. "What? I thought you said it was deserted out here." She straightened and glanced around, her brow furrowed.

"It is."

"So why the harrumph?"

"I'm staring."

Stacey blinked at him a couple of times as if trying to absorb what he said, then laughed. "Okay. So punch yourself in the nose if it pisses you off."

He laughed. "Float in peace. I'll avert my innocent eyes from your feminine beauty."

"Stuff it, Hatch."

He let her float, swim and relax, but Mason kept a close eye on his watch. He wanted to get back in time so they could both clean off the bay water smell before her family began to arrive. In the end, it wasn't necessary. She eased over near him after a quarter hour. In her eyes he saw an edge of weariness.

"You hurting?"

"A bit. My ribs."

"Come on. We'll head back. I'll give you a hand getting back on board."

He tried not to look. Really. But Lord was she perfect, or what? Winchester was a fool. Stacey should never have been his. She pulled Mason's shirt back on, but left her shorts off. He didn't want to pull his shorts on over his wet boxers, so when she started hauling in the anchor, he ditched the boxers and yanked his shorts on, going commando.

"Nice ass, Hatch."

He looked over his shoulder. "I can give you another look if you like it so much."

Stacey smiled. "Maybe later."

"I'll hold you to that. Why don't we set the spinnaker on the way back."

Stacey looked at him. "Okay, but I crew. You take the helm."

Mason chuckled. "This time, but I'll have you challenging Brandon in no time. Wait and see."

As it turned out, Brandon was already there when they arrived back. He stood on the dock, hands on his hips and his short blond hair lifting slightly in the wind. Stacey had already put her shorts back on, but she still looked disheveled, and Mason could see Brandon's gaze didn't miss the man's shirt she wore. His eyes, more green than Stacey's golden gaze, narrowed on Mason before going back to his sister.

She tossed him a line, which he slipped over the post on the dock while she and Mason finished securing the sails and setting everything in order. When Brandon helped her from the boat, she grimaced a bit in pain, and her brother's gaze once again darted to Mason. He'd been on the receiving end of those fuck-you looks before, but the last go around had been because of Lucy.

"What the fuck were you thinking, Hatch? Taking her sailing. Can't you see she's in pain?"

Stacey put her own hands on her hips and planted herself right in front of her brother. "He didn't take me anywhere. I wanted to go. In fact, I was the one who suggested it."

Mason put his arm around her shoulders. "You are tired, though. Come inside and get some of your meds before you shower."

Mason could feel the hostility boring into his back from the first of the Barlow-Barretts as they returned to the house. For a moment, he allowed his resentment to take hold. What the hell gave Brandon the right to have an attitude? Mason had been the only one around to help her. Where were they? One glance at the weariness on Stacey's face, though, and he decided maybe some of their hostility had been justified. She looked wiped out. Even if the sailing had been her idea, he should have kept better tabs on her energy level. Shit.

"Come on, honey," he told her. "Let's get you inside."

Brandon stalked along behind them, and Mason felt the anger radiating off him in waves but chose to ignore it, at least until Stacey was out of earshot. Brandon surprised him. He didn't open fire over the sailing. As soon as his sister had shut the bedroom door, he spun. "Why the hell didn't you call the police?"

Mason held up his hands. "Whoa! Not my decision. Stacey didn't want any kind of scene. It was all I could do initially to get her agree to go to the hospital."

Brandon scraped his fingers through his hair. "What the fuck's been going on, Hatch?"

"Exactly what I'd like to know too." Both men turned toward the door.

Chapter 9

Great. Now there were two of them. Seth stood in the doorway, making even Brandon look small.

"Where's Stacey?"

"In the shower, bro. Mason took her sailing."

"What?" Golden eyes so similar to hers zeroed in on Mason. "What were you thinking?"

Mason sighed. "She suggested it to get her mind off things."

Seth's stiff stance relaxed some. "All right. Is there anything you want to tell us while she's out of the room?"

"Winchester's made your parents believe she's developed a drinking problem and is close to a nervous breakdown because he wants to start a family and she doesn't. When Stacey called them earlier, your mother kept trying to find out where she is so they could come get her and check her into some posh rehab place."

Brandon's brows snapped together with fury, but Seth rubbed his jaw thoughtfully. "All right then. Winchester's shown his strategy. Once Phillip gets here we can work on how to counteract it."

Mason looked at the two men. "Look, I know she'll get into it, but you need to know so you don't scare the shit out of her when you find out. Winchester's not the only one who assaulted her."

"What?" Seth snapped, eyes narrowing like a lion ready to attack.

"It's his friend, Worthington, isn't it?" Brandon snarled.

"Yeah. This is so much worse than what you've already seen on the surface. I hired a detective…"

"But you didn't file a police report?" Bran questioned.

"Two weeks ago," Mason clarified. "Stacey came into the gallery with a severe bruise on her wrist. She was upset, wouldn't tell me what had happened. Said she'd fallen on her boat. I didn't believe her, plus I already had some suspicions something was going on. Winchester had moved Worthington into their home. So I hired a guy to start checking into them both."

"And what did you find out?"

"Enough to assume Worthington and Winchester were lovers and were somehow trying to get Stacey involved in a ménage with them."

"Oh Jesus," Brandon muttered, a grimace of distaste twisting his features. "That's just way more than I want to know."

Mason spun on him, his anger finally releasing. "If that's all you can handle, asshole, then you need to leave now because it goes downhill from there. But don't worry, I'll still be here. I'm not deserting the woman I love."

"Easy," Seth said, stepping between him and Brandon. "We need to work together. It would be easy to start pointing fingers about how this happened, and I suspect we all can take some of the blame, but we need to keep in mind the fault lies squarely at Jason Winchester's door."

His gaze suddenly went across the room. Brandon's and Mason's followed. Stacey stood in the doorway, her eyes wide, but her gaze strong and steady. Brandon strode over and pulled Stacey into his arms. "I should have done this earlier. God, Stacey, I love you. Whatever you need, we're here for you."

She hugged him back before pulling away to accept a bear hug from Seth. The elder brother held her a little longer, stroked her hair and whispered in her ear. Mason saw tears well for a second before she blinked them away. She hugged Seth again.

"Honey, you need some of your pain medication?" Mason inquired.

She nodded. "I think I tried to do too much. It's the bruising on my ribs." At the looks of fury on her brothers' faces, she explained. "I fell trying to get away."

A knock sounded on the door. Mason went to answer it and saw a younger version of Brandon at the door, but with Seth's additional size. Jesus, around these three he felt short. He held out his hand. "I'm Mason Hatch. I spoke with you yesterday."

"Phillip." The tone was clipped. This Barlow-Barrett might be dressed in jeans and a baggy shirt, but he carried a briefcase and obviously meant business. "I brought along some research and everything I need to go ahead and get information recorded." He glanced beyond Mason's shoulder for a second then returned his greenish gaze to him. "I can leave the briefcase in the car unless you think she's pretty positive she needs my help."

Mason stepped back. "Bring it. She's ready to nail him by the short hairs."

Phillip grinned. "Excellent. I never did like him. He's a prick."

"On that, my man, we are in total agreement."

"I see the elder statesmen are already here," Phillip remarked easily. "Have they frozen you with brotherly displeasure or prepared the skewer for your testicles?"

Mason chuckled. "Neither at the moment. I think I'm still in no man's land."

"Wow, they must like you. You know Seth bloodied the nose of Anna's husband the first time they met."

Mason arched a brow. "I think I can handle myself should the need arise."

"Did any of the wives come along, or are we going to overwhelm Stacey with testosterone?"

"The latter I'm afraid, but I think she can handle it. As a matter of fact, I think she will surprise all of you."

* * * *

She saw the worry in Phillip's eyes as soon as he entered the room, his gaze searching out hers. He was the only one of her brothers younger than her, but she would trust him to help her. Quieter than either Seth or Brandon, Phillip had doggedly gone his own way, letting their father know early on he would not be going into the newspaper business. Instead, he pursued a career in law. She knew he had another ambition as well, and that was politics. As she crossed the room to hug him, she whispered in his ear. "I don't expect you to help me if it will jeopardize your desire to enter politics."

"Screw that," he told her. "You want my help, you got it. I'll nail the bastard to the wall."

Stacey kissed him on the cheek, looked around the room and smiled. "You guys are the best. I need to take some meds. Can I get any of you something to drink?"

Everyone opted for sparkling water.

"I'll do that," Mason told her. "Just get your medication and get comfortable." He followed her into the kitchen, taking the opportunity to hold her for a second. "You okay?"

What a world of difference there was in the way he looked at her, spoke to her. "As long as you're here, Mason, I feel like I can do anything."

"I love the idea, but, Stacey, you can do anything you want to with or without me. You remember that."

She swallowed her medication and set the glass on the counter. "Are you planning on going somewhere, Hatch?"

"Only with you."

"Good."

Phillip poked his head in the kitchen. "Hey, what's taking so long?" His gaze flicked between them and he grinned. "You have anything to eat? I'm starved."

A quarter of an hour later, Stacey was stretched out on the couch. Mason had her feet across his lap and her three brothers were sprawled in chairs around them, two demolished bags of chips and a plate emptied of sandwiches sitting in the middle of the table. Phillip sat forward, cleared a space and opened his briefcase. He pulled out a small digital recorder and glanced at her with an arch of his brow. Stacey nodded, watching as he turned it on.

"This is the statement of Stacey Barlow-Barrett Winchester with regard to the sexual assault on her which took place on the morning of..." She took a deep breath as he continued with the opening, giving the date of the assault, the current date and who the witnesses were present to hear her statement. When he finished, he looked at her. "Are you ready?"

She nodded. She began with Brandon's wedding because for her that was when she had first noticed something off. As she recounted the overtures by Justin, the situation around the hot tub, the feeling she had of not being quite in control and the subsequent drinking she'd done, she saw her brothers shift. The clenching and unclenching of hands, the clunk of bottles as they were set down, all told her what they were feeling. Mason she had even more awareness of. When she hit a rough spot or hesitated, she would feel a comforting squeeze as he massaged her feet. When she mentioned the bruises on her hips and thighs, he went as rigid as though he had turned to stone.

"Could we take a break for a minute?" she asked softly. They had only reached the day she caught Justin and Jason together, so the worst was yet to come. "I need to collect myself."

After swinging her feet to the floor, she stood and walked along the hallway to the bathroom, leaving silence behind her. She knew they would talk while she was gone. That was okay. After splashing water on her face, she patted it dry and stared at herself in the mirror. She didn't look different. The same face had stared back at her last year, last month, last week and still stared back at her right now. But there was something different. Jason and Justin had manipulated her, thinking she was weak. Mason had nursed and nurtured her, knowing something else lay deep inside. She took a deep breath. It was time to get it on Phillip's tape recorder. Then they would decide where to go from there.

Mason was right. She could do this with or without him, but she was extremely glad it was with him.

* * * *

Stacey sat next to him again on the couch, but this time, all she did was reach over with her hand. Mason didn't hesitate. He took her fine-boned fingers in his, holding them with enough pressure to let her know he was there for her. Her brothers listened silently for the most part. Phillip interrupted every now and then with a question, either to have her clarify something or because he needed more information.

"Did you tell Jace you were going to your boat?"

"No, but that probably wouldn't take him much time to figure out. It's my getaway place, not his. Jace only ever came aboard reluctantly."

Phillip nodded and jotted a note on his legal pad. "So, you left Jace and Justin at the house Friday afternoon, but it was just before dawn Saturday when Jace arrived at the marina."

"That's right."

Phillip's glance swiveled to Mason. "What time was it when you left Stacey?"

He shrugged. "Midnight or after. I waited until she'd fallen asleep."

Phillip tapped his pen on the pad and pressed his lips together before he finally spoke. "Look, I'm sorry I have to ask this, but did anything sexual happen between the two of you?"

Stacey's hand trembled. Mason squeezed reassuringly. "No. She was upset and she'd been drinking."

She squeezed back. "He's being kind. I was plastered, Phillip. I tried, but he refused." Phillip made a couple of notes. "Is that a problem?"

"No. Just be prepared for his attorney to turn your presence on the boat into something, but if there's no physical evidence to back it…"

"There's not." Mason couldn't help the snarl that came through, but the thought someone would try to twist this in any way to make it seem like it was Stacey's fault crawled all over him.

"It's all right, Mason," Stacey murmured. "I'm ready for that."

He brought her hand to his lips and held it there for a minute. Jesus. He wasn't sure he could be as strong as she was.

Phillip set his pen on the table. "We can take a break for a few minutes…"

"Unless you need one," Stacey said, stopping him, "I'd prefer to get this finished."

Mason held her hand against his thigh, keeping an eye on her as she continued with waking to find Winchester in the cabin with her. She trembled as she recounted the details. Brandon stood restlessly and paced across the room to stare out at the dinghy bobbing in the water. When Mason turned his gaze on Seth, the only clue to his emotions was in the rhythmic tic in his jaw, as if the guy was clenching and unclenching his teeth. Even Phillip's grip on his pen had become white-knuckled. When he finally clicked the stop button on the recorder, Brandon spun.

"Fuck the legalities. Can't we pay the bastard a visit?"

Seth raked his hand through his thick hair. "I'm right there with you, Bran, but this isn't our call." He turned to Stacey. "What do you want to do?"

Stacey sighed heavily. "How strong do you think my case would be, Phillip?"

"You have plenty of physical evidence, but I have to tell you, without anyone else to place him at the scene…"

Mason jumped up. "For Christ's sake! He hurt her. The hospital took a rape kit on her. Even if he didn't actually do the deed, he tried. What more do they need?"

Phillip's eyes blazed. "I'm not the enemy here, all right? I'm just pointing out a good defense attorney could twist this into directions you really don't want to go."

"Like what?"

"Like the…evidence…was the result of consensual sex. Then you showed up. The two of you do have a history. It could be twisted so you become the attacker, not Winchester. People have seen the animosity between you."

"Fuck you!" Mason was nearly speechless with rage. As he took a step forward, Seth was suddenly in front of him with Stacey pushing her way in.

"Stop it!" she pleaded. "All of you. Please. Everybody, take a deep breath."

Mason took one look at her pale face and the fight drained right out of him. "I'm sorry, honey."

When he opened his arms, she stepped into his embrace. Mason's throat tightened, his vision going blurry before he blinked. God, the last thing he wanted to do was start boo-hooing in front of her or her ginormous brothers. Stacey cupped her hand around the back of his neck and rested her cheek against his shoulder. Mason took a deep breath, forcing himself to relax.

"What do you want to do, Stacey?" Seth asked. "We can get the police involved, but I don't think that's our only option. It depends on what you want."

She turned in Mason's arms and leaned against him. He kept his arms around her, his hands crossing over her stomach, her hands covering them. "I want my marriage to him to go away as quickly as possible."

"Divorce?" As soon as Phillip said it, Mason saw all of the Barlow-Barretts cringe. "The Church…"

"I want an annulment."

To Mason's surprise, Phillip actually smiled. "It's much easier to get a divorce. However, I think we can prove pretty easily you meet one, maybe even two, of the three standards for an annulment… Winchester's failure to disclose his sterility as well as his ongoing sexual relationship outside the marriage constitute both fraud and willful withholding of information."

"Can we prove it?" Brandon asked, returning from the window.

Phillip laughed. "The sterility without a doubt, and I suspect the mere threat of exposing the other will have him volunteering the information in closed court."

Seth leveled his golden gaze on his sister. "Is that all you want? Because I have to tell you, Stacey, if you don't go after him on criminal charges, you'll be running into him socially every time you turn around."

She stiffened in Mason's arms. "I want those pictures he took, and I want signed statements from him and Justin admitting what they did."

"Jesus," Phillip muttered. "And exactly what am I supposed to use for leverage?"

"Jason will do almost anything to avoid a scandal," Stacey said. "Just the threat of criminal charges would probably be enough, but if not, there's always the digital video from the security system that could go public."

Mason watched as Seth slowly grinned. "Jesus, Stacey. That's cold, but doesn't he know how the system is designed?"

"No. He's always assumed we had the run-of-the-mill alarm system. I never told him the rest of it. There will for sure be video of him and Justin in the study, and if the two of them decided to do anything in any other public areas of the house… Well, that will have been recorded too. There are cameras everywhere but the bedrooms and the bathrooms."

Mason laughed. He couldn't help it. Just the image of Winchester's face when he realized he wasn't the only one with damning pictures made him feel so much better. "Why did you go to such lengths with security?" he asked as he slipped around where he could see her expression.

"I was alone a lot while Jace traveled. In addition to my own valuables, I often had clients' belongings there on a temporary basis. So, when I brought the security guy in, I had him install the standard alarm, and also a digital video surveillance system. The cameras are sound- and motion-activated."

"It has audio?" Seth wanted to know.

She nodded. "Ambient sound, not directional, but unless there's a lot of background noise, it will pick up conversations too."

"Is it someplace he can access?" Phillip asked.

Stacey shook her head. "It's on a secure server. Since it was designed to assist with my business, I never told him the details." She bit her lip, her eyes sad. "I never expected...I would have to use it against him."

Mason squeezed her shoulder. "Do you have to access it from the house?" The last thing he wanted was for her to have to return to the brownstone.

"No. I--God--I could do it from here. It's internet-based."

"I have an office down the hall on the left. You can use my computer."

Stacey started to shake. "I-I don't want..."

"There's no need for you to see it," Seth said. "Give me the information. Brandon, Phillip and I will take a look to see if there's anything we can use. Is it configured so we can make a hard copy backup?"

Stacey nodded.

After she wrote down the information and her brothers had left the room, she leaned against Mason.

"Are you sure you don't want to have him charged?"

"Yes. It will be better this way."

He tightened his arms around her. "I don't like the idea he could approach you. Stacey..."

"Please, Mason. If he'll agree to the annulment and my other demands, it's enough."

He pinched the bridge of his nose and nodded. "All right. But I want you living with me or your brothers for your own safety. I don't trust him and I don't trust Worthington."

Chapter 10

Live with Mason or her brothers. That didn't sound much like a romantic relationship. Stacey felt her chest tighten with pain. Sure, she'd told him she needed to play the whole lover or friend idea by ear for a while, but suggesting she live with him or her brothers? Had she mistaken his interest? It had seemed pretty plain at the time. Now she wasn't so sure.

"What do you want, Mason?"

He paced away from her, rubbing the back of his neck with one hand before he turned back to her. "I want you here, with me."

Her heart beat heavily. "Just for my safety?"

"No, damn it. I want you with me…in my house, in my bed. If you can't feel safe with me, then you need to be with one of your brothers. I can't do this anymore. I'll take you however you'll have me. If that makes me sound pathetic, then too bad. I'm not risking having you anywhere I don't think you'll be safe."

Tears blurred her vision. She wiped them away. There'd been enough crying. She tried to smile, but her mouth trembled. For once in her life, she wanted to be able to stand up for what she wanted without feeling half sick because she was causing a scene. Fists clenched on either side of her, she took a deep breath.

"I want it like it was before Jace. I want you like I've never wanted any other man, but I can't do that right now. I can't…"

"Stacey…"

"No! Let me say it. I can't be with you right now, and I don't know when I will. I want to…but I just can't… And if you can't…"

He took her hands, sliding his fingers in and loosening her clenched grip. "I'll take you however you'll have me, Stacey. If that means just holding you, hell, if it means separate bedrooms…I can do that. I want you with me, yes, but I want you safe."

He pulled her toward him, wrapped her in his arms and simply held her. Stacey felt her tension, her fear, leave. "Will you come with me to get my things?"

"Him and the rest of us." They both turned to see Seth framed in the doorway. His eyes glittered in a face pale with fury. "Stacey, I want you to reconsider. I want you to think about pressing charges."

She shook her head, sticking her chin up. Phillip and Brandon now flanked Seth, their faces equally grim. "Please understand when I say this," Stacey said. "It's not because of what's been drummed into me for so long. I want to accomplish the specific things I've mentioned because I've seen what happens when the media gets hold of any of our family. I don't want a scene, not because I'm interested in avoiding a scandal, but because I want to put this behind me. I want my life back. Can you understand that?"

Brandon walked over to them. Mason backed away so her brother could take her face in his hands. "Baby, the scene in the study is on there, like you suspected, but it's not all."

Stacey's body went stiff. It had to be bad.

"There's video of you. Winchester left the door open. The three of you are visible in the background."

"I want to see."

Mason and Brandon both protested. "Baby, it's not just the video. The audio... Stacey, you just don't need to hear that."

She looked to Phillip and Seth. "I want to see and hear. You can't ask me to reconsider pressing charges without seeing..."

Seth was shaking his head, and Phillip had averted his gaze to stare out a window, but his mouth was tight and his jaw slowly clenching. She looked back to Brandon. He would understand. He'd always understood better than the others. Their eyes locked and finally he looked at his brothers.

"Move. Let me take them both back and show them."

"Fuck!" Seth swept past them, out the back door and down the steps.

Stacey was grateful for Mason's arm around her waist. They sat in front of the monitor as Brandon called the video back up. He didn't bother with the scene from the study. She'd seen and heard it in person. When he clicked on another camera, it was to replay digital recordings from the hallway outside her bedroom.

The images weren't the best, but the audio made it plain who the players were. It was like watching someone else. Stacey had to view it that way because to admit it was her would have driven her mad. From the tension radiating from Mason, she knew he couldn't be quite as objective. In fact, he stood in the middle of it and left the room. When Brandon stopped it, Stacey stared at the screen, numb.

"It's so obvious now when I watch it who the couple is and who the unwelcome third is. I never truly had a marriage."

"Oh, baby…"

"Until now, I might have been able to fool myself into thinking Jace at least liked me even if it was Justin he was in love with. But this?" She shook her head.

"Listen to me, Stacey." All the laughter was gone from Brandon's earnest hazel gaze. "This kind of stuff will screw with your head. Lucy has a friend…"

"I'll talk to her. You're right."

"And pressing charges?"

She closed her eyes. "I want to kill him--them--both of them, but I still just want this all behind me."

Phillip burst into the room. "You may have to get in line for the killing part. Mason just left."

* * * *

He would kill him. The idea kept repeating over and over in his brain as he aimed the Porsche back toward Georgetown. Stacey would be safe with her brothers. Mason had vowed to take care of her, and he would. Now, having seen the images on the security video, he was no longer content to simply discredit Jason Winchester and Justin Worthington. Allowing the two to fade from the scene was no longer enough. They needed to pay.

It hadn't been enough to get her drunk, to attack her. The two had humiliated her, carrying on so openly in her own home. Mason growled, saw the speedometer and forced himself to back off the accelerator. His pummeling Winchester and Worthington wouldn't preclude what Stacey wanted to accomplish, but it would give him a small measure of satisfaction. He didn't belittle what Stacey wanted to do, but inaction had never been part of Mason's make-up.

His cell phone rang. Mason glanced over, saw it was Stacey. He wanted to ignore it, so he could keep his single-minded concentration on the task of making Jace and Justin pay, but he couldn't do that to her. She'd been ignored enough. As the phone rang, some tiny bit of reason tunneled through his anger.

"What?" he barked.

"Mason," Stacey pleaded. "Please don't do this. Wait for us. Let us go together. Please."

He took a deep breath. "Are you following me? Stacey...you should be resting. Your ribs..."

"I can't let you do this, Mason."

"I can't not do it, honey." He stopped, jaw clenching as he forced himself to control the fury roiling inside him. "I can't let either one of them get away with what they did to you."

"Mason, listen to me! They won't get away with it, but this isn't the way."

He expelled his breath in frustration, knowing what he was about to say might hurt her, but unable to keep it inside him. "They hurt you, Stacey. Making him go away might be enough for you, but I'm finding it's not for me. I want them both to hurt. You come from a world where not making waves is important, but I've lived my life in a world of payback. Jace and Justin will find out what that means."

He ended the call. He didn't want to argue with her, didn't want to hurt her. He would, however, hunt Jason Winchester down. It would be so much easier to simply place a couple of phone calls, pull in some favors from years ago when his past had been a whole lot shadier, but that wouldn't do now. No, Mason needed the satisfaction of handling this himself.

He stepped on the gas again as he headed toward Georgetown.

* * * *

"He hung up." She looked around the room at her three brothers. "We have to stop him."

Brandon pursed his lips. "Personally, I wish I'd been able to get in the car with him before he left."

"You're not the only one," Seth growled.

"Guys!" Phillip snapped. "We don't need anything that might damage our case. We're getting in someone's car here and going after him--to stop him. Are we clear on that?"

Seth and Brandon grumbled. Stacey felt warm, cared for. Had she really spent so many years worried about proprieties she hadn't realized how fierce her brothers were? Even Phillip, who had now snatched the keys to Seth's SUV.

"I'll drive. You idiots will get us arrested if we get pulled over."

"And why would we get pulled over?" Brandon asked as he snagged Stacey's hand and pulled her along with them.

Phillip's grin was as sharp as a knife. "Because we'll be breaking every speed limit between here and Georgetown."

Brandon sat in front with him as Seth helped Stacey into the back seat. He buckled her seatbelt for her, then turned her chin so she had to look him in the eye. "When we get there, I want you to promise you will stay in the vehicle."

"Seth..."

"Darling, listen. You're already hurt. This will get ugly. If the cops show, I don't want you anywhere in the middle of it."

"But Mason..."

"He's a big boy, but he's facing two guys who are also no slouches when it comes to size or physical strength. We'll even those odds."

Phillip looked in the rearview mirror. "Seth! We are not brawling. We'll handle this reasonably and legally."

Brandon snorted.

"Oh Katie Christ," Phillip swore as he checked traffic before he merged onto the interstate.

"Phillip," Brandon said, "reasonable ended the moment we saw those videos. After we finish beating the shit out of him and his lover, then we'll get Jason to agree to our demands. Our beating the shit out of him doesn't have anything to with what he did to Stacey. You know that."

Phillip sighed. "You're right. Legally they are completely separate matters. I would however like us to keep anything we do well below felony level so I can keep my law practice, agreed?"

Seth and Brandon grunted their assent. Stacey worried her lower lip, her mind still stuck on the fact that right now Mason was going in on his own to face them. Two against one. Maybe it wouldn't be a bad thing if her brothers did help even the odds.

This wasn't exactly how she'd envisioned returning to the house for her belongings.

* * * *

Mason screeched to a halt at the curb in front of Stacey's brownstone. Reaching into his pocket, he pulled out the knife he normally carried and put it in the glove compartment. He wanted no temptation. No stranger to knife fights, he knew the odds would more than tip in his favor if he carried his knife, but killing the bastard wasn't his aim. Not really. Nor was spending time behind bars his goal for his relationship with Stacey.

Resting both hands on the steering wheel for a moment, he made himself take a deep breath. He was furious, but he also needed his wits because he knew he'd be facing two men, not one. When he was sure he had it together, Mason stepped from the car and slammed the door shut.

He was at the top of the steps in a couple of leaps and pounding on the door. As soon as he heard the deadbolt and the doorknob unlock, he pushed his shoulder against the panel and shoved his way in.

"What the hell...?" It was Justin.

"I've got a message from Stacey," Mason began, his voice low, and before Justin could get out another word, Mason swung, catching the taller man right in the gut. Sure he could have gone for his face, but he had no intention of taking either one of them down right away. No...Mason wanted to play. The oomph that rushed from Justin's mouth made Mason smile with satisfaction.

"Hatch!" Winchester sprinted down the steps, fury tightening his face.

"You want some too?" Mason snarled. "Come and get it. Both of you. Just fucking come and get it. You hurt her, you bastard!"

Winchester stopped far enough out of his reach Mason couldn't get to him, not with Justin between them.

"How dare you come in my house--"

"How dare you beat your wife!"

"I don't know what she told you," Winchester started, "but Stacey is very sick..."

"Shut the fuck up!" Mason snarled. He glared at both men. "I've had a detective uncovering all kinds of shit on the two of you. I know how far back you go. I also know about your problem, Jason."

"Get out!" Winchester blustered. "You don't know anything except what Stacey's told you."

Mason laughed. "Really? Don't be so naive. You're not the only one capable of taking illicit photos."

"Which I can still plaster all over the papers. Is that what you want? Imagine how many clients want to know you use their homes to have sex. Why don't you be a good boy and go back to the gutters you crawled out of."

"Fuck. You." Mason shoved past Justin and grabbed Winchester by the throat, but before he could throw the punch with his other hand, Justin jumped him from behind, grabbing his arms and giving Jason a chance to jerk away and throw his own punch. It caught Mason on the cheek, the signet ring Winchester wore drawing blood.

For a second Mason's head swam, but he shook it off. He'd been in a lot worse fights over the years and didn't give a fat baby's bottom he was outnumbered in this one. Kicking back, he caught Justin in the shin with the side of his foot then shoved an elbow in his ribs. With another breathy oomph, Mason was free and he leaped at Winchester, determined to wipe the self-satisfied smirk from his face.

"I'm going to beat the shit out of you. I want you to know what it's like to have your ribs bruised. I'll certainly stop short of what you attempted. But we're going to discuss that as soon as I'm through."

When he felt Winchester's nose smash beneath his fist, Mason grunted with satisfaction. Winchester kicked out at him, but Mason dodged out of the way, and the other man's foot barely missed his knee. Hearing a sound behind him, he spun to find Justin with a knife gleaming in his hand.

Mason laughed. "Why am I not surprised? Not enough it's two against one? Why would I expect a fair fight from either one of you?"

Justin held his ribs with one hand and the knife with the other. Gazing beyond Mason, he said to Winchester, "Call the cops. He's just bluster."

"I wouldn't do that if I were you." They turned. Seth nearly filled the doorway, and what he didn't fill, Brandon and Phillip did.

"Thank God you're here," Winchester started, but Seth cut him off.

"Save it." His razor glance took in Justin. "Put the knife away."

Justin glanced uncertainly from Winchester to Mason and the three blond giants with him. After snapping the blade shut, he shoved the knife in his pocket.

"I don't know what you've heard," Jason tried again, and this time it was Brandon who interrupted.

"Are you such a fucking idiot you think we'd believe anything that comes out of your mouth? That we would believe you over our own sister?"

Phillip shoved his way into the hall as well and Mason nearly growled out loud when he saw Stacey behind the three of them. The youngest, but certainly not the smallest of the three Barlow-Barrett brothers, Phillip glared at Winchester and Worthington with narrowed, hazel eyes. "And please don't insult us. We've got a lot more than hearsay. Perhaps we should take this into the living room. I've seen the video of what you two like to do in the study. I'm afraid none of us wants to step in there with that image in mind."

Mason nearly laughed when he saw Winchester's face lose its color. "Video?"

Stacey stepped forward, her brothers flanking her. "I had to bring plenty of valuable antiques home on spec, not to mention most of what's in here belongs to me anyway. Did you actually think I simply had a standard alarm system installed?"

Her chin was raised in a definite challenge. Mason felt so damn proud of her in that moment for standing up to Jason, he could have hugged her--but she wasn't through yet.

"I had the entire place fitted with video and audio surveillance as well--only the bedrooms and bathrooms were exempt."

While Mason pulled a handkerchief from his pants pockets and blotted the blood on his cheek, Phillip put an arm around Stacey's shoulders. "Please understand, Winchester, with what we have on tape, it would be an easy step to go to the police. We have enough evidence even the most reluctant of prosecutors would be chomping at the bit to pursue rape and attempted rape charges against you."

Winchester laughed. "Rape? She's my wife."

His size dwarfing Winchester, Phillip stepped forward. His voice was quiet, but his words were plain and succinct. "The precedent for marital rape is nothing new. So let me give you a bit of pro bono legal advice--I'd sit now and listen to what Stacey has to say because, unlike the rest of us, she's willing to keep this discreet. I would welcome the opportunity to face your counsel in a court of law because there's always civil court and divorce court."

Phillip's smile was broad, but it never quite reached eyes that glinted green.

Winchester's gaze shifted to Mason and the rest of the Barlow-Barrett men. "All right, but Hatch is not a part of this."

Mason couldn't suppress the growl that rose to his lips. He almost shook Brandon's arm from around his shoulders. "Come on, man. You and I will help Worthington pack his things while Seth, Phillip and Stacey talk to Winchester. She'll be protected."

Brandon glanced at Worthington. "Move it, asshole."

Mason looked over at Stacey. Her eyes met his, steadily and without any fear or hesitation. Flanked by the combined bulk of Seth and Phillip, Mason had no doubt she would be fine.

Chapter 11

As soon as the door shut behind the other men, Jace tried to make an argument again to Seth and Phillip, completely ignoring Stacey. If she hadn't been so tense, it would almost have been funny--and such a sad, sad commentary on what had been the sham of their entire marriage.

"Gentlemen, I don't know what she's led you to believe, but nothing..."

"Oh for God's sake, Winchester," Seth interrupted with a snap of impatience. "We've seen the damn security videos. We know exactly what happened, including video evidence of doubling the alcohol in her drinks. So please, quit with the poor Stacey's on the verge of a nervous breakdown bit. It doesn't wash."

Stacey took a deep breath. "Why me, Jace? Plenty of women probably would have bought right into your little triangle."

"I don't have any idea what you're referring to." Jace folded his arms over his chest, still refusing to acknowledge not only what she knew, but what her brothers and Mason knew to be true too.

"Let's have a seat," Phillip said. Once everyone had found chairs, he continued, "Stacey has some specific things she wished to discuss, and you, Winchester, would be advised to listen to what she has to offer."

"I want my attorney here."

Stacey rolled her eyes. Now her blinders were off, she felt like a fool for falling for his web of lies from the very beginning. What had happened to her good sense? Had she been so blinded by the need to be perfect for her parents she'd failed to see the obvious signs something wasn't quite right with Jason's timely proposal?

Phillip arched a brow. "Waiting for your attorney is, of course, your decision. However, our deal is on the table right now. If you don't listen to it, then the deal disappears and we'll allow the police to come in so they can conduct a criminal investigation..."

"You can't! My God, man, she's my wife..."

Phillip slapped his palm on the arm of the chair he was sitting in. The crack shut Jace up. "I have already explained this, Winchester. The mere fact you're married does not rule out charges for battery at the very least. You would do well to remember Stacey had a rape kit done at the hospital in Annapolis. Even if you didn't finish, there will be DNA evidence. It's doubtful many women scratch a man in the face in passion. You can listen to her offer, or Seth can make a call to the police. Your choice, but the offer is only good for the next five minutes." Phillip turned his wrist and casually checked the time on his watch.

She didn't want to do it, but Stacey forced herself to meet her husband's eyes. When he was the one to break eye contact, her confidence rose.

"I'll listen," Jace snarled.

Phillip caught her gaze and nodded. Seth's arm rested along the back of the couch behind her shoulders. Her breathing settled and her heart slowed. She could do this.

"There are four things I want," she began. "First, I want you out of this house tonight. Second, I want you to agree to an annulment, third, I want you to sign an agreement you will not contact me in any way again, and finally, I want the photos you took of Mason and me, plus a signed agreement you will never use them in any fashion."

Jace sat back as though what she demanded actually shocked him, and Stacey had to wonder if they inhabited completely different planets. Was he simply so arrogant and self-absorbed he didn't comprehend what he'd done?

"I need more time."

Phillip leaned forward. "Those are the terms. You can accept them, and give me contact information where I can bring documents for you to sign, or Seth can make the call to the police."

"That's blackmail."

"That's the deal."

Stacey leaned forward and set her hand on Phillip's arm. "I have something else I want to say."

Phillip leaned back and Stacey stared Jason in the eye.

"You threatened me, my family, and Mason in order to manipulate me into this marriage. I didn't love you, but I came into this relationship with the determination to make it work. You never did. You had no intention of ending it with Justin, and lied when you said you were putting our relationship before all others.

"More than that, Jace, you and Justin used me. You forced me and hurt me. I will never forgive you, but I'm not letting you destroy my life. So know this: I've given you my terms and if you don't accept them before I walk out of this room, I'll take the evidence I have and go to the police myself."

"Stacey...I never meant..."

"Don't, Jace. You did mean to. People don't happen to wake up one morning and think 'Gee, since I'm sterile, maybe I can get my lover to impregnate my wife.' They don't happen to sit in their study and get a blowjob from said lover, and they sure as hell don't step onto a boat, beat their wife and attempt to rape her! So help me God, if you try to bad-mouth me or Mason after this is over, I'll plaster pictures of you getting your dick sucked all over YouTube. You and I both know you cater to a clientele that won't tolerate that--at least not publicly."

She'd had enough. Stacey started for the doorway and saw Mason standing there. His dark eyes shone with pride and a faint smile played around his wide mouth.

"Bravo, honey!" He held his arm open for her and she curled into his side.

When she glanced at Seth, he smiled. "Take her home with you, Hatch. We'll take care of the cleanup here and talk to you tomorrow."

Mason kept her next to him as they went out the door and down the steps to his car. Only when they reached it did he turn and pull her into his embrace.

"I am so proud of you, Stacey. That's the woman I first met, the woman I fell in love with."

She leaned her forehead against his uninjured cheek. "God, that felt good." Leaning back a bit, she lightly touched the bruise and cut on his other cheek. "Are you all right?"

"It's just a scratch. You know it's not over with yet."

"I know. He's in shock right now, but I doubt he'll quit without a fight." Stacey leaned back so she could see his expression in the light from the streetlamps. "Mason, you know this could get a whole lot uglier before it gets better."

"I know. I also know I'll be at your side for all of it, if it's what you want."

She wrapped her arms around him, feeling how solid he was. He'd always been that way, would have been there for her, but she hadn't been able to trust herself, hadn't been able to assert herself.

"I don't want to face my parents. Do you know how infuriating that is? Mason, I'm thirty! Why is it so damn hard to go to them and tell them the truth, tell them how messed up my life was because I knuckled under instead of admitting to and defending what I felt? I can't help thinking, if I had only been brave two years ago, none of this would have happened."

"That kind of conjecture only leads to frustration. We have to play the cards we're holding, not speculate on what's already come and gone. Right now, I can tell you, I'll stand by you. I'll go with you to confront your parents, to tell them what's happened--because, Stacey, honey, you're going to have to tell them. You should tell them all of it. They need to share some of the pain their demands caused."

Leaning into him, she relaxed. "I know." She sighed. "Logically, I know this, have always known it, but it doesn't change the trepidation I feel."

Mason stroked a strand of hair from her face, making Stacey smile. He was tidying her without any regard to the fact his hair, which he normally kept so neatly confined at the nape of his neck, now hung in tangles around his shoulders.

"You make me feel so special," she whispered, holding his dark gaze.

"You are special. I want you to know that. Come back with me to my place here in town tonight. If you want to go back to the bay tomorrow, we can do that, but tonight, I need to hold you, Stacey, need to feel you against me and know you're safe."

She took a deep breath. "As long as we both know where we're at. I can't..."

He cupped her cheek. "I know. All we can do is take it one day at a time."

The knot of tension still coiled deep in her stomach eased, and she nodded.

* * * *

Mason was nervous as he settled her in his car. Stupid. He'd already had her in his home at the beach, so why should he be nervous bringing her to his brownstone? He knew the answer. The beach house had only glimpses of him in it, but this was his home. He'd decorated it. He'd picked the artwork. The home was the truest reflection of him. One glimpse of her townhouse, and her decorating hand had been obvious. It pissed him off to think a house she'd so lovingly furnished now held such horrendous memories--like her sailboat did. Jason Winchester had a hell of a lot to answer for.

As he slipped behind the wheel, Mason glanced her way. Judging by her expression, some of her thoughts must be following the same lines. She looked sad, wistful.

"I tried to make it a home, Mason, but it never really was--not when Jace could betray me the way he did."

Her words were little more than a whisper, but he was relieved to hear she no longer sounded as broken as she first had. He touched her arm to get her attention, waiting to speak until she met his gaze in the darkness.

"I am so damn proud of you and the way you stood up to him."

"Thanks. It's taken me some time to get there, but I think I finally understand how wrong it was to try to live my life solely in an effort to please other people. I mean, I don't want to be selfish, but I've always tried to please my parents, and it's led to nothing but heartache." She sighed. "I want to put this behind us. Is it even possible?"

"I'm not sure, but I do know I'd like for us to move forward together." He started the car and put it into gear, pulling out into the lighter nighttime traffic. "Is that possible?"

As she hesitated, the throbbing in his cheek grew more insistent.

"Mason, I can't imagine any place I'd rather be. I made such a mistake..."

"Shh... It's behind us, Stacey." Relief poured through him. "Come home with me. Let me show you how it can be. We had the sex right off the bat. Now let's see if we can have a relationship."

Stacey huffed out a heavy breath. "Maybe down the road, I'll be able to view Jace as just an unpleasant intermission in what should have been all along."

Mason took his hand off the shift and rubbed her shoulder. "It will be. Eventually we'll replace it with new memories."

"Then let's start now."

He pulled into the garage, accessible from the alley behind, and led her up the stairs into his spacious kitchen. With a flick of his wrist, he activated the overhead recessed lighting, then adjusted the dimmer.

"Let me how you your room." He started to move past her, but she laid her slender fingers on his arm. Mason stopped and raised his brows.

"Put me in your room, Mason." She was so nervous she vibrated.

He shook his head. "I won't push. I won't have you in my bed scared."

She squeezed his arm. "Not scared. Protected. I know I'm asking a lot, but until this is settled, I just... I would feel better if I knew you were right there. Is it too much?"

Yes. "No. I'll keep you safe." He covered her fingers with his, noting the contrast between her creamy skin and his darker complexion. An angel and a demon. "I've done a lot of things in my life, Stacey, that weren't always my proudest moments, but I've never..." He had to stop and take a deep breath. "I've never mistreated a woman, and I'll never mistreat you. I know those are just words right now, but time will show you."

He broke her gaze and glanced around the kitchen. "Would you like something to eat?"

She shook her head. "What I'd like is a hot bath and a bed."

He smiled, relaxing once more. "I can do that."

She feathered her fingertips over his swollen cheek. "First, let me clean your face. God, Mason. Will the pain Jace has caused never end?"

"It will. Sooner now." He grabbed her hand. "Come on. I'll get the first aid kit."

He set it on the wide wooden table, hooked a couple of the chairs and sat. "Do me."

Stacey gaped at him, then to his relief she laughed. He grinned at her. "Oh, Mason. I needed that. I need a washcloth."

"There are clean dishcloths in the drawer to the left of the sink."

He watched her as she found the cloth and started the water running. When the temperature suited her, she held the rag beneath it, wrung it out and turned off the faucet. She sat across from him and leaned forward, putting the fingers of one hand beneath his chin. She was gentle, but he still couldn't help the wince as she dabbed at the blood on his cheek.

"I'm sorry. The cut's not bad, but you're going to have a bruise."

"It was worth it." He held her gaze for an instant. "Get it bandaged, then I'll put some ice on it."

* * * *

Stacey was as gentle as she could be, but the blood had dried. She held the cloth in place and let the moisture soften it so she could wipe it clean. After daubing on antibiotic ointment, she covered it with a bandage and began cleaning. Mason rubbed his forehead.

"Head hurting?"

"A bit. I'm sure it's the stress as well as the punch."

"I'll get you some ice." She collected the first aid kit, dumped the trash in the compactor and stowed the kit in the pantry closet. "Do you have a cold pack or do I need to bag some ice?"

"There's a pack in the freezer."

She handed it to him, then paced restlessly around the kitchen. "I have this nervous energy. I-I don't know what to do with it."

"You could soak in the tub in the master bath. I'll bring you some wine."

She held his dark gaze, knowing she would be giving him permission to come in while she was vulnerable. "Okay. I'd like that."

She ran the bath, even found bubble bath to add to the water, then stripped off her clothes and slid into the fragrant bubbles. She smiled at the idea of Mason sitting amidst the suds. He knocked briefly on the door as though he'd somehow known how long it would before she settled neck deep in the water.

"Come in."

He had his hair pulled back and had changed into a t-shirt and some cotton sleep pants, his feet bare. In one hand he carried a glass of wine, in the other a dress shirt and some silky boxers. "I thought this would do you until we can get back to your place to get the rest of your belongings."

Stacey took the glass of chilled white wine. She hadn't given much thought to having to return to the home she'd shared with Jace. The idea of going in there again made her stomach twist in knots.

"I'll go with you, Stacey," Mason assured her. "You won't be alone."

"I can do it," she tried to assure him, but he cut her off.

"I don't trust him, honey. Until I'm sure he's going to leave you alone, I don't want you to go anywhere without either me or someone else with you."

She stared at him. "He's screwed up, Mason, but I don't think he'll try anything."

Mason set the clothing down and perched on the edge of the tub. "It's not just him. It's your parents. Until we have everything cleared, until they understand the truth and accept it, I don't trust them not to try something like an involuntary commitment either."

She rested her head against the back of the tub and sighed. "It's so complicated, and I just want it to be over with."

"It will be." He stood. "I'm going to call my assistant and let her know what's going on. As much as I'd like to keep this completely private, I want everyone at the gallery to understand they are to give out no information about either one of us. When you're through in here, come to bed. I want to hold you in my arms."

The door shut softly behind him, leaving Stacey alone in the subdued lighting of the large master bath. She sipped her wine and set it on the tile ledge next to the tub. She let her mind go back to her first time with Mason. He'd been rough and fast, trying to prove a point, but never had he done anything against her will. She had known even then his sole focus was in giving her pleasure.

And after the first time, they had never seemed to be able to get enough of each other. Stacey grabbed the washcloth, dunked it in the water then slowly drew it along her arm. It brought back a memory she'd pushed to the back of her mind after she'd broken things off with him. Late one afternoon, she was scheduled to meet a client at a house they were looking at for possible purchase. The current owners were out of the country, posted to an embassy in Central America, but they had left everything on--power, electricity--and all their furniture. Once the job appeared to be long term, they'd put the house on the market.

Stacey had arrived, but her clients were nowhere in sight. That was when Mason had walked around the block, grinning at her like a kid caught in a prank...

"What are you doing here?"

"It's a surprise."

"Mason! I have clients who'll be here in a few minutes."

"No they won't. I told them you had to reschedule."

She arched a brow. "A bit high-handed, don't you think?"

He grabbed her hand. "Come with me. Once you see what I have in store for you, I don't think you'll mind."

He led her inside, up the stairs and down the long hall to the master suite at the back of the house. Soft music played through the built-in speakers. When he shut the bedroom door, he led her to a small table near the window. Champagne and chocolate fondue greeted her. Stacey laughed.

"You're incorrigible."

He stepped behind her. "It will taste much better if we're naked."

She spun to look at him. "You're crazy!"

"Mmm. Maybe, but I'd like to lick the champagne from your breasts and the chocolate from..." He leaned in to whisper in her ear and Stacey's cheeks went instantly hot. Before she could say anything else, he began to strip her suit and blouse from her, then kneeled in front of her to tug her stockings down her legs, his lips touching the inside of each thigh. Stacey braced herself on his shoulders. He tilted his head to look at her. "Take your bra off, honey."

She had done it, cupping her breasts in her hands for an instant before letting the lacy undergarment fall. Mason hissed, put out his hands and ripped the panties off her. The sound of the tearing fabric followed by the flick of his tongue between her legs nearly had her falling to the floor.

"I want to see you," she'd gasped. "I want you naked."

"Whatever you wish." He had stripped for her. When he'd at last dropped his silky shorts to bare his hard ass, Stacey couldn't stand it any longer. She'd stepped forward, pressing along his backside while her arms wrapped around his front, teasing his chest, then sliding lower over his stomach to his rock hard erection. Her fingers had circled him, stroked. Mason had exhaled on a long groan. "That's it. Sweet, sweet Stacey."

He'd fed her fruit, dribbled chocolate and champagne on her, on him, and they'd laughed as they licked it off, and then he'd carried her into the bathroom, and while the tub filled, he'd slowly thrust into her where they'd landed on the thick bathroom rug...

Stacey shook her head, realized the water was cooling, and rose from Mason's tub. She had no idea how long she'd sat there daydreaming. That had been a beautiful afternoon, but she'd had to hurry away so she could get to a dinner with her parents, a dinner where Jace had been invited without her knowledge.

She dried off hurriedly and donned the clothing Mason had brought her. When she entered the bedroom, he'd brought in a tray of food and set it in the middle of the king-sized bed. He glanced at her entrance.

"I thought we could relax in here. There's TV..."

She shook her head. "Could we talk?"

Mason smiled. "Let's think of it like a first date. I can find out the important stuff, like your favorite color and what kind of dog you'd like to have."

"Blue." Stacey laughed. "And how did you know I'd like a dog?"

Mason took her hand and led her over to one side of the bed. After she sat, he handed her a glass. "Just iced tea," he assured her. "As to the dog, it's something I've always wanted so I hope you do too."

She eased back against the thick stack of pillows at the head of the huge bed. Tears stung her eyes. When one slipped from the corner of her eye, he brushed it away.

"Why are you crying?"

She shook her head. "It's stupid, but I guess until now, none of this seemed real to me. But somehow, the idea of getting a dog..."

He sat next to her. "We don't have to have one."

"No...I mean yes. I want one. Something that could come sailing with us...on your boat." She scooted over. "Sit with me. I think I'd like to feel your arms around me."

He eased onto the bed next to her, shifting the tray so they wouldn't spill it. "You sure?"

She nodded. "While I was soaking, I was remembering the day you surprised me at the house that was on the market."

Mason chuckled. "I remember that afternoon. Did it bother you to remember?"

Stacey sucked in a deep breath. "No. It makes me feel safer...saner." She set her tea glass on the nightstand and forced herself to meet his gaze. "I need to know, Mason. Does what happened make a difference to you?"

"Jesus, Stacey. No. If I thought for one moment you would even give me the opportunity to show you how little it does matter..."

"I'm giving you the opportunity."

Chapter 12

Everything inside Mason went utterly still. She wanted to make love? He took her hand, massaging the back with his thumb. This was something he'd wanted, more than anything, but he needed to know where her head was. He wouldn't be vengeance sex. He wanted her too much, loved her too much.

She was so serious, but she'd always been that. It had taken him some time to get her to loosen up with him and cast off the strictures drilled into her since childhood. Then when she'd broken it off, he'd seen, from a distance, how her social veneer fell back into place, even thicker and harder than before.

"Mason?" she prompted. "Say something here. You're making me nervous."

"I'm making me nervous," he admitted. "I don't want to scare you. I don't think I could stand that."

She smiled and leaned toward him. "Then start with a kiss."

Was it really so simple?

He framed her face with his hands and closed the distance between them. As gently as he could, he brushed his mouth on hers, nibbled at her lips and leaned back a bit to gauge her reaction. Her eyes were closed, her face relaxed. Oh yes. So far so good.

"I won't break." She opened her golden eyes and gave him a smile that was just a slight curving of her soft lips.

He leaned his forehead against hers. "Then I'll be happy to accelerate this a bit."

Mason moved the tray, setting it on the floor next to the bed. He stripped off his t-shirt, but left the sleep pants in place for the time being. He was already hard. While his body might be clamoring for him to rush this as fast as possible, he didn't want to go there at the moment. He wanted to give her time, woo her, as he'd never really done before. When he sat again, he pulled her into his arms.

"Lie down with me. I want to get closer," he murmured.

Her golden gaze locked with his. "I love you, Mason. I can't promise everything will go smoothly, but I want this. I want you."

"I love you. I won't scare you. So if you get to that point, you tell me. Is it a deal?"

"Yes."

Maybe it should have felt mechanical, but admitting what they were thinking made it feel like they'd put everything out there. For the first time, they were being completely honest about where they were and what was going on.

Mason ran his hands over the silky material of the shirt he'd loaned her, then gently back until he cupped her breasts with only the thin fabric separating his flesh from hers. Her nipples had hardened and he smiled.

"That's it," he whispered. "Just like that." Leaning in, he kissed her again, pleased to note she met him halfway, her mouth opening so their tongues could touch. Mason moaned. Man he'd missed this, missed her. Slow, slow, slow. But he wasn't listening. He pulled her hips into him, feeling her stiffen for an instant as her belly came in contact with his erection. There was scarcely anything he could do to hide his body's reaction. He was having a difficult enough time harnessing his need so he wouldn't rush or scare her.

She tangled her hands in his hair, obviously being careful to avoid the bruise on his cheek. Mason licked along the edge of her ear to her collarbone. When she arched toward him, he groaned.

"Sweet...so damn sweet, and I've missed you so much."

"Touch me, Mason. I want to feel your hands on me. I never ever forgot you, but all I could do was imagine your touch. Now I need it for real."

He flicked his fingers over the shirt buttons, releasing them and pushing the placket aside to reveal the pink, puckered tips of her breasts. Please, God, don't let him scare her. He cupped her again, stroking and squeezing before lowering his mouth to suckle her. When she moaned, his cock swelled until he ached with the need to be inside her. Slow. He had to slow down so he didn't frighten her.

"More, Mason."

He pushed her breasts together, licking first one nipple and then the other. Then, continuing to knead her with his fingers, he kissed his way to her belly, covered only by his silky boxer shorts. Mason laid his cheek against her and closed his eyes. His hands slipped to her waist, holding her in place while he swallowed again and again. Emotion had overwhelmed him and he simply couldn't do anything else as he fought for some control.

"Mason? Honey? Is something wrong?"

Uncertainty colored her tone, and he was sorry he'd sparked it. He shook his head.

"Then why have you stopped?"

"I'm so sorry," he grated, his voice thick and hoarse. "I let my anger blind me. I'd give anything to have been able to spare you this right from the very beginning. I should have trusted..."

She stroked his hair, squeezed his shoulder. They lay there like that until she finally spoke. "We can change it right now, Mason. Make love to me. Join your body to mine and let's make new memories. We can start again. I want to. With you."

He blinked the moisture from his eyes, leaned away so he could see her face. "I want you to see me, touch me, before we go any further. I have to know you're comfortable with..." He gestured to the thrust of his erection, tenting the front of his sleep pants.

She smiled, the most beautiful expression he'd seen. "Stand. Let me take them off of you."

Mason realized he was trembling as he watched the expressions flit across her face, and yes, there was a flash of fear, but then she moved beyond, as if her subconscious had awakened to whom it was standing so near. She rested her forehead against his stomach, her breath brushing the material covering his cock. Mason couldn't hold in the moan quaking through him.

"Oh, sweet heaven, Stacey. Touch me."

He was desperate, needy. He'd longed for this for the past two years, dreamt about it at night and then kicked himself for not being able to put her from his mind. She captured the ends of the ties at his waist, slowly pulling them undone while he shook. Then her hands slid into the elasticized waist and pushed. She eased back, her glance shifting between his face and his cock. When it finally sprang free, her gasp was soft--just a catch of breath.

"You're beautiful, Mason," she whispered, pushing his pants until they dropped of their own accord and he stepped free.

"Are you okay?" he asked, unable to tell from her expression where her head was in that moment. She didn't answer with words. Instead, Stacey touched him.

Mason went utterly still, tears running down his cheeks as he let her explore his body, afraid to move for fear he might frighten her. She wrapped her fingers around him, teasing him. Then her lips and tongue brushed him and he sobbed.

"Mason?" Worry colored her tone. "What's wrong?"

He shook his head, stroked hers, afraid to speak but hoping she would understand it was okay to keep going. She did. Her caresses gained confidence, so he let her continue to the point he feared he would lose control.

"My turn," he whispered, pushing her back on the bed and sliding the boxers over her slender hips and down her long legs. When she was bared to him, he knelt next to the bed. "You good?"

Her smile was a bit wobbly, but she nodded.

"I want you to watch. I want you to know who it is."

She opened to him, reached out and touched his cheek. "No one's done this since you."

Mason's hands clamped on her butt cheeks. Her husband had never given her this? What the hell? He turned his face to the inside of her thigh and softly kissed the tender skin. "Then let me love you this way. For this first time. All right?"

She nodded, her golden eyes glowing with anticipation. He remembered seeing her like that so often. With a final, soft smile, he raised her hips and began teasing her with his tongue. She was heaven--sweet, flowing heaven. Her moans and her taste had him hovering at the very edge of his own climax, but he held himself in check, intent on giving her the ultimate pleasure before he ever sought his own.

She cried after she came, wracking sobs he soothed with his body and his voice, and only when she was tucked against him and quiet did he begin to kiss her again. Mason shifted her so he could kneel between her thighs. She watched him as he guided his shaft to her opening, then smiled and laughed as he began to thrust long and slow.

Mason wished he could make it last forever, but it had been too long, and feeling her wrapped around him was more than he could resist. He locked his hands in hers, rested his weight on his elbows and held her gaze as he thrust, spilling himself inside her.

"I love you," she whispered and he answered the same way. She was back where she belonged. In his arms and in his bed. Now all they had to do was convince her parents it was the right thing. Mason knew Stacey too well. She needed that approval, no matter how much she might resent it.

* * * *

Jace shut the hotel door behind the last of his in-laws, who'd felt it necessary to escort him all the way to a hotel, and leaned his forehead against it as he turned the deadbolt. "You should go too, Justin," he murmured. His world was falling apart. "I don't care what they say. This is going to get ugly. Go back to the ranch."

Justin's arms slid around his waist, the comforting bulk of him pressing against Jace's back. "I can stand the heat."

Jace laughed, but it was choked and painful. "I'm not sure I can."

"Then let me help you."

If only it were that simple. Jace's mind raced as he tried to figure out if he could still avoid coming out. Publicly it might be possible, but could he avoid it even to his family? He shuddered. Being gay might not be a big deal in another place, or if he were another person, but Winchester men had always adhered to a certain code.

"Jace, let your sister's husband take over the business. Come back to the ranch with me."

He took a deep breath. "I can't do that, Justin. I think you were right the other day when you said you needed space. Maybe we both do."

"What are you saying?"

"Maybe you should go back to the ranch. I can't be what you want. I can't live the way you want."

"Can't or won't?" Justin had stepped back, studied him now with faintly narrowed eyes.

"Won't then." Jace hardened his heart.

Justin pressed his lips together. "I see. It's okay for us to sneak around and have sex on the sly, but now it's come to a point where we either bring our relationship out or deny it, you choose to continue living the lie."

"That's my choice."

"I'm sorry for you." Justin brushed past him, unbolted the door and stepped through it. "I'll be around for a few weeks so I can conclude the ranch's business here. You know where to find me."

The door shut quietly. Jace leaned against it again, but this time he made no effort to control the emotions that shook him with such force he eventually sobbed out loud.

* * * *

She must have slept. When she awoke, Stacey felt safe and rested, then realized part of her security might be due to Mason's arms wrapped around her and his powerful body spooning her. She breathed deeply, catching his spicy, masculine scent, and smiled.

Mason.

"You all right?" At his question, she realized she must have spoken aloud. His arms tightened, hugging her close.

"Yes. Yes, I am. God, Mason, I feel amazing."

He chuckled in her ear with his gravelly voice, sending a shiver of awareness along her spine. "That might be the best ego boost I've had in years."

She turned in his arms and buried her face against his neck, loving the feel of his scratchy beard, of his hair-covered legs tangling with her long, bare limbs.

"I know there are a lot of things we need to do," she told him, "but for a bit, I want to savor feeling like a normal woman."

She didn't want to discuss Jace, didn't want to mention the utter weirdness that had been her marriage to him. Maybe someday, she'd be able to look back on it with added perspective, but at the moment it was too painful and too humiliating.

"Wherever you are right now," Mason whispered in her ear, "leave that place. I can feel you tensing on me. The past is done. We're moving ahead. What's for you to decide is what you want to tackle first."

"If he's out of the house, I want to go get my personal belongings. As far as I'm concerned, the house can be rented or sold with its contents."

Mason stroked the hair back from her face. "Hold off until you get everything settled...at least the selling. I'll double check with Phillip, then you and I can drive over there to collect your clothing and whatever else you want to take."

An hour later, they were standing at the base of the front steps, where Stacey had stopped, unable to make herself move forward.

"I need you to go in first," she told Mason, handing him the house key. He put his arm around her shoulders.

"We're going to wait for Phillip and his assistant. They'll catalog everything, so there's no question of what was removed from the house. I trust Winchester as little as you do."

"All right."

Phillip pulled up in a couple minutes, rounding the car to hold the door for his middle-aged paralegal. After shaking Mason's hand and commenting on his bruised cheek, he pulled Stacey into a bear hug. "You all right?" he rumbled.

She hugged him back. He was as big as Seth, but not nearly as intimidating. Phillip had always been the Boy Scout of the family--serious and goal-oriented, he'd avoided the mischief Brandon had gotten into and the rebellion that had characterized Seth.

"I'm doing okay, Phillip."

He smiled at her. "We'll make this as easy as we can."

Phillip and Linda went in first, with her and Mason following. Walking in the front door brought back so many memories, few of them good. It had taken Stacey time, but in the back of her mind, she'd realized something was seriously wrong with her marriage. Maybe some of it was her fault. Even though she'd sworn to herself she would make her marriage work, in the back of her mind Mason had always been there. Jace had never come close to obliterating the memories of her weeks in Mason's arms.

As if he could read her thoughts, Mason turned her to face him. "Nothing you could have done would have made any difference, Stacey, so do not blame yourself. You might have entered into your marriage with good intentions, but Jace never intended to alter his lifestyle. Remember, it was him who split us apart to begin with."

"You're right." Stacey shuddered as she glanced around her. "Let's go to my office first."

This was the one space in the entire townhouse Stacey felt hadn't been violated by Jace's presence. He'd never come into her workspace. That she knew for sure thanks to the security she'd installed.

"If you'll tell us what you want to take with you from each of the rooms we go into," Phillip instructed. "Linda will record it, then we'll get copies of it to Jace before I bring in a mover. Where are you going to want it moved?"

Stacey hesitated. "My personal items can go to Mason's house, but this…"

Mason squeezed her shoulder. "There's room at the gallery, Stacey. I have an extra office you're welcome to make use of temporarily or long term."

Their gazes met. Stacey felt the tension that had been building start to release. She looked at her brother and nodded. "That sounds perfect."

As lunchtime approached, Stacey's cell phone rang. She glanced at the caller ID.

"It's Mother," she said.

"Take it," Phillip advised. "If she wants you to visit, I want both Mason and me with you."

Stacey nodded. She recalled her last phone conversation with her mother and hoped this would not be a repeat.

"Hello, Mother."

"Darling," she began in a tone she might use with a slightly hysterical child. "Your father and I hadn't heard from you and were worried. Are you feeling any better?"

Stacey lifted her chin. "Yes, Mother. The bruises are beginning to fade. Phillip and Mason are here at the house with me, helping me collect my belongings."

There was a long silence on the other end. "You've involved your brother in your disagreement with your husband? Is that wise? I can still make arrangements for you ..."

"Let me stop you before you continue along this same line, Mother. Not only is Phillip involved, but Seth and Brandon know what's gone on as well. In fact, all three of them assisted me last night in forcing Jason and his lover to leave. Phillip is filing the necessary paperwork petitioning for the annulment."

"But darling, the marriage is consummated. I think you're overreacting to Jason's desire to start a family."

Stacey pinched the bridge of her nose. "This is getting us nowhere. At the risk of inviting myself and my siblings to your home, I think it would be wise for all of us to discuss this."

"I think it's an excellent idea. I'll contact the priest and Jason..."

"Stop, Mother. I can assure you, should Jason be anywhere in the vicinity, your sons as well as Mason Hatch will beat him to within an inch of his miserable life. Please try to understand this. My marriage to Jason Winchester is over. Since you will not believe me, I will bring Seth, Brandon, Phillip and Mason to explain the details to you and Father. I had hoped to spare you that much, but you're making this into an impossible and very painful situation."

Phillip snagged the phone from her. "Good morning, Mother... Yes, I'm here with Stacey and she is perfectly sane. If you and Father have no other plans, please expect us around six tonight. I doubt the spouses will wish to be there, but in addition to Seth, Brandon, Stacey and me, you should also expect Mason Hatch... You'll recall him from Lucy's exhibition. Yes." Phillip grinned at Mason. "The one with the ponytail. Goodbye, Mother."

He punched End and handed the phone back to Stacey. She glared at him. "Why is it Mother never listens to any of her daughters?"

Phillip shrugged. "Maybe it's generational. It could be worse."

"How's that?"

"I'm not sure she's even aware we have a younger sister."

"Morgan does seem incredibly adept at fading into the woodwork or disappearing completely."

Phillip's lips tightened. "I hope this evening will be one of those nights. I'm not sure she needs to hear what we'll discuss."

"No. You're right about that." She glanced at everyone. "Let's go to the master suite. I'd like to get it over with."

* * * *

Mason kept an eye on her as they entered the room she'd shared with Winchester. It was hard enough for him, so he could only imagine what Stacey must be going through. She grabbed his hand, her fingers clutching. He pulled her to his side.

"You don't have to do this. I can do it for you."

"No. Just…stay with me."

Mason nodded, his jaw tight with controlled anger. He'd seen what was on the security video, and knew from Stacey's descriptions some of what had gone on had to have taken place here. He could only thank God it was truly designed as a suite--a living room area followed by walk-in closets and the master bath, with the bedroom beyond. Phillip halted at the door from the bath into the bedroom and glanced over his shoulder at his sister.

"Is there any need to go farther?"

Stacey's fingers trembled in Mason's grasp. "No. Everything I want is in the closet."

It took them another hour to go through the remainder of the house. Stacey refused to go either onto the deck or into Jace's study. After they left the kitchen, Mason stopped her.

"I think this is enough, Stacey. Let Phillip and Linda finish." He glanced at her brother. "Once we have Stacey's belongings out of here, have the locks changed. The property is in her name, so there's no need for Winchester to be in here without being accompanied by you or someone of your choosing. The sailboat you can put on the market as soon as we have Winchester's signature on everything. Until then, it needs to be secured for possible evidence, wouldn't you agree?"

"Absolutely." Phillip crossed the hallway and gave his sister a hug. "If I can talk Seth into driving, you want to ride out en masse to the house?"

"That might be a good idea," Mason interjected. "A show of solidarity."

Stacey took a deep breath. "All right."

Chapter 13

Stacey felt a bit like the president as they approached the front door to her parents' home. Dinners were never casual at the Barlow-Barrett mansion, at least when her parents were present. There had never been cookouts or informal family gatherings here. Those had always been saved for the beach or the house in Stowe. Here, the attire was dresses for women, at least a coat and tie for men. All three of her brothers were in suits. Even Mason had a suit on, though he'd paired it with a pink shirt and darker pink tie.

She slipped her fingers through his, smiling tightly when he squeezed reassuringly. He'd slicked his long hair back, but left it hanging loose to his shoulders. Stacey knew precisely why. It was a subtle way to draw her parents' anger from her to him, and she loved him all the more for it.

Seth and Brandon were walking side by side in front of them while Phillip brought up the rear. Yes, it was a bit like having the Secret Service surrounding her. And what a shame she needed such protection from her own family.

Forbes answered the door and informed them their parents were expecting them in the living room.

"Is Morgan here?" Phillip asked in a too-casual tone. None of them wanted their youngest sister present for what would have to be discussed.

"No, Mr. Phillip. Your sister has gone to the beach with friends."

"Good." Everyone relaxed.

Seth opened the living room door and stood aside for Stacey and Mason to precede him. As she walked past her brother, he whispered, "Chin up."

Stacey smiled slightly and did just that. She was tired of groveling to win favor from her parents, her mother in particular. As she glanced at her father's massive frame, she wondered sometimes exactly who was the boss in this family. Alexander Barlow-Barrett seemed, all too often, to simply allow his wife to run roughshod over their children. Yet, she'd seen him in action at Barrett Newspapers. He was not a man to sit idly by and allow events to simply happen. He wanted a hand in them. She pinned her hopes on that aspect of his character.

Her mother was the first to speak. "Was it really necessary to drag your brothers into this…this sordid mess?"

Before she could reply, Seth had lifted something from a side table. It was a business card with information scribbled onto it. "Already had a visitor today?"

"What do you mean?" Stacey asked, a knot forming in her stomach. Mason slid an arm around her waist, drawing her closer to him.

He flicked the card to Phillip, who snagged it and pursed his lips as he looked at what was written on it. "Looks to me like we're going to need to do another arm-twisting session with Mr. Winchester."

Brandon snorted. "Why don't we call the cops? We have plenty of evidence."

"Stacey wants this kept out of the press," Mason reminded them, "for the sake of your family, though personally, I see little reason for her concern."

Patricia Barlow-Barrett glared at him. "And what exactly would you know with regard to family, Mr. Hatch? Do you think we didn't have you checked out the moment those disgusting photographs surfaced? Why do you think we were so anxious for Stacey to accept Jason's generous offer? We would have done almost anything to prevent her association with you."

"That's enough." Stacey startled herself by stepping forward and speaking. "It might surprise you to know, Mother, Jason was the one who took those pictures. He was the one who sent them, who blackmailed you for money at the same time he was making his 'offer.'"

"Those are terrible allegations to make against your husband."

"He admitted it to me."

Her mother's smile was condescending. "You're hardly a credible witness. Jason told us…"

"Mother," Seth said quietly, "I had hoped we could hold off on this conversation until after dinner, but I'm afraid at least some of it must take place now. Phillip, do you have the pictures handy that were taken at the hospital? Before I listen to another word in support of Winchester, I want both you and Father to take a look."

Phillip set his briefcase on the coffee table and extracted a manila envelope, which he handed to his father. Stacey held her breath while he opened the envelope and pulled out the files. This was the moment she was counting on. She leaned into Mason, feeling his silent support as he rested his hands on her arms and gently squeezed. For as outspoken as he normally was, she was amazed at the control he was exerting now in not ripping into her mother, in particular. She leaned her head back against his shoulder and felt his lips brush her hair.

Her father's face flushed as he looked at the photos, passing them to her mother one at a time. "He told us you'd fallen..." he murmured as though to himself. "But I've seen enough pictures of abused women over the years."

Phillip handed Stacey a handkerchief. "Show them your arms, Stacey."

She took off the short matching jacket to her dress. When she turned around to face her parents, she saw doubt in their expressions, but this time it wasn't her word they questioned, but Jace's.

Her father looked at his sons, at Mason and finally at her. "From what I saw and what I read, I believe you're right. We should eat dinner first, then we'll take this into my study to discuss. I take it you have additional evidence?"

"We do," Phillip responded. "You also have the man here who found her and got her to the hospital."

Right now, the only acknowledgement her father was willing to give was a curt nod, but that would do. It was at least an acknowledgement that Mason was more than wallpaper.

"Under the circumstances," her father said quietly, "I suggest we forego the before dinner drinks and simply proceed to the dining room. We can do coffee and something stronger in my study afterward."

* * * *

Mason cupped Stacey's elbow as he followed the others to the dining room. Her mother was right concerning one thing--Mason didn't know anything when it came to families like this one. He'd been in several foster homes as a kid, and none were as cold and dysfunctional as this family appeared to be.

He regarded Stacey in an entirely new light. That she and her siblings had turned out as normal as they had said more for them as individuals than it did for any parenting skills on the part of Patricia and Alexander Barlow-Barrett.

"Don't stare at them as if they are bugs," Stacey whispered as they approached the table.

"They aren't?" he murmured in return, drawing a hastily stifled giggle from her. Glancing around, he found her mother's eyes boring into him. Mason dusted an imaginary piece of lint from his lapel and smiled at

Stacey's mother. In his years on the streets and now working with clients, he had met people--men and women--who did their best to intimidate anyone they felt was beneath their notice. Mason was immune.

He had come a long way since he'd had to do things he'd rather forget just to get a meal, so dining at a table set with Wedgwood China and Waterford Crystal was nothing new. Nor was the fact the walls were hung with original and collectible art anything to inspire awe, although he had to admit, he wouldn't mind making an offer to purchase some of it for his own collection.

"Forbes mentioned Morgan is at the beach," Phillip said, obviously trying to get some sort of conversation going that would span only neutral territory. "Is she sailing?"

"She went with some friends from the club. They're spending the weekend on the yacht."

Brandon chuckled. "I hope you reminded her she'll need to take her nose out of whatever book she's reading so she can pay attention to where she's sailing."

"Give her a break," Stacey murmured. "She's the best female sailor in this family."

"Give yourself a break," Mason said. "You do pretty well when you have a decent crew." He looked over at Brandon. "Like me."

"Is that a challenge, Hatch?" Brandon inquired, one brow arching.

"You sail?" Stacey's father asked, turning his first thorough look on Mason.

"Yes, I do," Mason told him. "In fact, Brandon and I were often on competing crews at Harvard."

Now, even Patricia gave him an intent look. Mason wanted to laugh.

"You attended Harvard?" she inquired.

He smiled. "Strictly scholarship, and what it didn't cover, I had to. In fact, that's how I got started sailing."

"He's good, Dad," Brandon told his father. "If he weren't such a shark in the art world, I'm sure he'd be captaining some well-funded racing vessel."

The conversation on sailing continued, and Mason was relieved to see Stacey settle down and finally eat some of her meal instead of simply shoving the food around the plate. As dessert was served, though, her hand tightened on her spoon. They would be heading back into dangerous territory soon. Even as he thought that, Patricia dabbed her lips on her napkin, set it aside and stood.

"Shall we?"

There was no doubt who the queen of this castle was, but Mason was damned if he'd let anyone else mistreat Stacey. He held her chair for her, then tucked her hand through his arm. As everyone else went ahead, he pulled her to the side of the doorway.

"Mason!" she squeaked. "What are you doing?"

"Reminding you there's more to life than this house and your parents' opinions." He tilted his head and brushed his lips across hers. When she responded, he tugged her closer and deepened the kiss, only breaking it off when he heard someone clear their throat. Seth regarded them with raised brows.

"I hate to interrupt, but I would like to get this over with so I can get back to my wife and child. Haunting these palatial surroundings isn't exactly my first choice of places I want to be."

"Sorry, man," Mason said. "I can see your point there. Just wanted to remind Stacey what matters."

She straightened the green jacket and sheath she wore and raised her chin. "You're right. Let's get this over with."

She had come a long way from the woman who'd flashed a diamond in his face and told him she was engaged to another man. Mason had the feeling this might be a Stacey he would have to get to know all over again as he watched her step into her father's study.

On the surface, her parents appeared unruffled, her mother asking Forbes to bring a coffee tray in and Alexander checking to see what everyone preferred in the way of after-dinner drinks. Mason was in with the rest of the men, preferring bourbon. Patricia shook her head, and Stacey requested sherry. As he observed her father, Mason noticed his hand wasn't quite steady. It would seem he, at least, had not already made up his mind.

Once everyone had glasses in hand, Alexander sat on the couch next to his wife and looked at Phillip. "I'd like to see what you have in terms of hard evidence against Winchester."

Stacey sat in a chair not far from her father. Mason leaned against the side of the upholstered wing, resting his arm along it as Phillip sat at the other end of the coffee table, briefcase once more in front of him.

"I think it would be best if I walk you through this as we go along," Phillip told his parents. "Some of what I have I would strongly advise you not to look at unless you feel it's absolutely necessary for you to get things straight in your own mind."

He set an envelope on the table. "These are the originals of the pictures you were sent two or so years ago. Do you still have the copies along with the note asking for money?"

Alexander nodded and his wife looked at him with shock. "You told me you were going to destroy them."

"They're in the safe. I thought it prudent to keep them in case something arose in the future...as indeed it has."

"As Stacey told you, Jace admitted to taking the original photographs of Stacey and Mason as well as sending the note demanding money. In addition, when she sought to leave an untenable marriage situation, he threatened her yet again with releasing the photos."

Pulling out a small, digital tape recorder, he played the message Winchester had left on Stacey's cell phone. When it was finished, her father's face was pale with anger, and her mother finally showed doubt.

"You've seen the photos from the hospital," Phillip said quietly. "I'd like you to read the report."

Stacey was trembling. Mason leaned down and took the sherry glass from her hand.

"Why don't you step outside on the terrace with me and let your brothers go through some of this?"

The face she turned to him made him even more determined to get her outside. As brave a front as she might be putting on, she was still only a few days out from a major trauma. Holding their glasses in one hand, he extended his other, careful to keep his expression neutral as everyone turned toward them.

"Stacey and I are going to step outside so you can go through this with your parents, Phillip. I see no reason for her to relive it. If you need me to add anything, we'll be on the terrace."

He didn't ask permission, nor would he ever. While Mason would be as polite as he could be to Stacey's mother and father, he laid a lot of the blame for what had transpired squarely at their door. As far as he was concerned, his job now was to look out for Stacey--whatever it took. He hoped it would not lead to any more distance between her and her parents, but if that happened then so be it.

As they stepped out the French doors onto the terrace running the length of the house, Mason handed her glass to her.

"You all right?"

She downed the sherry in one swallow, then brushed a loose strand of hair from her face. "I'll make it. I think hearing Jace's voice actually making a threat to go public with the pictures might have had the biggest effect so far."

Mason stared out at the rolling hills behind the Barlow-Barrett mansion and gritted his teeth in anger. No child should have to go to this length reliving such an experience simply so her parents would believe what she said. Curiosity ate at him.

"Your father seemed inclined to believe you from the very beginning. So what's with your mother?"

Stacey walked over to the balustrade, running her palm along the smooth stone. "Jace's mother is her best friend. The two of them were ecstatic when he took me to prom. You can imagine how the pressure grew exponentially when he proposed--coincidentally at the same time a mysterious blackmailer was threatening to publish nude photos of me with you. As far as Mother was concerned, everything had worked perfectly."

"Why does your father tolerate it?"

Stacey turned around and leaned against the railing. "I've asked myself that question a lot. You know, he infuriated her last year when he actually attended my niece's christening."

"Seth's daughter?" Mason asked, a bit confused.

"Anna's. Becca was born a year and half ago--and five months before she married the baby's father. You can imagine how well that went over in our household."

Mason snorted. "I keep expecting to see some family chapel with a shrine to the Pope. I mean, your parents kind of wear the whole Catholicism thing on their sleeves."

Stacey looked at him sideways. "You know she offered to have the priest meet with Jace and me."

Mason scowled. "When you talked to her on the phone?"

"Yup. I'm hoping Phillip will explain the whole annulment issue. That should make this situation somewhat more palatable. I know in her eyes divorce would put me beyond redemption."

Mason shook his head. "At the risk of being irreverent, I would simply like to see her face when it's finally made plain to her Jace's lover is another man."

Stacey shuddered, and Mason pulled her into his arms.

"Sorry, honey."

"That's all right." She leaned back a bit to look at him. "Is this finally over? Are we finally at a point where we can be together?"

He touched the end of her nose with his finger. "Wiggle your nose and wish it so. I have the feeling your brother will make it happen far faster than anyone else could. He's a bit of a bulldog. I don't think I'd like to have him on the other side of a legal battle."

Stacey snuggled closer. "I suspect he won't be in the courtroom too much longer. He's made noise as long as I can remember that he intends to go into politics, and made damn sure to stay squeaky clean so he can."

Mason arched a brow. "How squeaky clean?"

Stacey laughed. "He barely even dates."

"Wow."

A creak of wood against wood alerted them to the doors opening behind them. "We're through, Stacey," Brandon informed them, sticking his head out the doors. "Phillip's explained what you want to do."

When they stepped back into the room, Mason kept his arm around Stacey's waist. Patricia Barlow-Barrett sat like a statue on the couch, her face pale beneath her make-up, while Alexander stood near the fireplace, a scowl darkening his patrician features. When he spotted Stacey, he crossed the room and extended his hands to her. Mason felt her tremble before she left his arms to go to her father.

"We owe you an apology, Stacey. We owe you a hell of a lot more, but we'll start with the apology. Phillip's outlined what you've demanded of Winchester, and we'll support whatever it is you want to do. But I must tell you, I would be more than willing to pursue him to the full extent the law allows. What he did to you..." His eyes shifted for a moment to Mason. "And to Mason is inexcusable."

Stacey wrapped her arms around her father and laid her head against his chest. The older man's expression looked pained for a moment before he hugged her to him.

"Thank you, Daddy."

Chapter 14

Mason was quiet as he unlocked the door. He'd been that way the whole trip back to his apartment. As he shut the door and relocked it, Stacey took a deep breath. She wasn't going to tap dance around any man's moodiness anymore.

"What's wrong, Mason? You've been like a wall of disapproval since before we left my parents' house."

"Your mother. She never apologized. Jesus, Stacey, she never even hugged you! I know I'm not exactly the poster child for family feeling, but I've had more warmth from foster parents who were absolutely no relation to me."

"It's the way she is, Mason. The fact an apology came from either one of them is nothing short of a miracle."

"I have to tell you, I'm freaking amazed any of you are as normal as you are. I'd thought so earlier, but what I saw after we went back inside only solidified that idea. Nothing seems to warm your mother, and your father only unbent when we were discussing sailing."

She kicked off her heels and wiggled her toes in the thick pile of the large living room rug. "They've always been that way, particularly Mother. Her focus has always been on putting Daddy first. Everything revolved around him and the family's image." Stacey curled on the end of the couch while Mason continued to pace.

"She would have made a kick-ass press agent for someone, but it seemed to me, honey, she could have unbent enough to give you a hug and at least say you were right concerning Winchester."

Stacey laughed. "And tomorrow the sky will turn pink and the clouds will taste like cotton candy balls."

Mason stopped pacing and arched a brow at her before laughing too. "Not happening, huh?"

"Not likely in this lifetime. I think the most emotion I ever saw from her was when they brought Brandon back from Colorado after the plane crash. Then less than two months after that, Daddy had the problem with his heart. Sure, she wasn't crying and hysterical, but she never left his side. She's not a demonstrative woman…at least not with her kids."

Mason flopped onto the couch next to her and pulled her into his arms. "I am very much a demonstrative man, so if that's a problem, we should get it out in the open now. I like to touch, and I like to touch in public as well as private. That okay with you?"

Stacey stroked his cheek, already slightly beard-roughened again despite having shaved before dinner. "Very okay. Is this part of the finding out about each other process?"

"It can be. You could start with a thorough exploration of my person."

She giggled. "Mm. Likewise." She leaned forward. "Unzip me."

She held her hair to the side for him. His fingers brushed the nape of her neck, then the zipper snicked down and his lips followed. Cool air whispered over her skin.

"You have the most beautiful back." Mason's hands brushed her dress off her shoulders and she pulled her arms from it, letting it drop so only a lacy scrap of bra covered her.

"My back?" Stacey laughed. "Not exactly the place I would have picked as beautiful."

"Oh, but it is," he whispered in her ear. "But so is your neck and your ear. Then there's your collarbone." He pressed a kiss there and Stacey shivered with pleasure. "And your shoulder… Am I getting to know you?"

Her heart thudded and breathing was getting more and more difficult. "Oh, yes, but when will it be my turn?"

He chuckled. "Now seems like an excellent time." He stood. "I suppose I need to get a few clothes off?"

"By all means. I'll watch while you do that."

Mason grinned at her, dimples creasing his lean cheeks, and loosened his tie another notch. "Is that good?"

She shook her head. He removed the tie, shrugged out of his jacket and grinned, raising his brows in question.

"No way, Hatch. Keep going."

"If you insist." He unbuttoned his cuffs, slowly released the buttons on his dress shirt and tugged the tails from his slacks. After tossing the shirt on top of the jacket he glanced over his shoulder, one brow arched. "How about now?"

Stacey swallowed as she stared at the ripple of muscle across his back. "You're getting there."

He kicked off his shoes.

"Maybe you need to take something else off," he murmured.

Stacey stood and let her dress drop to her feet, leaving her in her bra and panties. "Seems I'm a bit more uncovered than you are right now."

"I can fix that." Still with his back to her, he undid his belt and a moment later his slacks pooled at his feet. His socks disappeared with a flick of his fingers, but Stacey barely registered that as she watched his butt flex beneath the silky material of his boxers.

"That's so much better." Her voice sounded breathless even to her.

Mason spun and pulled her into his arms. "Why don't we worry about the rest of it as we go? Hmm?"

"Sounds like a plan."

He eased her back on the couch, careful of her bruised ribs, and then he was cradling her near his chest. "Has anyone kissed you lately?"

"Not in the last thirty seconds or so."

He grinned at her. "Then let me fix that right now."

He nibbled and tasted and licked. For a man who did everything at top speed, when it came to kissing, to making love, Mason took his time. Stacey relaxed into him, enjoying the feeling they had all night, that this wasn't something he wanted to rush.

"I love you, Mason," She whispered in between him exploring her mouth and nibbling on her neck.

He gathered her even closer. "I'm afraid to hug you, honey," he whispered in her ear. "I love you so much."

This time she kissed him, pressing as tight to him as she could get, her good arm wrapped around his neck and her other hand stroking his chest. Her fingers tweaked his nipple and he groaned. While their foreheads were pressed close together, he flicked open the front clasp of her bra, brushed the lace away from her breasts, and gently massaged her. Stacey groaned at the sensation.

"So beautiful." He looked at her and grinned. "Touching you is like touching heaven. Can I see more?"

She laughed. "I'll show you mine if you'll show me yours."

"Deal... You first." And he joined her laughter.

They stripped off the last of their clothing, laughing and breathless. Stacey couldn't believe how carefree she felt. This was so different than anything she'd ever experienced...even their time before her marriage. More than the sex, they were learning to be comfortable with each other.

He leaned back on the couch, his erection lying heavy against his hard stomach, and watched her through slumberous eyes. His gaze stopped on her bruised ribs and his brows drew together slightly.

"We can go to the bedroom if it will be more comfortable for you."

Stacey shook her head. She wanted him right here, right now. Holding his gaze, she moved back over to the couch, loving the way his gaze followed her then slipped along her body, his lips parting and his breathing getting heavier. Just looking at his reaction was turn-on enough. She put one knee on the couch, then straddled his hips.

"That's it, honey." He cupped her bottom and rubbed her against him. Their bodies moved together in an easy rhythm, and their breathing grew louder and deeper.

"I need you, Mason." Wrapping her hand around his shaft, she guided him between her thighs, groaning as he pressed forward. He kept his hands on her butt, helping her move. The friction of their bodies made her flush with desire. "That's so good."

He raised one hand to frame her face so she'd meet his gaze. "Come for me, honey. I can see you're right there."

He lowered his hand, teasing her between her legs as he thrust. The added friction sent her over the edge. Stacey arched, grateful to feel his hand there supporting her. As the last tremors of her climax faded, Mason groaned, his teeth gritting together and his hands now holding her hips in place as he gave in to his own orgasm.

They froze, motionless for a moment and then Stacey slowly smiled and laughed.

Mason stared at her, a broad smile on his lean face.

"You're so incredibly beautiful," he told her. "You laughed like that the day I took you sailing. I thought then you looked so free, so different from how I'd ever seen you, and how I wanted to see you that way all the time. I love every aspect of you I've seen, but this laughing woman….this free woman… She's amazing."

She smoothed his hair off his face and leaned over to rest against his shoulder. "You make me this way. You make me feel like I can do anything."

"You can," he whispered next to her ear.

She turned her face to gaze at him. "Maybe. But no one's ever made me feel that way…except you."

* * * *

He pushed his fingers through her hair, overwhelmed by the love shining in her eyes. She loved the man he was now, but would she love the man he'd been?

"What's wrong, Mason?"

"Does it show?"

Worry clouded her brow. He didn't want that, but he did want her to know who he was.

"This is the part where we get to know each other, right?" he said, stalling.

"Yes." When she curled into him as if seeking warmth, Mason grabbed a throw from the back of the couch and spread it over her. Not exactly sure where to begin, he stroked his hand over the throw's velvety fabric. "You already know a lot about me."

Mason cleared his throat. "Yeah, so I guess it's only fair I let you know more of my background."

She rubbed his chest. "Is it so bad?"

"It's not something I like to revisit, but until now it didn't matter."

"You don't have to rehash it now. The man I love is the man holding me in his arms, and I love who he is now. If your past has helped you become that man, it's enough for me to accept it."

Mason's throat tightened and he closed his eyes as he softly kissed her forehead. "Thank you for that, but I still want you to know, Stacey, because I think some of my past might help you."

"All right. I'm listening."

"I was born in Baltimore. I have no idea who my father was, but my mother was a hooker who worked The Block." He grimaced. "I can see from the way you raise your brows you've heard of it. Mothering wasn't something she wanted to do. I bounced around foster homes, sometimes coming back to live with her for a few weeks or months when she was clean, then getting the boot again.

"Despite bouncing around from home to home, I did manage to stay in school." Mason sucked in a deep breath. "So many kids say they hate school, but it was a safe place for me, the one place where there was order and where I felt like someone gave a shit about me. I hated when summer rolled around. The only thing that meant was not enough to eat and trying to stay out of the way of my mother's johns."

Stacey's hand stilled on his chest. "Couldn't you go outside?"

Mason shifted. "Damn. I just don't want to go here, but I need you to know… It wasn't that some of them thought I was in the way. They…they didn't confine their interest to hookers."

"Mason?" Her arms crept around his chest, hugging him as closely as she could.

"Baby, I know how you felt when I found you on your boat because it happened to me too, only it was more than attempted." His throat ached with every word that came out of his mouth, and he waited for her reaction. He'd only ever shared it with one other woman, and she'd walked out on him.

The silence stretched until he feared he'd misjudged her...that she wouldn't be able to handle it either. And if that was the case, then she might as well know it all.

Voice tight, he continued, "It...wasn't always rape. I was hungry and they had money and food."

Stacey shifted then and he feared she was going to leave. Instead, she framed his face and stared at him, her expression fierce. "Just because they gave you food and money for you to have sex with them doesn't make it any less a rape. You were a kid, Mason! What happened to you was not any more your fault than what Jace tried to do to me."

He buried his face in her hair because he couldn't do anything else. For several minutes, they simply sat locked in each other's arms, rocking slightly.

"God, Mason," Stacey finally whispered in a voice sounding as tight as he felt. "How the hell did you get out of such a life?"

He released a breath, letting some of the tension ease out of him. "My high school PE teacher. He was the football coach too and encouraged me to go out for the team. After practice one day, he noticed the scar on my ribs and started grilling me for details."

Stacey ran her fingers along it. "I've wondered about it too."

Mason's jaw tightened. "I got it when I was thirteen from a john who wasn't very happy when I told him no."

"And he cut you?"

"It was mutual. My mother got him off me, got hold of the police. I was permanently removed from her care after that."

"So what did the coach do?"

"Besides getting me involved in football, he made me toe the line on my school work. His wife was an art teacher. She made an attempt to turn me into an artist, then settled on giving me a deep appreciation for it instead. They turned my life around."

"Where are they now?"

"Retired. Living out in Arizona. I fly out there a couple times a year. I guess if I had to identify what makes a good family, it's them."

"I suppose they're behind you getting a scholarship to Harvard?"

Mason smiled, stroking his hands along her arms. "Completely. They gave me the confidence to believe I could be something more than where I'd come from."

"I am curious about one thing. You said if I didn't want to go to the police about Jace, you could make a few phone calls. Where do those connections come from?"

Mason laughed. "A very satisfied art customer from an unnamed city out West. He was so happy with the work I acquired for him, he told me he owed me. Anything I needed...and he meant anything... He was the man."

He shifted her on his lap so he could look at her. "Stacey, I had a juvenile record. It involved some of what I just told you, but I cleaned up my act. I've been tested--I do that routinely...because of my past--and I'm clean. If it makes a difference...I'll understand."

"Not one damn bit. I'm guessing it helped clue you in with regard to Jace. You suspected long before I knew, didn't you?"

He nodded. "Almost from the moment I first met him. But I was so damn angry and hurt...I'm sorry, honey. If..."

"Don't." She laid a finger across his lips. "No 'if onlys'...okay?"

Mason glanced at his watch. "Let's go to bed."

"It's still early."

He grinned. "I know. I can think of a few things to do before we go to sleep."

Stacey arched her brows. "You're going to help me go through paint samples for my newest client?"

Mason grimaced. "Not exactly what I had in mind."

Chapter 15

Mason woke her the following morning as he rolled out of bed. "I need to go into the gallery today. You're welcome to poke around here, or you can come in with me."

Stacey sat with legs crossed in the middle of the bed. "My ribs are feeling better. I think I'd like to go in so I can accept your offer of office space, if you don't mind. I already bring so many clients through your gallery, it makes sense."

"That's what I thought. Go ahead and grab the bathroom. I'll get the coffee started."

Stacey smiled when she saw the spacious shower with its multiple heads. Mason might have started life on the wrong side of the tracks, but he'd certainly learned how to enjoy the luxuries he'd earned.

She'd rinsed the shampoo from her hair when he stepped into the bathroom.

"Coffee's brewing. Mind if I join you?"

"Not as long as showering's all you have in mind."

He stuck his lip out, making her laugh. "One kiss then, if you're going to be stingy."

"All right."

Mason stepped under the spray, pulled her into his arms and proceeded to kiss the living daylights out of her. Breathless and flushed, she finally eased back.

"I thought you said one kiss."

"That was one."

Stacey stepped from beneath the spray and grabbed a towel from the warming rack. "Mason, Phillip mentioned going to his office after lunch today to handle the paperwork. Do you have time to go?"

He stared at her, his dark eyes serious. "I'll make time."

Stacey was fine until they actually entered the gallery. She halted just inside and he glanced back at her curiously, one hand draped casually in his slacks pocket. "You okay?"

She took a deep breath. "Yes. I guess it's just hitting me how much is changing. I'll need to contact a lot of my clients. Mason, are you sure this is what you want to do? I don't want to interfere with the gallery's business."

He stepped back to her side. "I want you here, and I have the room. Come upstairs. I'll show you the office I have in mind."

No one else had arrived yet. As they mounted the steps, Mason flicked on the light switch, illuminating the two-story entry with cool, recessed lighting. He led the way along the landing to a door at the corner. After opening it, he stepped back. "Take a look and tell me what you think."

The first thing that struck her was the light pouring in through the large windows. The room was empty as if waiting for someone to develop its potential, and Stacey's decorator instincts soared. A blank canvas.

Mason walked to a door on the wall opposite the windows. "This adjoining room could be used for clients or as a sort of conference room."

"It's perfect."

Mason laughed. "It's empty."

Stacey wandered into the room he had suggested as a conference room. She could already envision it with comfortable furniture that would put her clients at ease.

"It's a decorator's dream...empty with white walls. I can start from scratch."

"If you have a few minutes, why don't you put your things in the gallery's conference room, then we'll take a look at some of the artwork I have in back. Take your pick of what you'd like."

She glanced sideways at him. "A little cross-promotion?"

"If one of your clients likes a piece, it can be theirs."

They spent the next half hour going through the storage area until Stacey had picked out several pieces. "You have paintings?" she asked eyeing the canvases stacked near one side.

"New additions. Take a look. It's an artist I signed an agreement with to sell his work."

"Mason's has always been known for three-dimensional art."

"I'm branching out a bit. In fact, the building next door just came on the market, and I'm thinking of buying it in order to expand the gallery." When she raised her brows, he shrugged and grinned. "Business has been good."

They went back upstairs to his office area. Stacey already knew his employees, so Mason explained she would be working from the gallery for the foreseeable future. "Until she gets her space arranged to suit her, she'll be using our conference room."

When the door to the conference room shut, Mason took her in his arms and waggled his brows. "We could christen it."

Stacey hugged him. "I think a kiss would be enough for now."

He complied, nibbling at her mouth until she was the one who deepened their embrace. He had backed her to the table when her cell phone bleated.

"Shit."

Stacey dug in her purse. "You were trying to cheat, Hatch. Besides, it's Phillip."

"I'll get him for this."

Stacey answered the phone. "Good morning, Phillip."

"Good morning to you too. You sound upbeat."

She glanced at Mason who lounged in one of the conference chairs, his suit coat open and his thumbs hooked in his belt. "I am."

"I talked with Jace. He is willing to sign the paperwork, but he has requested you be there as well. Says he wants to apologize in person."

Stacey frowned. Being away from her husband for even a short time had made such a difference, and she really didn't want to see him.

"Sweetheart," Phillip said. "You have the control here. If you want to tell him to go to hell, then that's fine. If he balks, I can turn the case over to the police."

As though sensing something was bothering her, Mason stood and dropped his hands to her shoulders, gently massaging.

"I don't trust him, Phillip. I'm sure you can understand that. But I also want closure. Maybe this will provide it...so, okay. I hope you'll understand if I bring Mason with me."

"Absolutely. Be here at noon. He's scheduled to arrive at twelve-thirty, but I want you to be here first."

"All right."

As soon as she hit End, Mason turned her to him, his brows drawn together and his lips tight. After searching her face for an instant, he growled, "You've agreed to see him, haven't you?"

"He requested it."

"Stacey...honey..." Mason stopped, spinning around and walking over to the window, his hands jammed in his pockets.

She could feel the anger rolling off him, but she wouldn't back away. "I need closure."

He whipped around, eyes flashing. "He hurt you, dammit! You don't have to answer to him. All you have to do is say the word and you can send the bastard to jail. I don't..." He paused, closed his eyes and sucked in a breath before he continued, "I don't understand how you can be so calm. Just thinking about it makes me want to strangle him...and Justin."

She set her phone on the table and went to his side. "You've seen the world I was reared in. As laid back as you seem to think I'm being, do you truly think this won't eventually come out? Mason, he's ruined. He might have hurt me. He might have humiliated me, but he is ruined around here. An annulment will hurt him far worse than a divorce ever would have. While prison would have been bad, he wouldn't have to face--day in and day out--everyone who will question why our marriage ended. Someone will talk. Someone will see him and Justin together and begin to add it up."

She looked out the window at the busy street, the trees dotting the sidewalks. "He has a very traditional client base. It's his father's client base. Jace will lose them, and he can't afford to. It wasn't his money that supported us. It was mine. The only thing he brought in was the damn Winchester diamond. I discovered after our marriage even the boat had been financed based on his marriage to me and the money I would bring in. What's left of the Winchester money is mainly tangled in trusts that dole out a pretty small allowance. Nice, huh?"

Mason sighed. "And you want to see this scum one more time?"

Stacey lifted her chin. "I do. I want him to see how little he's affected me."

Silence stretched while Mason searched her face. "All right. And I will go with you, but I won't promise to behave myself if he says or does anything out of line."

"Fair enough."

* * * *

Phillip's office was only a couple blocks from Mason's gallery, so they walked the short distance. Mason held onto Stacey's hand the entire way. He'd tamped down his temper for her sake, but he knew his fuse was short. If Winchester did anything, Mason wasn't sure he could hold himself back.

When they entered the office, Phillip's assistant waved them toward the door at the end of the hall. "He's expecting you. Go on into his office. I believe he's planning on meeting in the conference room once Mr. Winchester arrives."

Stacey nodded and smiled, obviously familiar with where she was headed. Mason followed. One thing was for sure, no one could fault any of the Barlow-Barretts he'd met for their taste either in decor or art. He grinned, and like many of his siblings, Phillip's interest in sailing was obvious from the choice of both. Only Stacey's home had been without any obvious sign of a love for the ocean. He wondered if that was her, or an attempt to please Winchester.

He decided right then if they chose to live in his home, he'd give her a free hand to redecorate any way she pleased...the bay house included. Hell, he'd build her a house if it would make her as happy all the time as the glimpses he'd seen recently.

"Mason?"

He realized with a start she'd halted right outside what he assumed was the door to Phillip's office. He grinned. "Sorry. I was thinking."

"You looked mighty fierce."

He cupped her neck with his hand. "I'm feeling a bit that way."

"Settle down, please, because I need you rock steady."

"I'm here for you."

She nodded and opened the door. Phillip stood from behind his desk and came around to give her a big bear hug. "How you doing, sweetheart?"

She glanced back at Mason then looked at Phillip. "So much better. I'm ready for this, Phillip. I'm ready to get this over with."

He motioned them to seats at the conference table on the other side of his spacious office. "I'd like you to take a look at what I have outlined before Winchester arrives."

"Is he bringing an attorney with him?" Mason asked.

"He said not. I think he's doing his damnedest to keep this as quiet as possible."

Stacey nodded. "He will. You and I know that won't happen, Phillip, but he'll try. The circles our families travel in are simply too small. When word gets out we've split, people will start poking around until they find out why."

"So you expect this to eventually hit the media anyway?" Mason asked. Stacey was surprising him more and more. He could never imagine the woman he'd first met being so calm about the idea her name--and very possibly pictures of them both--could eventually become public fodder.

Phillip nodded. "It will happen."

Stacey laid her hand on his arm. "I know you have political aspirations. If you think this will harm your chances of seeking office in the future, you still have time to separate yourself."

Phillip smiled and patted her hand. "I'm good, but thanks for the concern, sis. I figure I'll be tied to it anyway simply through our relationship. So why not take an active role as the one who jumped through the legal hoops to get you out of an untenable situation."

Stacey shook her head. "Always working an angle, but I appreciate your help."

"Not a problem. Either of you want something to drink? Coffee? Water? Something a bit stronger?"

Mason shook his head and Stacey did the same. He took the seat on Stacey's right, while Phillip sat to her left and began showing her the papers. In addition to the agreement for the annulment, there were statements for Jace to sign admitting what he and Justin had done, an affidavit affirming he had turned over all photos of Stacey and Mason in his--or anyone of his knowledge's--possession and finally an agreement to stay away from Stacey or any other member of the Barlow-Barrett family. She looked over all of them, touching them with slightly trembling fingers.

"Do you want me to add a promise to say nothing to the press?" Phillip asked.

"Yes. That's probably not a bad idea. His finances are not nearly as flush as he would like others to think. If something goes wrong with his relationship with Justin, he could decide to capitalize on it," Stacey murmured.

"And most likely at a time that would be the most inconvenient for you or your family," Mason added.

As they considered that, the interoffice phone buzzed.

"Mr. Winchester has arrived," Linda said over the speaker.

"I'll be right out to escort him back," Phillip replied. He looked at his sister and at Mason. "Ready?"

"As much as I can be." Beneath the table, Stacey reached for Mason's hand. He held it in his, squeezing slightly to reassure her.

When the door shut, he leaned over and kissed her. "We'll get through this."

She nodded. "Thanks for coming with me."

He squeezed her hand. "I wouldn't be anywhere else."

As the door opened, he felt her tense and tremble. Winchester looked a little the worse for wear. Mason kept his expression neutral, but it warmed him to know he'd gotten in a few good punches. The more he saw Stacey's soon-to-be-ex spouse, the more obvious it became to him Winchester was teetering on the edge. The man looked bad, and not just from the punches Mason had landed.

"You should have informed me Hatch would be present," Winchester snapped at Phillip.

Phillip leveled a stare on him. "You made no requests that she be on her own. It was her decision to bring Mr. Hatch with her."

"I want him out," Winchester insisted.

Stacey leaned forward, bracing her elbows on the table. "If he goes, then so do I. Your choice, Jason."

Winchester glared at them both, but sat, leaning back and crossing his legs. Phillip outlined the documents as well as a listing of what assets were held separately and what assets would need to be either assigned or sold so the proceeds could be divided.

"You can keep the house," Stacey said, "if you'll agree to assume payments and reimburse me for my half of the equity."

"You can keep the boat." Winchester smirked. "That should cover the equity and then some."

Mason felt Stacey shiver and he nearly leaned across the table to grab Winchester by the front of his shirt.

"I neither want, nor will I accept the boat as an asset. As far as I'm concerned, it could sink tomorrow." She leaned back in her chair and raised her chin. "What I will tell you, though, is if you continue to antagonize me, Jason, this conversation and this deal are over. I'll make the phone call to the police myself--right here and right now."

Winchester's face, already pale and haggard, lost even more color. Mason wasn't sure whether it was with fear or anger, but once again, pride in Stacey flowed through him. At this moment, she had no idea how much she resembled her hard-driving brothers and her hard-nosed father.

"That's hardly necessary. I'll sign the damned paperwork. Sell the house. It's too big for me anyway, and I've always detested your taste in decor."

"That's enough, Winchester," Phillip cut in. "Taking this to a personal level gets us nowhere, and may well land you in jail."

The atmosphere in Phillip's office was as tense as any Mason had ever felt without some sort of violence bursting forth. Even Phillip, who appeared to be the most levelheaded of Stacey's siblings, was on edge. His pale face and tight-lipped countenance might have appeared like a poker face to some, but having seen him more relaxed, Mason knew he was wound as tight as him.

Stacey signed her part of the paperwork, then sat back and waited on Winchester.

"With your consent to the annulment," Phillip told him, "we should be able to get this through the courts fairly quickly. There will be no need for you to appear since you've already agreed to it." He stopped his perusal of the documents in front of him and glared at his brother-in-law. "In fact, you would be well-served not to be there. Should the judge put anyone under oath for any additional inquiries, what you're hoping to keep under wraps would come out in open court. Do you understand?"

"I am not an idiot."

Phillip merely arched a brow. "Sign the papers and save any further comment. You have no friends here."

Mason stroked Stacey's hand as it trembled in his grasp. The sooner this was over the better.

"I see no division of the joint bank accounts here," Winchester growled. "Half that money is mine."

Stacey leaned forward again. "Save it. You and I both know who was earning the money while you sat around on your ass. Try actually working the company your father left you, Jace. It might help keep your mind on something other than getting a blowjob from Justin."

"Stacey…" Phillip said in a warning tone.

Her head whipped sideways to glare at him. "I'm sorry, Phillip, but I'm done here. I see now what the whole purpose of requesting my presence here was…no more than a pitiful attempt to stick his fingers in money I earned, and the assets I brought into this marriage. That's not happening." She stared, narrow-eyed, at Winchester. "Take what's outlined or walk out now."

Winchester looked down his nose at her. "You know I used to pretend you were Justin so I could get hard enough to fuck you."

Mason was across the table before he could stop himself. Chairs clattered as he grabbed the taller man and began punching him. If Stacey and Phillip had had enough, Mason was long past the point where he could pull back from beating Winchester like the dog he was.

Winchester was swearing at him, but Mason no longer heard anything other than the satisfying crack of his hand against the other man's face. He wanted to pound that aristocratic nose and those well-bred cheekbones until he heard things crunch under his fist. Winchester needed to pay, needed to experience even a fraction of the pain and humiliation he'd caused Stacey. Vision narrowing, Mason went in for another punch only to feel strong hands dragging him back. He twisted in Phillip's hold, but the bigger man refused to let go.

"Leave it, Mason," he ordered. "We cool?"

Mason blew out a breath in frustration and shook off Phillip's hands. "Yeah."

Had Phillip not stepped in to pull him off, Mason wasn't sure he could have stopped. As it was, he didn't want to. Only Phillip's level gaze kept him from going back again, like a terrier after a bone.

Phillip looked at his sister. "We're done. Get Mason and yourself out of here. I'll finish this and send Winchester on his way. We clear? The last thing I need is to have to call an ambulance and the police. There would be no way to keep this quiet then."

Stacey tugged at Mason's arm, dragging him toward the door. As soon as the door shut behind him, he leaned back against the wall and sucked in a deep breath through his nose. Once his breathing settled, so did some of his temper.

"I'm sorry," he finally murmured.

Stacey stroked her hand over his chest. "It's all right. It's over, Mason."

Was it? He wasn't quite so sure. There'd been something wild in Winchester's expression, as though the man felt he had nothing left to lose.

Chapter 16

Jace stared at his reflection in the hotel bathroom mirror. There wasn't much hiding the bruised cheekbone and the faint black eye. Still that wasn't what stuck out to him. It had been two days since his meeting with Stacey in her brother's office. Two days, and he still had heard nothing from Justin. They'd had their share of differences over the years, but Justin had always come back. They'd always apologized and managed to move forward. This time, it occurred to Jace Justin might truly have meant it.

He might actually be leaving, going back to the ranch for good.

Jace wandered out of the bathroom, slumped into the chair near the window. He could have gone back to his family's home, but doing so would entail too much of an explanation to his mother. She was vacationing with friends in the Hamptons, but her staff would no doubt inform her he was there, so home wasn't an option.

He'd already tried Justin's condo. The line had been disconnected. He'd left voice mail on Justin's cell. It had gone unanswered. With a deep shuddering breath, he pulled his phone out and tried again. It rang and rang.

"Hi, this is Justin. Leave a message."

Justin was never far from his phone. He simply wasn't taking Jace's calls. The beep sounded.

"Justin. It's me. I really need to talk to you. I'm ready to listen, to make some changes." He paused and took a deep breath. "Please call me."

He continued to hold the phone in his hand as he stared out at the river view outside his window, but his phone didn't ring. The following day, Jace was allowed back into the house to collect the rest of his belongings. He'd hired a couple people to take care of furniture, clothing, that sort of thing, but his office he packed himself. He pulled open the top drawer and stared at the small .22 caliber Ruger resting inside. It was a tiny gun. He'd

Laura Browning

originally bought it thinking Stacey might want something she could carry, but he'd never given it to her. Now, he tucked it in his pants pocket.

When he was finished, he returned the key to Phillip's assistant, gave her a polite smile and directed the guys driving the box truck with his belongings to the storage locker he'd rented. The gun, he kept.

* * * *

The rest of the week seemed to fly by. Stacey was so relieved to have everything with Jace behind her. Of course they had the annulment hearing to go through, but Phillip assured her it would be only a formality since the grounds were there, and Jace wasn't contesting it. As a peace offering to her mother, Stacey was even beginning the annulment process through the church.

In the meantime, she was moving on. With Mason's help, she had already furnished her office and discovered it was infinitely easier to run her business through an office not located in her home. Having Mason in the same building with her was somewhat of a distraction. Stacey grinned. But they had found several places to be private. And being so close to him also gave her an added sense of security--something she needed even if she hated to admit it.

"Hey!" Mason startled her out of her reverie. "Brandon and Lucy called to see if we wanted to join them for dinner."

"Where?"

"There's a new place that's opened two blocks from the penthouse. If we head home, we'll have a chance to change clothes and we can walk there."

Stacey glanced out the window. It was a beautiful summer evening. "That sounds wonderful."

"Let me straighten a few things and I'll meet you downstairs in five."

She stared at the empty doorway for an instant, realizing she had a silly grin on her face. As she started straightening her desk and saving computer files before logging off, it dawned on her none of her brothers had extended similar invitations during her marriage. Had even they realized something was off? She shook her head. She refused to think about Jace now.

A wonderful evening awaited her with Mason, Brandon and Lucy.

* * * *

Justin opened the door to his condo, setting his fishing gear just inside and snagging his mail off the floor. Enough renovations were finished he could stay there. More importantly, it was done enough he could sell it. Rubbing a hand over his hair, he let his gaze travel over the interior.

Stacey had done an incredible job with her suggestions. Someday, he might be able to apologize to her, but he doubted it would be anytime soon. Before she could ever forgive him, he would have to reach the point where he could forgive himself.

He'd made so many mistakes since Jace had first told him he was going to marry her. They both had. He'd realized that over the past few days. Getting out on the river again where he could fish and think had helped him. Now he had to find Jace. They had to talk.

After showering and shaving, he dressed in jeans and boots. He was tired of playing city boy. If Jace wasn't ready to make changes, Justin would get on the next flight to Denver then make a connection to Billings. From there, he'd drive to the ranch. He was done.

Punching the power button on his phone, he began to go through his messages. There were one or two from his parents and one from his older brother, but the rest were from Jace. After listening to the last one, Justin frowned and hit Save. Jace said he was ready to make changes, but there was something off in his tone. Justin shoved his phone in his pocket and hurried out his door and to his car.

Jace didn't answer his phone, so Justin opened the GPS application they'd both downloaded. At the time, they'd laughed over being able to always know where the other one was. Now Justin hoped it would help him find Jace before he did something foolish.

* * * *

Mason was looking forward to the evening as much as Stacey. Not only would he be able to spend time in a relaxing atmosphere with Stacey, he'd also be in the company of people he considered friends. After changing, he waited in the open living room for Stacey. She'd chosen a sundress and flat sandals. He grinned. One of the things he liked about her was her confidence she could wear flats and still have great looking legs. Sure, he liked what heels did to the line of a nicely turned leg, but he detested seeing women teetering along, barely able to walk.

"Why are you staring at my feet, Hatch?"

He glanced up. "I was thinking what great-looking legs you've got."

She stared at him for a moment as though surprised by the compliment. "Thanks."

"Let's go. I suspect the place will be packed."

It was a pleasant walk, the waning sunlight casting long shadows along the sidewalk and the faintest of breezes lifting a tendril of Stacey's hair now and then. He loved that about this new Stacey. No more sleek chignons and French twists. More often than not, she left her hair loose to wave about her shoulders. He snagged her around the waist and drew her to his side as they walked. Tall as she was, their strides matched, and he enjoyed being able to turn his head and look her in the face.

"Stacey, as soon as this is settled...will you marry me?"

She stopped dead in her tracks and grinned at him. "Was that seriously your proposal, Hatch? No hearts and flowers? No bended knee? Really?"

He shifted. "You want that?"

She hugged his arm and leaned her head on his shoulder. "No...and yes, I'll marry you as soon as we get this untangled."

They walked a few more steps.

"You want a ring?"

She shuddered. "No. I don't need a ring to remind me of you. You're in my mind and my heart every second of the day."

This time it was Mason who stopped. He blinked a couple of times, slightly embarrassed by how much that touched him. Cradling her face in his hands, he leaned in and kissed her right there on the sidewalk as people walked past them and cars rolled along the street.

"Let's find Bran and Lucy. I feel like proposing a toast...to all of us."

* * * *

Stacey eyed the crowd of people spilling onto the sidewalk and knew it would be a while before they even got through the door. Fortunately, they spotted Brandon and Lucy arriving at the same time. She wasn't sure they could have found each other once inside.

"I'd say this place is already a hit," Brandon observed then gave Stacey a hug before clasping hands with Mason. "How's it going, Hatch?"

"Great." He glanced at Lucy. "He treating you all right?"

Lucy was as tall as Stacey, but built a lot more voluptuously. Strangely enough, Stacey found that no longer bothered her. Mason had helped her gain the confidence her childhood and her marriage had damaged to the point of near destruction.

"Brandon always treats me fine," Lucy said with a laugh. "After all, he owes me."

Brandon gathered her close. "I thought we were even after I fished you out of the bay."

"Okay...then he treats me fine just because."

They settled into a discussion of artwork as they waited to get into the restaurant. Around this crowd, even Brandon's status as COO at Barrett wasn't opening any magic doors. Once they were finally inside, a harried waitress ushered them to a table on a side patio. It was slightly less noisy and the atmosphere was a lot more relaxed. Stacey settled in, enjoying the conversation, which swung from art back to sailing. Since Lucy was nearly as avid a sailor as the two men, it was a conversation everyone could enjoy.

God, this was so different. Stacey hated to keep making comparisons between what life had been like during her marriage and what it was like now, but she supposed that was inevitable. Living so closely with Jace had limited her viewpoint so she began to think everyone lived the same way. One glance at Mason's laughing expression was enough to smash her misconception to smithereens.

Mason would never sit in judgment. He would be there to support her. And if they disagreed, there would be no smothering disapproval. There might be a heated argument, but never the feeling she was facing a judge and jury.

Stacey leaned back and sipped the wine she'd ordered, glancing casually around the patio. She nearly knocked her glass over as she reached for it at the same time her wandering gaze settled on Jason standing, alone, on the other side of the patio. Mason grabbed her glass, stopping it from spilling its contents right in Brandon's lap.

"Stacey? What's wrong?"

She could barely speak. Irrational, she knew, but her immediate gut reaction to the surprise of seeing Jace once more was to recoil in fear, to flee. Now she fought the flight response, taking a deep breath to calm herself.

"Jace... Over there."

She cringed as the other three turned their heads as one to look.

"We can go somewhere else," Brandon murmured.

"No," Stacey said. "I knew this was inevitable when I chose the path I did, but I won't go back now."

"There's no need to climb all your mountains at one time," Mason said for her alone. "It's okay if you want to leave."

All three were watching her. "No. I won't have my life circumscribed by him anymore." She raised her head and smiled. "I'm sitting here with people I love, and I have nothing to make me feel ashamed."

"Thatta girl." Brandon reached over and patted her hand.

The conversation turned once again to Lucy's work.

"I've rented space in a studio with several other potters. It was a whole lot less expensive for now. We've discussed eventually getting a house out in the country, but staying right here around the district for now makes sense."

"A little tough to get your kiln in Brandon's townhouse," Mason remarked.

He laughed. "Yeah, not sure the neighbors would have appreciated being so close to the heat, and we felt like Lucy's house was a bit too cozy."

They were talking and laughing, Mason's arm draped around her shoulders, when a sorority sister and a fellow debutante stopped at their table. Stacey stiffened, noting immediately the way the other woman's gaze soaked up how intimately she and Mason were positioned.

"Stacey! It's been ages since I've seen you." She glanced around the table. "I saw Jace across the way. How are you two doing?"

It was one of those moments where it seemed, to Stacey at least, the entire restaurant had stopped and was holding its breath waiting for her answer. The quickest way out of this situation would be to simply say fine and let Deirdre move on. But doing that made it seem she was somehow ashamed of her relationship with Mason, and really only delayed the inevitable. People would figure out soon enough her marriage to Jace was over.

She smiled to soften her words. "We've split, Dee."

"Oh! I'm sorry to hear that. You always seemed like such a well-matched couple."

God, and how did she address that? Feeling as though her smile was now pasted on her face, she said, "Looks can be deceiving. Jason has taken a new direction with his life, and I have with mine. We're both better off that way."

She didn't want to say too much. In fact, she wished Dee would move on, but Stacey didn't want to be rude. The other woman's gaze shifted to Jace, and Stacey nearly groaned aloud as she saw Justin wending his way through the crowd toward him.

"Well…how interesting." Dee offered a generic smile. "I'm sure I'll be seeing you around the club."

"Not if I can help it," Mason muttered under his breath. Stacey elbowed him as Dee finally took the hint from the lack of invitation to join them. With a mumbled "have a good evening," she was off.

Brandon's narrowed gaze followed her. "Is that the one who couldn't keep her mouth shut about anything?"

"The same." Stacey watched the other woman already bending someone else's ear. When that person's gaze shifted to Jace and Justin, who was now speaking intensely to him, Stacey sighed. "There's no keeping this quiet. She's already taking great pleasure in spreading the word as quickly as possible. We might as well have splashed it over the front of National News."

In just a few minutes, a chill went down Stacey's spine. She found Jace glaring at them. Justin, dressed like he was already back on the ranch, had a hand on his arm.

"Judging from the look coming our way," Mason murmured, "I'd say your friend did a little speculation of her own on what busted your marriage."

Brandon threw two twenties on the table. "I think we should go someplace else." He raised a brow as he looked at Stacey. "I don't see this as hiding or running. I see this as ratcheting down a situation with the potential to get nasty."

"Too late," Lucy murmured. "The trouble is headed our way."

Jace was winding his way through the tables, his brows drawn together and his lips pinched. Stacey raised her chin, refusing to avoid his gaze. Justin followed him, but it looked, judging from his expression, like he was trying to cool Jace's temper--to no avail.

As he reached the table, both Mason and Brandon stood. Brandon was slightly taller than Jace, and what Mason lacked in height, he made compensated for in sheer muscle. As the men glared, Stacey rose to her feet as well.

"What the hell did you say to Deirdre?" Jace snarled.

"Only that we'd split," Stacey replied in a cool tone. This time it wasn't her imagination, the tables around them had gone eerily quiet as Jace's volume increased.

"I thought the agreement was to keep this quiet!" Jace's face went from flushed to pale with anger. It reminded her so forcibly of their last argument that Stacey shrank away. She heard murmurs from the tables around them, and Justin frantically whispering at Jason to keep it down.

"She had to say something," Brandon snapped. "Get real. The woman could see for herself Stacey was here with us while you were across the freaking room."

"Let's go, Stacey," Mason said in an even tone. "You don't need this grief."

"So were you fucking her the entire time? Did you even stop?" Jace asked, and Stacey felt almost physically ill. She'd shaken off many of the strictures drilled into her by her mother, but this was beyond anything she'd experienced or even knew how to handle. Jace was spilling everything into far too public a forum.

"That's enough," Mason growled. "You seem to forget she's done you a favor. You also seem to have difficulty recalling exactly what your part was in this entire situation."

Stacey tugged at Mason, not wanting a repeat of the scene in Phillip's office and terribly aware they were drawing more and more attention from other guests. Taking matters into her own hands, she turned and began walking away, relieved to feel Mason's hand at the small of her back. She knew it was his touch, didn't need to turn to see that. As they exited the restaurant, she was relieved to see the crowd at the door had thinned.

"I'm sorry," Stacey said, feeling like she needed to apologize. "Why don't we pick someplace else within walking distance…?"

"Don't walk away from me, Stacey!" Jace's voice cut in from behind them. He was making no attempt to lower his volume as he left the restaurant…shaking off Justin's hand.

He started for them, and Stacey suddenly found both Brandon and Mason standing between her and Jace. In the distance, the faint whine of sirens punctuated the pause in what was going on.

"It's time to back off, Winchester," Mason warned, his tone now a deadly monotone she'd never heard before.

The sirens grew louder. Had someone called the police? Stacey squeezed her eyes shut for a moment in sheer mortification. They would have been better off to simply take the entire thing through the courts at this rate and invite the media into front row seats.

"Stay the fuck out of it, Hatch. You think I don't know how you sabotaged us? You couldn't leave her alone could you?"

Stacey had endured enough. She pushed between Brandon and Mason and faced Jace. He was obviously drunk. The man she'd known would never create a scene like this on a public street. "Don't lay the blame at Mason's door. You created this situation. No one else. You blackmailed my parents and blackmailed me into a marriage I never wanted. And for what?' Stacey raked him from head to toes with her gaze, then looked beyond to Justin. "So you could continue to carry on your own affair. You want to make this a public scene, Jason? Then suck it up big time because I can air a whole lot more dirty laundry than you."

The police sirens had cut off, but she barely registered the fact.

"I tried to keep this quiet. I gave you the opportunity to get away without any penalty for what you did, but you're the one choosing to air this now, not me. I'm done, Jason. Those papers you signed? They don't mean squat. My next call is to the police, so maybe you need to hock the Winchester diamond and hire yourself a good attorney."

"You can't do that!" Before she could walk away, Jason had pulled a small pistol from his pocket. Stacey stared at a bore that loomed so large she thought it would swallow her. Everything happened at once. As her mind registered the metallic slide and click of the semi-automatic cocking, Brandon and Mason both shouted.

Doors slammed. Additional shouts now from officers who had arrived at the scene. Their words didn't register. Time slowed so even the voices sounded sluggish and from afar. Jace raised the pistol, aiming at her. Stacey's gaze was glued to the barrel's gaping hole and then Mason was there between them at the same time several cracks split the air.

To her side, she watched Brandon pull Lucy to the ground beneath him. Several uniformed officers rushed forward, but it was Mason and Jace she watched in horror. As Mason twisted, grimacing, she caught a glimpse of Jace behind him. Jace jerked a couple of times. It appeared at least one of the cops' shots had struck him. His gun clattered to the pavement, and Jace crumpled to the ground.

Justin fell to his knees beside him, and Stacey turned away from them. Her only thoughts now were for Mason, down on one knee and gasping.

"Mason! Oh my God. Are you hurt?"

He closed his eyes, nodding, his hands clasping his side. More sirens whined, tires screeched and suddenly they were surrounded by police. As an officer tried to pull her away, Stacey shouted at him and yanked her arm from his grasp.

"No! Let me stay with him. He's hurt!"

Brandon pushed his way to her side. Words were exchanged that she paid no attention to, her eyes on Mason and the blood darkening his shirt and his hands. A gap opened in the wall of police and emergency personnel. Now she was being helped to his side. He sat on the pavement, his face pale and his thick hair escaping from the ponytail at his nape.

He'd taken a bullet meant for her.

"Oh, Mason. God, I'm so sorry…"

His gaze was filled with pain. "Are you all right?"

"Yes. Oh how can you even ask that?"

"He was going to shoot you. Christ Almighty! I had to do something." Mason turned his head, looking at where Justin was crouched next to Jace. "Is he dead?"

"I don't know. I…"

Paramedics arrived. One team went over to Jason, and the remaining two began working on Mason.

"We need you to step back, ma'am."

"No. I…"

"She stays," Mason growled. "She stays or I'm outta here, even if I have to crawl to do it."

Brandon and Lucy were on either side of her. Stacey looked at both of them, trying to assure herself they were all right. Brandon wrapped her in a hug, holding her tight. She heard his sigh of relief, a sigh that sounded as though it had come from the deepest part of him.

"I've got you cleared to go with them. We'll follow in our car to the hospital."

Stacey slipped from his grasp, back toward Mason who was now strapped to the gurney and being pushed toward the back of an open ambulance. As she stepped away to follow, she looked back at her brother.

"What about Jason?"

"They're stabilizing him," Brandon responded. "Beyond that, I don't know."

Stacey sucked in a deep breath, not sure what she felt at the moment, just knowing she didn't have time to examine it. The man she loved was being loaded inside an ambulance, and she was going with him. She'd go with him wherever he went because he'd already followed her to hell and back--and they'd both more than paid the price. As the doors of the ambulance began to close, shutting her in with Mason, she saw Justin being allowed to climb in another ambulance.

For a moment, their gazes locked. She saw pain, regret, and the same worry she was feeling being reflected back at her. If he felt a fraction for Jace of what she felt for Mason, maybe they would be all right.

Epilogue

Three months later…

"That's it, Stacey! Around this buoy and you've got him."

Wind tore at the hair she had tucked into a worn cap. Mason was working swiftly at her command, her crew as she made the turn around the buoy and left Brandon in her wake. She laughed with the sheer joy of it. As they crossed the predetermined finish line, Mason ran toward her from the bow and grabbed her into his arms.

"Christ! That's some of the best sailing I've seen. You nailed Brandon. Hah! And look at your father. You can see his grin even from here."

Leaning back in Mason's arms, she turned her head toward her father's yacht, feeling absurdly close to tears when she saw him wave. Morgan wasn't quite so subdued. Even from this distance, they watched her jumping up and down and laughing.

From their starboard side, Brandon shouted, "I concede. Dinner's on me tonight."

"We'll meet you back at the marina," Mason shouted back.

He turned Stacey into his arms, lifting her hand and kissing the thick gold band resting there, a slightly smaller version of the one on his own lean finger.

"I will never let him live this down." He grinned at her.

Stacey twined her arms around his neck. "Oh, Mason. I love you so much."

"Back at you." He tucked a strand of hair under her cap. "Every day I open my eyes next to you, I see the woman I love and wonder what I've done to deserve you."

She rested her head on his shoulder. "I'm the one who should be wondering."

He put his hand over her heart, his expression somber. "The day I saw you at Brandon's wedding, I never dreamed we'd be back together. You were so brittle...so broken...and I felt such helpless rage..."

"It's over. Father told me Jace's attorney managed to cut a deal. He's being allowed to go to Montana with Justin. I'm almost at the point where I feel sorry for them," she whispered.

"I'm not sure I can be that forgiving, honey."

She smiled. "I can because it gave me you. It made me stronger, and you healed what was broken."

"We healed it. In both of us."

Meet the Author

I live in the rolling country of central North Carolina in the middle of a small farm along with my husband and son. My background with horses and journalism was the initial impetus for this series (Bittersweet and Balancing Act), but as each of the Barlow-Barrett siblings has found his or her voice, I've discovered winning the love of their lives was only half their battle. Each of them must also find how they fit into a powerful and wealthy family where private lives are seldom private.

Turn the page for a special excerpt of Laura Browning's

Winning Heart

Can love beat a lust for revenge?

Nelson Anderson is one of the richest men in America, but his life has become a quagmire of bitterness and the need for revenge. Wynter O'Reilly is a gutsy girl determined to make her life better–and she just may be the tool Nelson needs. All she needs is a little polish.

To his surprise, a girl from the wrong side of the tracks helps heal emotional scars that all the money in the world can't fix. But just when Nelson realizes that, his own plot for revenge may cost him not only Wynter's love but her very life.

On sale now!

Chapter 1

Three hundred dollars would stretch a long way, but pinching pennies wasn't anything new for Wynter. She and her mom had done it their whole lives. The problem was, she was down to her last little bit of cash, and as she stared at the help wanted ads, finding a job still seemed far away.

She was either over-qualified or under-qualified. With no address since she gave up the room she'd rented, some employers tuned her out right away. Wynter also had no references and no expectations the Southards would provide them. They were the only people for whom she'd ever worked.

Her mouth tightened. She stared out the windshield at a farm across the road. She wasn't ready to give up her dream. She would get into Duke. She would make her mother proud. But damn it, she needed a job.

Hell, she'd already squared everything with the high school so she could graduate, but if she didn't get a job soon, she would have to go home and admit defeat. Her options were running out.

Horses grazed in the pasture across the street, and she watched them wistfully. Wynter understood horses. She always had. It was what had landed her a job on Southard Farm. All she needed was another shot, and this time she wouldn't screw up.

She'd driven north of Durham that morning to get out of the city and weigh the choices. Right. Who was she kidding? She rationed out the last cigarettes a week before. Now she was on her last tank of gas, had just a couple of dollars left and still no job. She thought if she left town it would clear her head, so she could make a decision. Gamble one more time finding a job or go back.

She thought about her mother, how hurt and disappointed she would be. Wynter loved her, but she couldn't go back. Irene had struggled her whole life to give her daughter opportunities, and Wynter had repaid her by getting in trouble and losing a scholarship that might have changed both their lives.

Somehow, she must make it right. She would not call it quits. There must be something someone would hire her to do. She looked over at the horses once again.

On a whim, Wynter cranked the ignition and the old truck rumbled and coughed. After checking both ways along the narrow state highway, she drove across the road and down a long, neatly-manicured drive toward the barns in the distance. Bradford pears lined the smooth asphalt, mulch in neat mounds around the base and the grass mowed and trimmed. The whole farm was a showplace that screamed money.

So what are you doin' on it, trailer trash?

Stomach rumbling, she pulled into a parking area in front of what looked like a business office. Nerves or hunger? Did it matter anymore?

She stepped from the truck and slammed its door. After a quick check to make sure her hair was still in a neat braid, Wynter smoothed her palms over her jeans. They were worn, but at least this pair didn't have any tears. It was still cool, so she pulled on the sweater Mama had knitted. It was the best thing she owned.

Her knock was hesitant. Nervousness tingled and tickled the pit of her stomach. Hunger, not nerves, was making her belly as jumpy as a hoppy toad.

"Door's unlocked. Come on in."

The words were tinged with an accent she couldn't quite identify. Wynter turned the knob and pushed open the door. It was much darker inside and took a moment before her eyes adjusted. Two men sat in the room, but she directed her attention to the one sitting at the desk right in front. He was older. Besides, the other man worked on a computer toward the back and didn't even glance up when she came through the door. All she saw of him was gray-streaked hair and broad shoulders. Probably some techno-geek working on the system.

"What can I do for you, miss?" the older man asked. Wynter shifted her gaze. Her lips trembled and curved into a smile as she identified the accent as Scots. His face was round, with light blue eyes and receding gray hair. On the desk, a tweed driving cap lay as though it had just been tossed there.

"I was wondering if you might have any jobs available."

The Scotsman assessed her from the tips of her sneakers to her slender arms and legs. "Have you worked around horses, lass?"

"Yes, sir," Wynter confirmed. "I worked for a family, grooming and exercising their field hunters. I took care of the barn too, feeding and mucking out stalls."

"We don't need any grooms or riders right now," the Scotsman remarked. The last hope drained away, but she fought to keep it from showing. He hadn't said no yet.

"I do need a stall mucker." He eyed her again. "You seem a might skinny. It's a lot of heavy work. We're a training-and-show facility with twenty-five horses in active work."

"I can do it," Wynter assured him, hope rekindling.

The Scotsman's eyes twinkled. "We could try it and see. Do you have a letter of reference?"

Hope crashed back to earth with a dull thud of despair.

"No, sir, I don't."

"How about a phone number, and I'll give them a call."

She shook her head and bit her lip. At this point, Wynter felt more than saw the other man stop what he was doing while he watched too. As always, when she drew attention, heat seeped into her cheeks.

"Do you not know the number?" the Scotsman asked. "That's all right. Just give me your employer's name, and I'll ring them up."

She looked back up at the older man and cleared her throat. "The Southards fired me, sir. They won't give me a reference." He shook his head, so she continued on, "Thanks anyway for your time."

Wynter turned on her heel and hurried out the door. She'd almost made it back to the truck when she heard a younger, deeper voice.

"Wait!"

The other man stood on the porch. Her eyes widened when she saw him lean on a cane. His face was pale, as if it had taken him a great deal of effort to get outside. In the bright light outdoors, she saw brown hair streaked with gray and deep blue eyes shadowed with pain and something else she couldn't quite pinpoint, but it was the eyes that stopped her. So dark, so deep, she felt she was almost drowning in them.

"Please come back up here on the porch. I hate yelling at people." His voice held a quiet command impossible to ignore.

He moved aside, so she could sit in one of the rocking chairs out front. When she moved past him, Wynter caught a faint scent of horses, leather and some spice she couldn't quite pinpoint. For a moment, it reminded her of her friend, Wythe, but was different. His scent was familiar, comfortable. This man's scent made her stomach flutter. She shook the thought away. The man remained standing, although he supported his weight against the porch railing behind him.

"I'm Nelson Anderson. You are?"

"Wynter O'Reilly," she supplied with a challenging tilt of the chin, not sure why they were having this conversation but feeling compelled to answer him.

"I own Pheasant Run," he supplied as though that would clear things up. So, not a techno-geek. Wynter watched him warily. He also seemed a little uncertain. "What did you say the family's name was who fired you?"

Her eyes narrowed. Hypnotic blue eyes be damned! Wynter's experience with blue-blooded horsey families was they stuck together in their own clique, and it was small enough most of them knew each other. For all she knew, Payton Southard might have decided to press charges against her.

"Southard," she mumbled.

Nelson Anderson's beautiful eyes narrowed, any trace of warmth vanished. "Where did they live?"

"Southside Virginia."

There was a long pause. Anderson's gaze moved from her face to work-roughened hands. She gripped her knees, shifting with nerves, but refused to hide her hands.

"If—if there's nothing else, Mr. Anderson, I should leave." Right, because she had so many appointments in her day planner. No, it was his eyes she needed to get away from. They saw far too much.

"Wait here, Wynter." It wasn't a request. Despite the quiet demeanor, it was obvious Nelson Anderson was a man accustomed to being in charge. Leaning on the cane, he limped back inside the office. The right leg was the one he favored. Wynter stared after him with a touch of resentment. Why should she wait if they weren't hiring her? She still needed a job, and standing around waiting wasn't getting her any closer to employment.

She was about to leave when the door opened again, but it wasn't Anderson who came back through it. It was the Scotsman.

"Come with me, Miss O'Reilly. We'll try you a week and see how things go."

She jolted with surprise. "You will?" She jumped up and grabbed his hand and shook it. "You won't be sorry. I'm a hard worker and a lot stronger than I look."

He eyed her with one bushy brow raised. "I hope so. My name is Thomas Sinclair. You can call me Thomas like everyone else does. I don't stand much on ceremony, but I do expect an honest day's work for an honest day's wage."

As he spoke he headed down the steps. For a short man, he walked briskly, and Wynter found herself hustling to keep up. When they entered the barn, he glanced at the sneakers she wore. "Do you have any other shoes?"

"Just my paddock boots."

Thomas shook his head and rolled his eyes. "Manure'll ruin your boots. Look in the wash stall there to your left. See if there's a pair of Wellies to fit you."

He waited while she checked a couple of pairs before finding a fit. When she'd slipped them on, he was off down the barn, talking over his shoulder while he explained the daily routine and what her duties would be. As they reached the end of the aisle, he handed her a pitchfork, pointed to the wheel barrow and said, "You can start right now."

By day's end, Wynter was exhausted. She wanted nothing more than a hot shower and a soft bed. One out of two wasn't bad. Earlier she'd noticed a shower off the tack room at the front of the barn. She'd given up the small boarding house room in Durham, so it looked as though she would be sleeping in the truck until she got paid and found someplace to live. She scrounged up enough change to grab a couple of packs of nabs and peeked out front. There was still a light in the office but no cars in sight. Wynter grabbed the small bag containing shampoo and other toiletries, snatched up clean underwear and a t-shirt and sprinted back to the barn.

She paused as she entered, savoring the noises of horses settling in for the night. The rhythmic chewing of hay and the rustle here and there when a horse moved around its stall were as soothing as any lullaby. It was good to be back among animals she understood. All they asked was for someone to look after them and treat them well. They had no ulterior motives.

The shower room wasn't much, but it did offer a stack of clean towels on a shelf in the dressing area. In addition to the shower, the large tack room contained a washer, dryer and a toilet. Wynter grinned. She could almost live here, she thought as she stripped and turned on the shower. When the hot water washed over her, she sighed in relief. She would be sore tomorrow. Although cleaning stalls was nothing new, she'd never cleaned so many. But it felt good. She'd found a job. Things would be fine again.

* * * *

By Thursday afternoon, she wasn't so sure. She didn't get paid until the next day. Her whole body ached, and she hadn't eaten. Wynter drank water to squelch the hunger pangs, but after a while, even that didn't work. Her muscles ached even more than usual, and she couldn't wait until the end of the day. She wanted a hot shower, and then she planned to wash and dry her clothes in the tack room.

She lingered over sweeping the aisle and hanging the hoses, waiting for everyone else to leave. It was a warm spring night, and some of the amateur owners still hung out, laughing and gossiping. There was a show coming up at the Hunt Horse Complex the next week, and everyone scrambled to get ready. She looked forward to it for another reason. She might be able to pick up extra cash at the show braiding manes and tails. At last everyone cleared out, and she walked to the front entrance of the barn.

As usual, the light in the office was on. She figured they had left it that way because she never saw anyone. She grabbed her duffel bag and the sheaf of financial aid papers she'd picked up from Duke. Her grades and test scores were good enough that they were going out of their way to find the money she needed to start classes. But unless they covered almost everything, she'd have to lower her sights.

Wynter didn't linger in the shower. She wanted to get the laundry done and leave before anyone became suspicious. When she had given up the room in Durham, she had used some of her precious store of cash to buy an old sleeping bag at the Goodwill. She secured it under a tarp in the back of the truck. Although a little cold at night, it had been dry, so she'd found an old farm road in the woods just down the road where she parked the truck and slept in the back of it. Wynter wanted to wash the sleeping bag too, and it might take a few minutes longer to dry. She didn't bother separating any of the clothes. Everything she owned fit in the large capacity washer with room to spare. It was used to wash horse blankets, so it had to be big.

As the washer spun, she looked around the tack room. She was so hungry. Against the wall was the refrigerator where Thomas kept horse medications. She checked for something edible, but her stomach rumbled in protest when all she saw were vials of vaccine and boxes of horse wormer. Out of the corner of her eye, she spotted a crumpled potato chip bag sitting on top of the trash can. Wynter hesitated a fraction of a second to get herself past the gross-out factor before grabbing it and shaking it. Hallelujah! It had something in it. She almost cried with joy when she discovered someone tossed out half a bag of chips. Wynter slipped two fingers in and grabbed one, savoring the salty, starchy taste.

The washing machine beeped when it finished. Setting the bag of chips next to the papers from Duke, Wynter slipped into the laundry area and shifted the clothes and the sleeping bag from the washer into the dryer. The machine hummed as it started. Wynter settled back in a comfortably shabby overstuffed chair with the garbage can chips and the Duke paperwork. The chips were gone in pretty short order. It blunted the edge off her hunger.

She checked the dryer, took out the t-shirts, underwear and her oldest pair of jeans and restarted it. The rest of the jeans and the sleeping bag were still damp. While she waited for them to dry, Wynter tried to concentrate on the paperwork, but she was just too tired. In no time, she found herself drifting off.

* * * *

"Are you worried about the lass too, sir?" Thomas had asked Nelson that afternoon when he'd once again caught him staring after their newest stable hand, Wynter O'Reilly.

Nelson glanced behind him. "She looks thinner."

"I'm afraid the job's too much, sir, though she's giving it her best. I won't be responsible for her hurting herself or one of the horses."

Nelson had watched the girl struggle to guide the wheelbarrow down the aisle and out to the manure pile. She was tall and slender, now bordering on thin. When she had returned and passed the two men, she had smiled tiredly at them. Nelson's eyes had followed, resting on the dark auburn braid hanging from underneath the beat up baseball cap perched on her head. It swayed when she walked in the same easy side-to-side rhythm as her slender hips.

Nelson frowned. "Do what you think's best. I trust your judgment."

He had more things to worry about than the fate of one stable girl. But when he got ready to leave the office late that night to return to the house, he noticed her truck was still there. Wynter O'Reilly would not be dismissed, no matter what he might say. But now the question nagging at him was what she was doing in his barn so late? Still turning that over in his brain, he limped to the tack room in the barn. As soon as he had eased open the door, he spied her sleeping in a chair on the other side, one hand tucked beneath a cheek and her legs curled beneath her, as innocent-looking as a baby.

On her lap, resting beneath her other hand, was a sheaf of papers. Even from here he saw the Duke University logo. Now his curiosity sharpened.

As a general rule, stable girls were drop-outs or runaways. *Which are you, Wynter O'Reilly?* He limped over quietly and was rewarded when she continued sleeping undisturbed.

He saw financial aid papers, a summer school application sticking out from them. Nelson looked at the dark circles under the half-moons of her sooty eyelashes. Was this why she worked so hard? Trying to get into Duke? He glanced at the full name on the application, and noted she had put Pheasant Run's address under place of residence. He frowned again, sharp eyes taking in the still damp hair and the sound of the dryer from the laundry room.

There was a lot more to Wynter O'Reilly than had first appeared. While he whispered her name and shook a slender shoulder, Nelson wondered if the girl might be of use. She seemed to dislike the Southards. Perhaps he should find out more about her connection to that family.